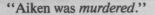

"Aiken was *murdered*."

"Indeed he was," Stryker agreed gently.

Kate looked at the others, at her own hands, looked again at Stryker. It's *terrible*. He was stabbed, mutilated."

"Yes." His voice was even.

"*We're* terrible," she went on. "Sitting here bickering and bitching at one another, being obstructive and smart-ass and...in this room, here...all of us...is it always like this? Are people *always* like this?" she demanded, appalled.

Stryker smiled. It was a gentle, forgiving, kindly smile.

"Only those with something to hide," he said.

——————————— ★ ———————————

A Forthcoming Worldwide Mystery by
PAULA GOSLING

BACKLASH

MONKEY
PUZZLE

PAULA GOSLING

TORONTO • NEW YORK • LONDON • PARIS
AMSTERDAM • STOCKHOLM • HAMBURG
ATHENS • MILAN • TOKYO • SYDNEY

This book is dedicated to my daughters,
Abigail and Emily.
May their lives be safe from tigers.

MONKEY PUZZLE

A Worldwide Mystery/September 1990

Published by agreement with Doubleday, a division of
Bantam Doubleday Dell Publishing Group, Inc.

ISBN 0-373-26056-3

Printed in U.S.A.

It would be foolish of me to deny that I went to an American university, because it is a matter of record. But it was *not* the University of Grantham, for no such place exists. Nor do any of the characters I have placed there exist, outside of my imagination.

Now, when I set my imagination going, it is on the strict understanding that it plays by the rules and does only original work. This is particularly true when it comes to the creation of characters. But memory is an odd thing. Random, disconnected fragments dart about there in a snipe-like and insistent fashion. Sometimes one or two will settle on a fertile patch of imagination and pretend to be something new. What is worse, you believe them.

It is this kind of behaviour that makes authors old before their time.

All I can say is, I have done my best. As far as I am concerned, the characters in this book bear no resemblance to anyone living or dead.

If old friends or mentors recognize a gesture here, a nose or an elbow there, they have only themselves to blame. Had they been dull and ordinary they would have been forgotten long ago.

ONE

HE ALWAYS TOLD HIMSELF it was like watching a silent movie. Safe and solitary in the dark vastness of the closed university library, the security guard looked across at Grantham Hall. It was mostly in darkness now, except for the reception areas in the forward corner of each floor, including the English Department, in the penthouse addition.

The guard drank some coffee and picked a stray piece of ham out of a back molar. He'd gotten into the habit, once he'd made his first round, of sitting and casting a benign eye over his kingdom. Immediately before him lay the snow-covered Mall, then the bulk of Grantham Hall, and beyond it in the distance the glittering spider's web of the downtown area, lights strung gracefully between the surrounding hills.

At this hour it was, of course, a largely uninhabited kingdom. Earlier there had been the cleaners. They were usually good for a laugh; dropping things, reading people's mail, tripping over their buckets, scratching their crutches and picking their noses because they thought they were alone. Everybody over there thought they were alone—but they weren't. Not while *he* was watching.

Now there was only the one light left—that of an office halfway along the penthouse floor. One of the offices of the English Department. It was like a television screen, suspended over the blackness, tuned in especially for his entertainment.

Within the office a man sat, looking at photographs.

"Oops, almost caught you, didn't he?" the guard said, suddenly sitting up with interest. The door of the office had opened and the man had turned the pictures face down on the desk. Obviously the visitor hadn't bothered to knock. Well, well—a little something to look at after weeks and weeks of boredom. The guard was delighted. Amateur observer though he was, it was very clear that an argument was developing over there—wild gestures, red faces, wide-open mouths.

He took another swallow of coffee and belched gently. His faith was being rewarded. This was really funny. The two of them were getting crazy over there. Maybe one would have a heart attack or something.

Maybe tonight would be different.

TWO

"FOR CHRISSAKES, I can handle it!"

Lieutenant Jack Stryker plucked at the shirt over his waist. "I'm getting fat hanging around here moving paper. Look at that."

Captain Fineman and Sergeant Toscarelli examined Lieutenant Stryker's waistline with owlish concentration. A fold of shirt, yes, and perhaps a small flare of flab above the belt, but no more. Stryker was pinching air, doing a fat-man act. His bright blue eyes whisked from captain to sergeant like a spectator at a tennis match, wondering which one had the weakest defense.

"I'm fine, I tell you," he insisted. "Hell, how bad could it be up there? So some kid got a lousy mark on his term paper, lost his temper and offed his professor. Big deal! It's not as if I were going to rip open the rotten underbelly of our sick urban society, is it?" He pronounced this bit of journalese with sarcastic relish. "They're not exactly bums in universities, you know. They're civilised people."

"Exactly," Fineman growled. "And you'll roar in there like Attila the Hun, getting up their noses—"

"Oh, come on," Stryker pleaded, switching instantly from anger to placation. "I went there for two years myself. I even still take a night course now and again. I've *got* manners—I just don't waste them on you guys, that's all. Have I stuck it all these years just to end up with my ass parked permanently behind a desk? It was only pneumonia, you know, not the bubonic plague. Put me back on the street, Fineman, help me avoid premature hypertension. Let me catch a small killer now and again. *Soothe* me."

Fineman's mouth twisted into a reluctant, one-sided smile. Maybe it was time to turn Stryker loose. He'd been out of the hospital for nearly a month now. "All right, all right," he muttered. "It's yours."

"Hallelujah!" Stryker headed for the office door.

"But Stryker . . ." Fineman's voice was cautionary.

"Yeah?"

"Be nice."

Stryker's eyes widened into vast blue innocence. "A natural charmer like me? How could I be anything else?" He grinned and shot through the door before Fineman could change his mind. Beyond the glass they saw him grab coat and hat, scrabble in his desk for a decent ballpoint, finish his coffee, knock over his desk lamp. He was suddenly very busy.

Fineman peered over his glasses at Toscarelli. "He still looks lousy," he said bleakly.

"He *feels* lousy," Toscarelli replied.

Fineman boiled. "Goddammit, he told me—Stryker! Hey! Stryker!" he shouted through the half-open door.

But Stryker was gone, humming down the hall like a top, his sneakered feet slapping the terrazzo with dedication, his curly hair fluttering over his receding hairline, his scarf flying high. He was alive again.

Toscarelli sighed and prepared to follow him. He was a huge, dark, steady man. He'd been Jack Stryker's partner for a long time, his bulk a necessary ballast to Stryker's often self-destructive forward motion. He was in the habit of picking up the pieces, and Stryker counted on him to be there. They were an effective team, and Toscarelli, too, had fretted at Stryker's forced inactivity due to an injudicious all-night wait for a no-show informer and a following guest appearance at the hospital. Stryker had almost got away from Toscarelli then, and he wasn't about to let it happen again. He loved the little bastard like a brother, and had long ago reserved the right to strangle him himself—no interference brooked. As he swung toward the door, Fineman's voice caught him over a frantic rustle of paper.

"Here, dammit, in this memo. Look. In black and white. 'The medics have given me the all-clear to return to full-time duty.' He says it right here. He *signed* it."

Toscarelli's big shoulders rose and fell. "He lied."

STRYKER SCOWLED out of the car window as Toscarelli wound through the one-way system that surrounded the campus and finally drew up at the foot of the Mall. As he got out of the car he grunted slightly at the impact of the cold air. He pulled his tweed cap down over his forehead, then tilted his head back to glare up at the face of Grantham Hall. One of the new ones. In the old days the English Department had been haphazardly housed in a couple of the graceful old houses on Lafayette. The expanding university had taken over block after block of these old houses through the years. But now, with the possibility of becoming a state university as a carrot, it had mulishly begun an architectural blitz, razing the old to raise the new. To Stryker the university had become an in-human place. The proportions were wrong. The new buildings might have won architectural awards, but how could you curl up with a good book inside a T square? He didn't know how the kids could study or feel a part of it. Sure, the place was full of air and light—cold air and cold light. In the old English Department he might have suspected the butler did it. This place? Maybe a robot.

They took one of the two lifts marked FACULTY ONLY up to the penthouse floor. The doors slid open into a white-walled reception area lined with square plastic benches behind square chrome-and-glass tables.

The only colour was provided by a huge abstract painting that glowered down in conflicting shades of arsenic green, yellow, orange, shocking pink and black. A small plaque beneath said it was entitled "Struggle" and had been a gift of the Art Department.

"Who were only too glad to get rid of it, I'll bet," muttered Stryker, unbuttoning his coat.

"What?" Toscarelli was staring around.

"Nothing." Stryker crossed the lobby. "Hey, look, the stinkers had a party and didn't invite me." He peered through the glass walls that enclosed an area proclaimed FACULTY LOUNGE in gold letters on the glass door. "Faculty this and faculty that—they sure like to draw the lines, don't they?" The chairs within looked only marginally more inviting than those in Reception. On two of the tables pushed against a side wall there was a litter of empty plates, scattered toothpicks and a few dried triangular sandwiches that lifted their corners beside overflowing ashtrays. The windows on the far side of the glass cube overlooked the empty Mall and the blank lines of the Library. Below, under the black lacework of the leafless trees lining the Mall, a lone bus growled its way over the crisp half inch of new snow that had fallen during the night, leaving glistening black snail-tracks behind it. Even through the insulation of dead air and glass, Stryker could hear the asthmatic engine and the hiss of air brakes as the bus slowed for the lights at the next corner. He took a deep breath, felt emptiness clutch at his chest, and turned it to a cough. "Well, where's the bod?" he asked abruptly, thrusting his hands into his pockets.

"Down here," Toscarelli said, having made a quick reconnoitre while Stryker was communing with the leftovers from the party. Could it be, Stryker thought as he followed the big man, that the corpse is a leftover too?

They went down a narrow corridor that ran parallel to the Mall, doors on either side. Offices overlooking the Mall had to be the choice ones, Stryker concluded. The ones on the inside would have been gloomier, and reserved for peasants, starvelings, and Baconians, no doubt.

The scene of the crime was one of the offices overlooking the Mall, and a uniformed officer stood by the door. They stepped over the long thick ribbon of partially dried blood that curled over the doorsill. The room was about fifteen by ten, walls white, floor grey linoleum. Book-filled shelves were hung on both end walls. Filing cabinets stood against the inner wall, which backed onto the corridor. The outer wall was bare save for the radiators under the windows. A couple of neutral paintings hung over the filing cabinets, but otherwise the place was workmanlike and rather bleak. It would have been cold, too, if it hadn't been filled with men. Between them he caught his first sight of the body—and of Bannerman, the medical examiner, crouched over it.

That was something, anyway. Stryker liked Bannerman, who still retained a sense of humour, despite having to deal with customers who were no longer in a fit state to laugh at his jokes.

Stryker then cast an eye over the two junior detectives who had been despatched immediately following the uniformed officer's call. The older one, Pinsky, he knew and trusted. He was relieved to see he'd been assigned to the case. Pinsky was a tall, shambling man of about Stryker's age. He had a long, lived-in face and always looked as if he were wearing a larger man's clothing picked up by accident in some steam-fogged Turkish bath. The other one was a new face—Neilson? That was it. He'd come onto the strength while Stryker was still in hospital. Young, dark, well-dressed and sleek, he looked like a smart-ass, but Stryker reserved his judgement. With training many smart-asses turned out to *be* smart. (Some of course turned out to be just the other half.) Pinsky seemed able to put up with him—so maybe the kid had something.

Stryker glanced at Donovan, the photographer. "Don't forget my extra prints," he reminded him.

"So you can get everything backwards? I won't forget," Donovan grinned. Every time, on every case, Stryker asked for two sets of photographs, one normal, one reversed, in which left became right. He claimed you saw things differently that way. He'd read it in a book somewhere. Nothing had come of it, and probably wouldn't this time either. But Donovan always obliged, to keep the peace, because Stryker could be an awful nag.

Stryker went over to stand beside the body. "Messy," he observed.

"More than you know," Bannerman said, looking up. "The killer went overboard on this one. At least ten wounds in the chest—probably from that knife." He gestured toward a brass dagger visible through folds of a clear plastic bag. Stryker recognized Pinsky's small, backhand script on the tag. "Paper knife or letter opener, looks like," Bannerman said.

Stryker stepped over the legs of the corpse and bent down. "Quite an item. Belong to the deceased, you reckon?"

"Probably."

"Odd thing for a college professor to have." The knife was actually a heavy brass dagger, the handle in the shape of an erect human phallus, life-sized and fully detailed.

"Here's another odd thing—for a college professor *not* to have. Take a look," Bannerman said.

Stryker and Toscarelli bent over the body. Stryker said nothing, but Toscarelli gave a choke of revulsion and turned away, making quickly for the door. "Sorry," Bannerman apologised. "I forgot about Toscarelli's stomach."

"You might have spared a thought for mine," Stryker said, looking around. "Have you found it?"

"Not yet."

"What does it mean?"

"Damned if I know. Done after death—fortunately for him. I make him dead sometime between eleven and one, pending the postmortem. The windows were left open, and the heat goes off in this place around eleven—the cold made him stiffen up faster. Even so—I'd say no earlier than eleven."

"Did he put up a fight?" Stryker asked.

Bannerman shook his head. "Nope—at least, I don't think he did. Has a hell of a dent on the left temple—probably knocked out before he was stabbed."

"From the front or the back?"

"Could be either."

"Windows opened by the killer, you think?" he asked, going over to inspect the catches, which bore traces of fingerprinting powder.

"Maybe," Bannerman said. He was rolling the corpse over, and the outflung right arm, stiffened by rigour, rose over his shoulder to point to the ceiling. For a moment Stryker was visited by the whimsical notion that the corpse was waving at him, trying to get his attention.

"No prints on the window latch," Pinsky said. "Only smudges."

"Gloves?"

"Why not? It's winter, isn't it?"

Stryker looked down at his own hands. He was wearing gloves himself. Did that mean the killer had come in from outside? The victim was not dressed for outdoors. He wore a beautifully soft grey suit which looked like cashmere, an ivory shirt, crimson tie, black shoes and black socks.

"Is that a red tie or—"

"Red tie," Bannerman nodded. "The blood ran down over it, but the tie was also red to start with." He pulled back the jacket and showed Stryker the stab and blood pattern. "He was half on his side when the killer finished with him—position of postmortem lividity confirms that. These are big wounds. If he'd stayed on his back, most of the blood would have remained in the body. Turned on his side, facing the door, the poor bastard just drained to death."

"You mean, after all that, he wasn't dead?"

"Oh—dead within a few minutes, sure. They're big wounds, but none hit the heart. They were delivered straight down. You have to go under and up behind the sternum or in this way, between the ribs, to really nail the heart."

"Straight down," Stryker echoed.

Bannerman rocked back onto his heels and wiped his sleeve across his face. It was a long face, with acne scarring high on the cheeks, and the general aspect of a friendly horse. "I figure he was on his back when he was stabbed, okay? The last thrust went into the sternum—the breastbone—and stuck there. The killer had to rock it and pull hard to get it out—you can see the wound is different from the rest. In doing it he turned the victim over slightly. I guess the killer was getting tired by then. Slowing down."

". . .'All passion spent'?" Stryker asked.

"Something like that."

"Man or woman?"

"No way of knowing. There are small men and big women—and he was unconscious, remember."

"Then, why all the anger?"

Bannerman shrugged. "You tell me. Maybe it started out to be one stab and then the killer snapped—got into a frenzy, kept going. It can happen like that."

"I know," Stryker murmured. "I've seen it happen."

Bannerman's face was bleak. "You mean you've felt it happen. That's how babies get bashed and wives beat up. It's very scary."

"We stop ourselves after the first blow. The killer didn't."

"That might be the only difference between him and us," Bannerman said, starting to repack his case.

"Anything else I should know?" Stryker asked.

Bannerman stood looking down at the dead man. "He was in his middle to late sixties, well preserved and well nourished, probably drank a bit too much."

"That wasn't his only vice," Pinsky said. "Take a look at those pictures on the desk, why don't you?"

Stryker went over to the desk and picked up the sheaf of pictures that lay face down on the blotter. Porn glossies. The usual thing—saucy poses with coy expressions, legs spread, hands busy, eyes inviting. He'd seen thousands like them. With one difference.

These were all men.

"Oh, swell, a pansy," Stryker growled, dropping the pictures back onto the blotter in disgust. "Is this the reason for the mutilation, you figure? Male homos often mutilate when they kill."

Bannerman shrugged again. "I wondered about that, but they usually cut off the obvious thing, don't they? He's intact below. I never had one with his tongue cut out. Never before read of one either.

"Maybe it was to keep him from talking," Neilson suggested facetiously.

"Funny," Stryker said.

But he didn't laugh.

THREE

STRYKER WAS LISTENING to Pinsky finishing his preliminary report when Toscarelli spoke from the hall. "Somebody's coming." Stryker went out.

Neilson looked after him, and raised an eyebrow. "You mean to tell me *that* is the 'Jumping Jack Flash' you guys kept telling me about? He doesn't look so much to me."

Pinsky gave him a dirty look and Bannerman said, defensively, "He's been sick."

"I *guess*," Neilson said with a laugh.

Donovan was putting his cameras away. "I'd be careful, kid," he said mildly. "You'll see him jump eventually—and if you aren't looking, it could be onto your back. He doesn't like sloppy cops." He had the satisfaction of making the kid blush as the brass knife slipped into its plastic bag and hit the floor.

"It's the blood on it—it's slippery," Neilson protested.

Bannerman nodded. "So's Jack Stryker. Watch yourself."

In the hall, Stryker and Toscarelli watched with interest the approach of five-foot-nothing of icy-eyed lightning, whippy and fast-moving. It was a man, but it looked more like a grey-haired boy. "I'm Stark, the chairman of the department. I had a call from Campus Security. They said there'd been a killing here. Is that right?"

"That's right," Stryker acknowledged, producing his identification. "I'm Lieutenant Stryker, this is Sergeant Toscarelli. We'll be in charge of the investigation."

"In here?" Stark demanded, looking toward the open door.

"Yes. He—" Stryker was too slow. Stark was past him and into the office before he could finish the sentence. Bannerman was kneeling again beside the body, unfolding a body bag. He and the others all suspended their activities momentarily, as if playing a game of statues.

Stark stood over the body, looking down. His face seemed to tighten all over, but his expression remained neutral.

"Well, sir?" Stryker asked, coming up behind Stark. "Is it him?" Meaning the man whose name was on the office door.

"Is it *he*?" Stark corrected him automatically. "Yes, it's Aiken. Obviously not suicide." His tone was dry.

"Struck on the head, then stabbed repeatedly," Bannerman volunteered.

"Indeed," Stark said blankly.

Bannerman opened his mouth to go on. Behind Stark, Stryker shook his head violently, but Bannerman didn't notice. "And his tongue was cut out," he continued. "Afterward."

Stark stared at him for a moment, then turned on his heel and shot out of the door. Stryker caught up with him halfway down the corridor when the small figure stopped in mid-step and seemed to shiver momentarily. "Did he say . . . ?"

"I'm afraid so, sir," Stryker said. "He shouldn't have said anything until the autopsy was complete, but—"

Stark peered up at him. "Why not?"

"Well, these details often—"

"I'd hardly call that a *detail*, Lieutenant. Dear God, how Aiken would have hated the thought of his appearance being mutilated."

"Well, it won't show with the mouth closed," Stryker pointed out helpfully, thinking of the funeral arrangements and trying to be practical. "They'll make him look normal."

"He'd hate that even more," Stark snapped, and hurried down the hall. He began talking fast, half to himself, making a lifeline of words to hold onto, stringing out small items of interest as if to keep himself afloat. "He has no family. We'll take care of the arrangements. I'll have to notify the dean. And his lawyer. I think I'm currently one of his executors."

"Currently?" Stryker asked.

"He could go on and off people, like a neon sign," Stark said. "You never knew from one week to the next." They'd reached the foyer, and Stark's glittering eye fell on the detritus left in the Faculty Lounge. He clucked impatiently. "That looks debauched. I must do something about that before Monday."

"There was a party last night?"

Stark shook his head. "Not what you'd call a *party*. This has been Registration Week, you see, and we have a traditional gathering at the end of it. Sherry and so on. Nothing wonderful."

"And how late did this gathering last?"

Stark considered. "Most of them were gone by six. But we stayed on."

"We?"

"My assistant chairman, Arthur Fowler, and the members of the Honours Committee. There were things to discuss."

Stryker got out his notebook. "Was Aiken Adamson one of the members?"

"Yes."

"And the others?"

Stark took a deep breath. "Aiken, Arthur and I, Pinchman, Rocheleau, Underhill, Heskell, Heath, Grey-Jenner, Trevorne, Coulter and Wayland."

"Twelve."

"That's right."

"And they all stayed on—until what time?"

"I don't know, exactly. About seven-thirty or eight."

"What does this committee do, exactly?"

"It's a new thing we're trying. Special programme for promising English majors—taking them out of normal classes during their junior and senior year and giving them intensive individual attention on a tutorial basis." Stark was becoming fretful. "I really must notify the dean immediately."

"Of course," Stryker agreed. "And you can call the rest of them, too, while you're at it."

"The rest of them?" Stark demanded. "*All* of them? Do you realise there are over sixty members of faculty in this department, plus secretaries and student assistants? English is the biggest single-subject de—"

"Take it easy." Stryker consulted his notebook. "I only want Fowler, Pinchman, Rocheleau, Underhill, Heskell, Heath, Grey-Jenner, Trevorne, Coulter and Wayland."

"On a Saturday? Some of them are the most senior and—"

"I want to talk to them," Stryker interrupted, unperturbed. "I don't care if they can recite Shakespeare backwards, went to Mass with Tom Eliot or split logs and infinitives with Robert Frost. This is murder, Dr. Stark. These people stayed late, they were the last to see Adamson alive. Maybe one of them was the *very* last."

Stark was horrified. "You don't think—surely you *can't* think one of *us* . . ."

"I don't think anything yet," Stryker lied. "I'm just a vacuum cleaner sucking up facts and impressions. That's part of my job. One of them may know where Adamson planned to go after the meeting, or why he stayed on here *if* he stayed on here. Or why he went away and came back, if *that's* what he did. He might have said something to one of them, or been overheard saying something. *He* sure as hell isn't going to tell me, is he?"

"None of them are Catholic," Stark announced abruptly.

"I beg your pardon?"

"Couldn't have gone to Mass with Eliot." His eyes brightened suspiciously. "We *do* have an associate professor on the faculty who claims to have made spiritual contact with William Wordsworth, though."

"Sounds daffy to me," Stryker said, straight-faced.

Stark raised an eyebrow. "Oh, *very* nice. Do you suppose—"

"Call them. I want them here as soon as possible. Unless you think they'd find a trip to the police station more of an intellectual challenge?" Stryker smiled at Stark. It was a charming smile, a warm smile, a salesman's smile.

Stark was neither charmed nor sold.

He eyed Stryker, assessing him. Tough, he decided. And bright. And not easy to impress. Why should he be? Our authority extends to the edge of the campus—his is everywhere. And authority does things to people. It's done things to me, made me someone I never set out to become. But if I'm careful, if we're *all* careful, and cooperative, there's no reason why the entire matter shouldn't be settled quickly and safely with no harm done to the department or the university. My God! The dean will go berserk when he hears about this. He's always looking for a chance to sit on English. The vote at the state capitol is due in a few months, and we have a murderer loose on the campus. Hardly a qualification for state university status. Or funding—unless it would be a disaster area. He'll blame me, somehow. All my work, everything I've done, will be dust. Unless we can get it settled fast. Damn Aiken. *Damn* him.

"Very well, Lieutenant, I'll call them," Stark agreed.

TOSCARELLI JOINED Stryker in the foyer as Stark went down to the main office to call the dean and the members of the committee. Stryker sent Pinsky with him, then stared out at the traffic on the street below. It was heavier now. The black asphalt glistened, and car wheels had begun to throw a dirty lace cover of slush over the brilliant white slopes of the snowbanks that lined the street.

"This is not neat," Toscarelli announced.

"I know," Stryker agreed. He told him about the meeting of the previous night. "Stark says they finished around eight. The victim could have left with the others or stayed on or gone out and come back. This place isn't locked up until eleven, when Campus Security does a patrol."

Toscarelli snorted. "They *say*."

"Yeah." They reflected on the general unreliability of anyone who wasn't a serving police officer.

"Some nut could have come in, waited in the john until the patrol went past, then made his move."

"How could he know Adamson would be here, unless he had some kind of previous arrangement with him? And if he had an arrangement, why hide in the john?" Stryker took out a battered silver cigar case, glared at it, put it away. "And why *here*? Say it was some kind of sex thing—I can think of a hundred better places than that office."

"Okay. Maybe it was business."

"What business?"

"*I* don't know, do I? I'm only thinking out loud."

"Yeah." Stryker's eyes fell again on the remains of the refreshments in the Faculty Lounge. "Twelve little professors had a party, and when it was over, one of them was dead. What's the odds on it being one of them?"

"Oh, come *on*," Toscarelli's tone was derisory. "The guy was a fag, right? He had funny friends. Maybe he went out, found a pickup, brought him back here, and the guy changed his mind and stiffed him. Happens all the time."

"Uh-huh. *All* the time."

"Well, it *does* happen."

"Sure. In gay bars, known haunts. Not in universities."

Toscarelli was irritated. "Look, just because they're so smart it doesn't necessarily make them so smart, you know?"

"I agree—that's what I just said. I don't buy the fag angle at all. It had to be something else." Stryker fumbled in his pocket. "Seal this floor off—nobody in unless invited. These are the invited." He gave Toscarelli his notebook to copy the names. "Next, send Neilson over to Records. I want class lists for all Adamson's courses last year—and final marks. I want to know anybody he failed, or even gave a 'D' to. Then get onto Vice and get somebody to cover the gay scene to pick up what they can about Adamson's habits, contacts, everything. Schuster is into all that, poor bugger—you should pardon the expression." He took off his tweed cap, rolled it up and jammed it into his coat pocket, rediscovered his cigar case, opened it, took one out and stuck it between his teeth. He began to search for a match. "Next I want—"

"You're not supposed to smoke," Toscarelli reminded him.

"I'm working, for Chrissakes," Stryker protested.

"The doctors—"

"Screw the damn doctors," Stryker growled, then looked away from Toscarelli's reproachful glance. "Okay, I'll compromise, I'll give up matches, okay?"

Toscarelli looked skeptical. "Until you forget."

"I won't forget. *Jesus* it was *me* that nearly died, not you, remember?"

"Just so long as *you* remember."

"You should have been a Jewish mother, you know that?" Stryker said belligerently. "You probably were, in a former incarnation. Get off my back, Tos. I got a case here."

"You *are* a case," Toscarelli said.

"Funny. Ha ha." Stryker made another circuit of the foyer, pausing at last before the painting. "God, that's awful. Really awful."

"Anything else you want done?" Toscarelli asked, ignoring the art critic. Stryker's cigar jutted upward as he chewed it.

"I want some coffee and a Danish. They've got good Danish at the union." He whirled on Toscarelli before the big man could speak. "If I can't smoke, I'll eat, okay?"

"Good. You should build yourself up, anyway. You're due for your annual check-up in two months. They'll catch you at that."

"I'll be fine in two months," Stryker snarled. "I'm fine *now*." He glared at the Faculty Lounge. "I bet one of those turkeys did it. I don't think it was a thief, I don't think it was a fag, I don't think it was a student with a grudge, I bet it was one of them. Feels like it already."

"You haven't even *talked* to them," Tos objected.

"Listen," Stryker said. "That office was searched—you saw the open drawers and the papers everywhere?"

Toscarelli nodded, and Stryker continued.

"None of the papers were under the body, but some were scattered over it. Now, if Adamson had come back and surprised a thief, there would have been papers *under* him. God knows they were everywhere else. No—whoever did it killed Adamson and *then* messed the place up to make it look like a thief. *But* thieves aren't messy—not professionals. They don't kill, either, come to that."

"They do if they're on drugs."

"What would a junkie expect to find in a goddamn professor's office?" Stryker wanted to know. "A first edition of *Confessions of an Opium-Eater*?"

"What's that?" Tos asked, momentarily distracted.

"A book."

"You don't *eat* opium, you smoke it."

"It was a Victorian— Oh, the hell with it." Stryker was walking impatiently around the foyer in circles as he talked. The lab men, coming down the hall, skirted around him. Donovan raised an eyebrow at Neilson and jerked his head back at the pacing figure.

"Told you," he muttered. "He's starting to jump already."

"But I grant you the possibilities," Stryker went on, not seeing the technicians or even Toscarelli, but only his own sneakered feet below him as he moved around. "I will grant you the possibility of a fag killing, I will grant you the possibility of a psycho with a grudge, I will grant you the possibility of *suicide* if you want it. It's wide open, sure it is. Have I ignored anything?"

"Only my vast experience and sound counsel," Tos said. "I'll bet you twenty it was an outside job."

Stryker's cigar went up and his eyes glittered. "You're on, fuss-pot."

"Don't call me that."

"Then, don't tell me how to run my lungs," Stryker snapped, and started down toward the Department Office. "And tell the guy who goes for the Danish it should be cheese or apple."

"Prune would be better," Toscarelli said. "You gotta keep up your fibre, you know."

But Stryker was too far gone to hear.

FOUR

KATE TREVORNE, jammed halfway up an exit ramp from the freeway, drummed her fingers on the wheel and glared at a fat woman in a station wagon who was trying to force her way into the line.

"Sorry, madam, my need is greater than yours," Kate muttered, putting her foot down and darting forward to close the gap. She ignored the irritated blare of a horn and, gaining the upper road, turned left and accelerated toward the faculty parking lot. Rolling down the window to insert her plastic card, she looked around and noted the few cars that were there. Some were covered with snow—others had been swept or blown clear. She picked out Pete's Colt and Jane's Lincoln, then turned into a space of her own.

She switched off the engine and stared out at the back of the Science Building. A murder, right here on campus, right in the English Department. Aiken *dead*. It was unbelievable, but hardly the kind of joke Dan Stark was apt to play—so it must be true.

So much for being safe here, she thought.

Not that this was the kind of danger she'd thought she was escaping when she'd come back from her abortive foray into the crass and commercial world of advertising. She'd come back to recover from Tony, caught up with old friends who convinced her to stay, and had come down here to the university one fresh spring day to plead her cause with Dan Stark. Years before, he'd begged her to stay on when she'd finished graduate school—but she'd caught the sweet scent of expense-account living. The stink had come later. She'd been back two years now—and she loved it more than ever. The bustle and energy in the halls, the students struggling toward a degree and, with luck, a little wisdom.

Had one of *them* killed Aiken?

She got out of the car and nearly fell flat on her face. The night's snow had fallen on frozen ground already coated with old snow and ice. Under the fleecy mantle of fresh flakes was a treacherously pocked and pitted landscape designed to bring down both the meek and the mighty.

Kate had a feeling that what lay ahead in the English Department would be the same.

As she crossed the wet street and picked her way carefully over the unswept paths, she wondered again what Richard was doing and thinking. She'd tried to call him at the fraternity house, but they'd said he'd already left. It would have been so much better if they could have talked it over between them. At least they'd been together last night. At least she needn't worry about *that*.

If only Dan had told her what *time* Aiken had been killed. But his voice on the phone had been tense, the words of explanation brief, as if someone had been standing over him, listening.

Probably someone had been.

The police.

Her mouth tightened as she stopped and looked around the Mall. Two or three students were walking on the far side, their bright clothing labelling them clearly. Four more were having a snowball fight on the Mall, their shouts thin and bright in the icy air. So the police were back at Grantham. Oh, my children, may you stay untouched in the middle of the young day, laughing and free. The fuzz cometh, and you haven't the least idea what that means, have you?

But *I* do.

I'm not the forgetting kind.

She took a deep breath and forged ahead, walking outside of Grantham Hall, hugging her shoulder bag tightly against her body, ready to swing it if necessary. But no policeman barred her way into Grantham Hall, although there was a Campus Security guard in front of the faculty lifts.

"Ah, there you are, Miss Trevorne," he said. "They're waiting for you upstairs."

"Are they indeed?" Kate said with a wry smile. "Obviously *they* didn't have to drive in through the crowds heading downtown to the January sales."

"No, ma'am." The guard looked as if he'd like to smile under different circumstances. He pushed the button and held back the lift door for her. She noted the name on his uniform and paused.

"Do you know anything about this, Mr. Jackson?"

"No, ma'am!" he said defensively. "I made my rounds at eleven, just like always, and there wasn't *nothing* wrong then. I *told* them that. But you know cops—they don't think much of us Campus Security people. Think we're duffers and has-beens. If I'd seen anything, don't you think I'd have reported it? Done something about it?"

"I'm sure you would have," Kate said warmly. "You caught those vandals last year, didn't you?"

He looked gratified. "Yes, ma'am, I did. You remember that, do you?"

"Of course. Three of them, weren't there?"

"No—only two. But *big*." He hesitated. "And drunk."

"Do you think it was somebody like that who did this?"

A uniformed police officer appeared down the hall, and Jackson's expression became a little hunted. "I don't know. I'm not supposed to talk about it, you understand. You go on up, Miss Trevorne—they're waiting, all those *smart* cops."

His outrage was concealed with difficulty. Obviously the police had given him a hard time. Kate leaned forward and held the lift door open. "Jackson?"

"Yes, ma'am?"

"Up theirs!"

He looked startled, then his face broke into a grin. "Right on, miss. I forgot all about you and them others. You was—"

The lift doors closed on his memories but left Kate with her own. She'd been trying to forget for a long time, had become staid and sensible, a member of the Establishment. But now she could feel it rising up in her again. They were still pigs, were they?

Nothing changed.

The doors slid back on the foyer of the English Department. Dan Stark was standing there next to a stocky, dishevelled man who seemed vaguely familiar. He wore a scarred leather jacket over baggy slacks, a long scarf trailing down over a shirt and a sagging pullover, and dirty sneakers. He needed a shave.

But his eyes, when he looked up from his notebook, were alert, intelligent, and so direct they were unnerving.

She felt violated by those eyes as if he'd reached down her throat and plucked at her gullet. There was an air of suppressed energy in his stance that made her instantly wary—as if he were about to spring. His mouth was soft, but his voice was hard, with a metallic edge of annoyance.

"Sorry—faculty only," he barked. "Didn't that dumb guard downstairs even—"

Dan interrupted. "This is Kate Trevorne, Lieutenant, one of our instructors. She only dresses like that to lull her students into a false sense of identity."

"Oh. Okay. You can go in." The blue eyes flicked back to his notebook. She was dismissed.

"Go where?" she asked sweetly.

"Conference room." His voice was bored.

"Don't I get a police escort?" she asked. "I just *love* big strong policemen. They make me feel all *gooshy* inside . . ."

"Now, Kate," Dan said warningly. "Stop that right now."

Stryker had looked up again at the sarcasm in her voice. He seemed more startled than angered. Once more, the blue eyes raked her from crown to boots, and she knew she'd been filed away under "Trouble." Again.

Lifting her chin, she glared at him. "Don't hit me, officer—I wear contact lenses."

"Gee whiz," Stryker said with mock amazement. "*Do* you? They *hardly* show. You should wear a sign around your neck, so's we'd all be *careful*. Wouldn't want anything to happen to those big, beautiful grey eyes, now, would we?"

"Cop," she said. It was an accusation.

"Virgin," he snapped back involuntarily.

"Dear me," murmured Stark as Kate whirled and marched down the hall, her hips flicking angrily from side to side in her tight jeans.

Stark cleared his throat. "I'm afraid Kate has rather an unfortunate attitude toward the police. It's only bravado, you understand. She—"

"Not a bad ass, for a teacher," Stryker said absently.

"Yes. You see—"

"Then, let's get it on," Stryker said, following Kate down the hall.

Buoyed along by her irritation, Kate strode down the hall. She'd almost forgotten how the real ones were. Dealing carefully with Inspector This or Lord That in the classic novels of detection had dulled her recall. This one brought it all back—the tear gas, the wagons, the shouting and the fists. Machines, that's what they were. Destructive, mindless machines, fueled by their own sense of power, protecting and protected by the System.

She strode into the conference room and dumped her shoulder bag onto the table. "Greetings, fellow suspects," she announced. "I gather somebody's finally bumped off the old bastard."

Behind her, Stryker's voice was sharp.

"Did you say 'finally,' Miss Trevorne?"

FIVE

Stryker stood at the head of the table and looked at the faces around it, one by one. He recognized some from his undergraduate days, although their faces had been blurred by time. Once, they had terrified him, held his future in their hands.

They didn't scare him now.

If anything, they looked scared of him. All except those two at the end, of course. The Viking and the Virgin. He realized why she'd fooled him at first. The long straight hair had become short and curly, the big glasses obscured half of the heart-shaped face and hid the grey eyes with their attendant lines. Time had passed, lady, he thought. Only the ass was the same. *That* I remembered.

And the guy next to her—still tall, blond, bearded and incredibly handsome. Was there a change there, too? Or not?

"Okay, ladies and gentlemen, we've got ourselves a murder here. I'm Lieutenant Stryker, and this is Sergeant Toscarelli. We'll be in charge of the case, assisted by Inspectors Pinsky and Neilson, over there. Normally I'd talk to each of you separately, but as there are so many, I thought this would save time. Any objection to that?"

"Would it matter if there was?" the Viking asked.

"Who are you?" Stryker demanded, looking down at his list.

"Richard Wayland," the Viking said.

Stryker met his eyes and his attitude head on. "If you'd rather withdraw from the general discussion, Mr. Wayland, I have no objection. We can go into your reasons later, down at the station, where you can make an individual and private statement."

"Like that, is it?" Wayland drawled.

"Wasn't it always?" Kate asked scornfully.

Stark spoke suddenly, his voice sharp and very angry. "Now, the two of you are to stop that right now. This is a murder investigation, not a protest meeting. Aiken is dead. Horribly dead. We are grown-up people, not children, and we are going to behave like grown-up people. Is that clearly understood?"

There was a moment of uncomfortable silence.

Kate, blushing, ended it. "Sorry, Dan."

"Can I trust you?"

"Scout's honour," Wayland drawled, holding up three fingers.

Stryker, taking this in, realized it was totally foreign to Wayland's nature to knuckle under. His tone of voice indicated that to one and all. He would be polite—as barely polite as possible—only out of deference to his boss. Kate Trevorne, on the other hand, looked truly contrite. The look that passed between her and Stark held affection as well as respect.

"Now, before we talk about last night," Stryker said, "I'd like to get all of you straight in my mind. Mr. Rocheleau?"

"Here." A man halfway down on the left raised a hand. He had a sad clown's face, with quirky eyebrows, but his expression was benign and kindly. He'd been the one who'd winked at Kate Trevorne a moment ago. Next to him sat Jane Coulter, who answered Stryker's call with a nod. He remembered *her*, all right. Looked like someone's granny but had a mind like a razor, and had nearly flunked him out of freshman English. She'd also taught him a lot.

One by one he identified them, either through memory or by reference to his notes.

Edward Pinchman was the old guy with two tin legs whose aluminum crutches leaned against his chair. Arthur Fowler, now assistant chairman of the department, was bald and fussy. (He *had* flunked Stryker.) Lucille Grey-Jenner was new. Sleek and elegant in her Italian-knit two-piece, she looked out of place among the others. Then came Stark, small and watchful.

Beside him was Mark Heskell, dimpled and gleaming. Frank Heath, a Negro, came next. Tall and bulky with beautiful hands carefully folded on the table before him. Then another beard— Chris Underhill, poet in residence. He'd won the Rademaker Prize, but at present appeared to have slept in his clothes. He was struggling to light a pipe. His hands were shaking. All these were new to Stryker.

At the foot of the table, one arm draped negligently across the back of Kate Trevorne's chair, was Wayland. Nothing about *him* was new to Stryker—all very old news.

Kate watched Stryker sorting them all out. He's pigeonholing us, she thought. Flick, flick, flick, one by one we're dropping into his categories. It's not what he sees that worries me, but what he *doesn't* see.

When he looks at Richard, does he see the gentleness and sensitivity hiding within? I doubt it. Does he see Jane's uncompromising intellect as well as her sweet expression? Probably not. And what about Edward's humour? I don't suppose he'd guess a man with no legs would have such a wry, delicious store of laughter in him—or such a gift for teaching. Can he glimpse Mark Heskell's conceit? Or Chris Underhill's religious fervour? Or Lucy Grey-Jenner's sexuality? Or Dan's compassion? Or Frank Heath's dignity and immense store of knowledge? Or Pete Rocheleau's incredible ability to nurture a small sprout of ability into a vast tree of talent?

No. And why? Because he's a cop, that's why.

Cops only look, rarely see.

Why should this one be any different?

Stryker, alone at the head of the table, felt momentary weakness and exhaustion sweep over him. He glanced at Tos, and saw concern in his eyes. If he gave in now, he wouldn't get another case for months, and that was certain. He'd *have* to hang on, he'd have to take hold of this and shake it until it rattled and the answer dropped out. If he didn't make it now—

"All right," he said, turning away from the table and walking to the windows that overlooked the inner courtyard. Grantham Hall was L-shaped, and the two arms protected a garden area of trees, benches and flower beds between it and Science Hall, some six hundred yards away. "At some time between eleven and one last night, Aiken Adamson was killed in his own office here in this building. The body was discovered this morning by the security guard making his normal rounds. The office was apparently searched, but at this moment we have no way of knowing what, if anything, was looked for or taken. He—"

"How was he killed?" That was from Wayland.

"He was stabbed."

A rustle of movement went around the table, and several of them drew in a sharp breath of shock. Then Wayland spoke again, his voice ironic and thin. "In the back, presumably. How very apt."

Everyone at the table looked away, as if embarrassed.

"Stabbed?" Pinchman quavered, his face quite pale.

"To be precise, he was hit on the head, then stabbed several times in the chest with his own paper knife."

Stryker dropped the facts like pebbles into a pool, watching the ripples spread.

"Fingerprints?" This was from Kate Trevorne.

"On the knife? No. Lots of others around the office, of course. We'll need to take your fingerprints later, for purposes of elimination. Obviously we would expect to find your fingerprints in a colleague's office. It's the odd ones we're after."

"You left something out, Lieutenant," Stark said pointedly.

Stryker glared at him. He'd hoped to keep it back, but it was obvious if he didn't tell them, Stark would. "Sometime after death, Adamson's tongue was cut out," he said flatly.

"Oh, God." Lucy Grey-Jenner's hand went to her own mouth, and lingered there.

"Christ," Heskell said in a husky croak.

Stryker was watching them all, but the ripples hit no rocks. Their horror seemed genuine. He didn't know what he'd hoped for—a sudden accusation, a pathetic confession? That was in books. These people knew books—did they know life? "We haven't found the tongue yet," he added conversationally. "Could be anywhere."

"Who so keepeth his tongue keepeth his soul," Underhill murmured.

Arthur Fowler began to giggle, almost uncontrollably, his eyes widening in horror at what his mouth was doing. "Oh, God," he managed to say, and clapped his handkerchief over his mouth. "I'm sorry," he said after a moment. "Forgive me, it was just—" his voice wavered again, rebelliously.

Stryker took pity on him. "It's the shock, sir. It happens to a lot of people when they're told of sudden death."

"Oh. Oh, I see." Fowler wasn't certain if he wanted to be connected with "a lot of people," but he subsided.

"Was he robbed?" somebody asked. The voice had been soft, and Stryker thought it had come from Heath.

"We think his watch and a ring were moved—and perhaps his briefcase was taken."

"Then, it *was* robbery." That was Pinchman.

Stryker shook his head. "I don't buy it—although that's apparently what the killer wanted us to think. Adamson's wallet was still in an inner jacket pocket, and it had over two hundred dollars in it. There were also lots of small items left in the office that a thief would have taken because they're easy to sell. A transistor radio, a quartz alarm clock, brass bookends, a tape recorder, and so on."

"Perhaps the thief was interrupted," suggested Dr. Coulter.

"If he had time to mutilate his victim, I'd guess he had time to search him," Stryker said. "Now, you were all here last night at this meeting—" He stopped at their murmurs of protest.

"You don't suspect one of *us*, surely?" Mark Heskell's voice squeaked with indignation. "That's ludicrous."

"No, it's quite logical," said Kate, her voice slow and reflective. They all turned to look at her, Stryker with the most surprise of all. "Aiken had no family, Mark. *We* worked with him every day, *we* were with him last night. Except for muggings and robberies, people usually know their killers well. You have to *know* someone before you can hate them enough to..." Her voice trailed off as she became aware of their concentrated regard. She looked up, her eyes darting from one face to another. When her gaze met Stryker's she blushed, deeply and uncontrollably.

"Perhaps I should make it clear that I've asked you all to come here *not* for purposes of accusation, but elimination," Stryker said. "There's no need to get uptight about it. Now, first off, I'd like to know exactly when each of you left the building last night."

Immediate chaos.

They all started speaking at once—either to him, in protest, or to one another, seeking verifications. Nobody wanted to have been the last. Kate watched and listened to them in a kind of daze, then looked again at Stryker. He was watching them intently, and she could almost hear his mind clicking and ticking over. He *does* suspect one of us, she thought, in sudden horrified conviction. It's true, it's real. Look at him, he's like a dog at a rabbit hole, waiting to see who makes a mistake, who makes a run for it. Their eyes met again, and it was his turn to look away.

"People, people, *please*," he said, raising his voice. "Can't we just get it together without all this cra—without all this confusion? All I want is a simple timetable, is that so terrible? I've only got one pair of ears, you know."

"Could have fooled me," Richard Wayland said, glancing at Toscarelli, who was taking notes so quickly it could only have been in shorthand.

Stryker shrugged. "Okay, *two* pairs of ears. Big deal! Now—one at a time, please?" Even down the length of the table, Kate could feel the depth and quality of Stryker's basic emotion. It was neither an intellectual fancy for puzzle-solving, nor a noble dedication to duty, nor a hunter picking up the scent.

It was anger. The man was angry because someone was dead. But that's how it *should* be, she thought wonderingly.

It took a while, but eventually the pattern was established.

Pete Rocheleau had left first—at a quarter to seven.

Underhill had been next, at seven-ten.

"With a flea in your ear," Heskell said.

Underhill glared at his colleague. "Thanks a *lot*."

"Only trying to help," Heskell said lightly, gazing out of the window and ignoring Underhill's glower. Stryker glanced at Tos, who met his eye and nodded, his pencil racing over the page.

Jane Coulter had gone down in the lift at seven-forty, with Kate Trevorne and Richard Wayland. Heskell had just missed them and had taken the stairs, beating them to the bottom. Frank Heath and Lucy Grey-Jenner had been next, at around eight. They had gone down in the lift together.

Stark's secretary, Karen Lasterman, had left just after them, and Stark himself, along with Fowler, had left at eight-twenty.

And so it turned out that Edward Pinchman had been the last of the group to leave the building. At nine-thirty. And when he'd left, Adamson *had* still been in his office. "I went by his door and said goodnight. He was on the telephone, but he raised a hand to acknowledge me."

"Why did you stay so long after the others, sir?" Stryker asked.

"I always do all my work here. Aiken was the same. Never took any work home. Can't carry anything home with me because of my sticks, you see. Place was deserted when I left, except for Aiken. Even the boy had gone."

"Boy?" Stryker asked sharply.

"Boy on the switchboard," Pinchman said.

Stark explained. "I'd forgotten him. I'm sorry. But he went home *long* before we did last night, because there were no classes—"

"What boy?" Stryker asked evenly.

"During the term time we have a student on the switchboard until nine o'clock Mondays through Thursdays, and until seven on Fridays. We don't have any evening classes on Friday, so—"

"He was here last night?" Stryker interrupted.

"Only until six-thirty. Registration Week isn't exactly—"

"Name?"

Kate spoke up. "Longman. His name is Jody Longman. I have him in my murder class." When Stryker scowled at her, she lifted her chin. "I teach a course on the history and development of the crime novel."

"There you are," Richard Wayland said, stretching luxuriously. "No need to worry, Lieutenant, you have a resident expert right on hand. Just ask Kate—she'll solve it for you. No doubt the butler did it.''

"Shut up," Kate hissed through clenched teeth. She supposed he thought he was being funny. The worse things got, the more facetious Richard became. It was an old habit.

"I see." Stryker nodded, and he looked at Kate. "Of course, it's a well-known fact that the odds on the butler having done any given homicide are three thousand, six hundred and forty-two to four against, particularly on a Friday, as I'm certain Miss Trevorne will verify. Being an expert and all. How many of you have keys to this building?''

Silence. Then Stark spoke. "We all do. Why?"

"According to Campus Security, this building is locked up at eleven," Stryker said. "They make a round then, another at approximately three in the morning and another at six. The guard who made the eleven o'clock round claims there were no lights on in any of the offices, and he saw and heard nothing unusual. All of the offices up here were locked at eleven, including Adamson's.''

"So Aiken left his office before eleven?"

"Presumably. Did he mention his plans for the evening to any of you?" Stryker looked around the table. "No? Did he mention having an appointment or a date of any kind?" His eyes went to Heskell. "That amuses you, Mr. Heskell?"

"Aiken would hardly confide his social schedule to one of us," Heskell said uneasily. "We weren't on that kind of footing with him. We were only colleagues, you see. *Not* friends."

"Was it a generally known fact that Professor Aiken was gay?" Stryker asked. "Or was that his little secret?"

"Well, *really*," Pinchman huffed. "I hardly think that sort of thing should be discussed here—''

"Oh, we can take it if you can, Edward," Jane Coulter said. She smiled at Stryker. "It was generally *assumed*," she told him. "Nothing was ever said."

"It was none of our business," Fowler said prissily. "The man had a right to his privacy."

"Which is more than he granted anyone else," Heskell snapped.

"Why do you say that, Mr. Heskell?" Stryker asked.

"He was a Paul Pry, a Nosy Parker, he loved knowing things other people didn't," Heskell said defensively. He looked around the table at the others. "Well he *did*, didn't he? I don't see any point in being mealymouthed about it. The man was a menace."

"Did he menace you?" Underhill asked, leaning forward.

"No. No, of course not!" Heskell said testily. "You know what I mean. And don't try and read anything into it, either." Heskell's voice was becoming shrill as Underhill grinned maliciously at him.

"Obviously he frightened someone, didn't he?" It was Heath's soft, dark voice, somehow cutting across the others without being raised at all. "In a manner of speaking, that is. The man's dead, gentlemen. The man's *dead*."

There was an odd emphasis on the last word that made the statement seem something like a warning. Both Heskell and Underhill subsided abruptly. Fowler cleared his throat and addressed himself to Stryker, demanding his attention.

"You say the security guard made his rounds at three in the morning?"

"He was supposed to," Stryker said, irritated at Heath for distracting the others from what had promised to develop into a nice, revealing little argument. "Unfortunately, it began to snow about eleven-thirty. As Miss Trevorne will no doubt verify, burglars *never* work in the snow. Therefore, neither do Security Guards. Not this one, anyway."

"But he *did* come around at six?" Fowler pursued the details with the enthusiasm of a connoisseur.

"Oh, yes. At six he came around."

"And everything was locked up then, too?"

"Everything was locked then, too."

Fowler seemed confused. "Well—I mean to say—what made him look in Aiken's office? He must have had to unlock the door to get in. Were the lights on?"

"No, the lights were out."

Fowler looked around with a show of bewilderment. "Well, then—was he tipped off? Was there a noise? What made him investigate that particular office at six in the morning?"

"Why, the blood," Stryker said cheerfully. "The blood that was running out under the door. Wouldn't that make *you* curious, Dr. Fowler?"

SIX

THE SECURITY GUARD, coming out of the library, stopped when he saw the collection of police and official cars parked in front of Grantham Hall. He lit a cigarette, taking his time, and watched the men moving in and out. Passersby, on foot or in cars, slowed to look and wonder.

Well, now. What should he do?

Of course, his duty was clear. It had been clear the previous night. He hadn't fulfilled it then, and he was hesitating about fulfilling it now. During the course of the dawn he'd kept an eye on the events across the way, safe behind his blank windows, alone in the echoing hollow cubes of the Library. Reality had come in with his relief man, at eight-thirty.

They'd asked him why he hadn't said anything last night. Why hadn't he raised the alarm? There would be anger and accusation—maybe a lot of trouble.

Some students passed him, going into the Library, buzzing about what might or might not have brought the police to Grantham Hall. One was of the opinion that a faculty member had been busted for sniffing coke, the other was certain it was murder—he'd seen the emblem of the Medical Examiner's Department on one of the cars.

Well, the kid was right. Murder it certainly was.

The security guard began to walk slowly toward Grantham Hall, crunching across the uncleared snow of the Mall and going in by the side door. He went down the empty hall, his footsteps echoing off the green metal doors of the lockers. He passed the closed doors of empty classrooms and the study area behind the lifts without encountering anyone. But when he rounded the corner, there was Jackson in front of the lifts, and uniformed cops everywhere.

"Hey, what's going on?"

Jackson turned, cast a wry glance at the uniformed cops and lowered his voice. Murder was going on. Upstairs, in the English Department. Adamson, the one with the limp wrist. Hell of a thing. Had *he* seen anything last night, for Christ's sake?

The security guard took a long last drag of his cigarette, dropped it, ground it to tatters under his heel. "Naw. Nothing. You?"

"Nothing. Did my rounds—nothing." Jackson flushed. "Skipped my three o'clock, and didn't they haul my ass for that? Jee*sus*, it was snowing. You're all right over there. Me, I gotta go *out* to get here, right? It was *snowing*."

"They're cruds," the security guard said, not bothering to keep his voice particularly low. "I wouldn'ta gone out either."

"Well, then," Jackson said self-righteously. "I bet I get fired. You watch. You wait—they'll fire me."

"Talk to the union. That three o'clock round is whadya call it—discretionary? The timing is up to you, see? They can't do zip to you."

"No kidding?" Jackson was mollified.

"Talk to the union," the security guard said. "If they try anything, I mean. You know. Like firing you."

"Okay."

The security guard left Jackson guarding the lift and walked down the hall toward the door at the far end. It would be locked, like the other secondary door, but he had a key. They all had keys.

As he went, he listened to himself, trying to figure out what he was up to, inside. He'd done it now. Told Jackson he hadn't seen anything. If the cops asked him, he'd have to say the same thing, wouldn't he? Now, why had he done that?

He *had* seen something.

Godammit, he'd seen *everything*.

He should tell them, they could make use of it.

Unless, of course, *he* could make use of it first.

He paused, hand upraised with key hovering to unlock. He smiled. So *that's* what his subconscious had been up to.

The little devil.

SEVEN

STRYKER BEAMED at his little group.

"Now, what was this meeting all about?"

Jane Coulter stirred, releasing a waft of lilac and lavender perfume from somewhere beneath her rather worn and venerable mink coat. She shrugged it onto the seat behind her, and bent to retrieve a fur-backed mitten that fell from one pocket. She was annoyed. Since Dan was so obviously knocked over backward by all this (look at him, just *sitting* there!) and Arthur had begun to flutter, it was up to her as senior member of faculty (now that Aiken was out of the ranking) to take charge.

"One of our regular ritual gatherings, Lieutenant," she said, beaming back at him. "The brave, loyal band of soldiers rallying around their leader. We huddle together at irregular intervals in the face of the general animosity of the student body. It reassures us."

"We always have a meeting at the end of Registration Week to see if there are going to be any problems," Stark muttered.

"I see. And were there any?" Stryker asked.

"Nothing important."

"I think you'd better let me—" Stryker began.

"Be the judge of that?" Wayland finished for him. He hugged himself. "How classic of you."

Fowler made an impatient clucking noise. "Pay no attention to him, Lieutenant. Ever since making a nuisance of himself over Vietnam, Richard feels compelled to argue every point, deliver judgement on every utterance, and flout every authority. He feels keenly his position as resident dissident."

"Why, Arthur, a rhyme. How delightful! Resident dissident. I love it—quick, somebody write it down."

"Someone is writing it down, Wayland," Peter Rocheleau said with a warning glance in Toscarelli's direction. "Unless you're auditioning for Aiken's role, I'd cool it."

"Aiken's role?" Stryker asked quickly.

"Resident gadfly," Underhill explained. "A step up from resident dissident, perhaps ... but without benefit of rhyme."

"And far preferable to resident hack," Heskell put in.

My God, they were already becoming caricatures of themselves, and we've only been here ten minutes, Heskell thought. Their lives are bounded by this department, this university, this city. It was pathetic. None of them has any idea of what life is really about. Well, he amended, maybe Kate does. What a couple they'd make! But she preferred Wayland. Wayland *looked* wonderful, of course. He envied him that long, lean body and that negligent charm. Having to watch your weight and all the rest of it was so *wearing*, but where he was headed, appearance was important. One day he'd be president of this university, and then he'd be ready to step onto the larger stage. Academics went into government all the time. And the *money*—

"At least I *can* hack it," Underhill snapped. "I hear you can't, any more. True?"

"Now, now, children," Stark said. "Play nicely."

Stryker's expression was baleful. "If only out of consideration for the dyslexic constabulary. Could someone define 'gadfly' for me—in this context?"

Pete Rocheleau smiled and obliged.

"You're beginning to sound like one of us, Lieutenant. Watch yourself. Aiken was a wasp, a stinger. He loved making pointed remarks, sarcasm being his strong suit. He felt it his mission in life to keep us all alert. Make a wrong attribution in a lecture or make a misquote in an article and he was on you instantly—preferably where the audience was large. He liked to hurt. He *claimed* it was all in the line of maintaining literary and academic standards. It wasn't . . ."

"He wasn't above a personal attack, now and again, just to keep his hand in," Frank Heath murmured. "Or perhaps one should keep to the image and say proboscis."

"Was he a good teacher?" Stryker wanted to know. He'd never had Adamson when he'd attended Grantham. If his recollection was correct, Adamson had been the kind of man who *swept* down a hall, rather than walked, usually trailing a small convoy of students in his wake.

"Yes," Stark volunteered. "Very good."

Heskell stirred again. "He required the adulation of the young. He bought it by siding with them, hating the things they hated. Playing up to them was his biggest weakness—and his marking was easy. They're quick to spot that."

"He had the ability to impart knowledge painlessly," Jane Coulter said. "That is a gift not given to all."

"Ah, a defending voice," Stryker said. "I was beginning to despair."

"I wasn't defending him, merely pointing out a fact," Dr. Coulter said imperturbably. Stryker looked at her. With her tight grey curls and apple cheeks she could have been someone's granny. As he watched, she took a small black cigar from her handbag and leaned forward as Rocheleau lit it for her. Well, he amended, maybe not *everyone's* granny.

"You'll gather that Aiken was not one's *favourite* colleague," Heskell said.

"Wow!" Stryker said in a disgruntled voice. "I can't *wait* to see if you people hold a funeral or a jubilee. If I catch this killer, I suppose you'll all chip in to pay for his defense, is that it? Or crown him with myrtle?"

"Only if Myrtle doesn't mind," Wayland said laconically.

"Please forgive my family, Lieutenant," Stark said, looking around reprehensively. "It must be the shock."

"Or it might just be the truth," Rocheleau said. "You were always too ready to forgive Aiken his trespasses on other people's corns, Dan. The man was a son-of-a-bitch to work with and you know it. We might be academically weaker for his loss, but by God we'll be happier." Ah, friends, lose not your cool, he thought. Let us be dignified, for God's sake, and help this intruder to do his distasteful duty quickly and neatly, and then get the hell out of here. More to the point, let's help him get rid of Aiken once and for all. He destroyed so much while he was here, let not his evil live after him.

"Amen," Edward Pinchman murmured, as if he'd read Pete's thoughts.

"I think we should be flattered that the lieutenant thinks any of us capable of murder," Wayland drawled. "I've never thought any of us had enough nerve to kick a cat, much less slaughter a fellow human being. *If* you could stretch that description to fit Aiken. We're all such *sensitive* souls."

"Rubbish," Kate said briskly. "Anyone is capable of murder, under the right circumstances."

Richard regarded her with glee. "Even you?"

"Even me."

"Especially you," Underhill pointed out, but without malice. "Look at the shelves in your office—three hundred and sixty-five ways to kill without being caught, all at your fingertips."

Kate smiled sweetly. "And at everyone else's. People are *always* borrowing my books."

"If you're talking about crime novels, I might point out to you that they only deal with failures at the art of murder, not successes. At the end, whatever means used, the killer *always* gets caught. That's where they differ from real life," Stryker said.

"Is that supposed to give us hope, Lieutenant?" Heskell said archly.

"Does it give *you* hope, Mr. Heskell?" Stryker asked.

"One always has hope," Heskell said majestically.

"My God, Aiken would have loved this," Lucy Grey-Jenner said suddenly. "It's almost a shame he isn't here to join in."

"Considering his tongueless state, he wouldn't have much to say," Wayland pointed out.

"Why aren't you questioning Aiken's family? His friends?" Fowler asked petulantly. "Why *us*, first of all?"

"Aiken's friends will be taking to the hills," Heath said.

"Without even stopping to put on their eyelashes," Wayland added, inspecting a thumbnail and ignoring a jab from Kate. "Doesn't postmortem mutilation usually have a sexual connotation?"

"Even more likely, a ritual connotation," Jane Coulter said, leaning forward. "You have only to consult Fraser or—"

"Dear me," Pinchman murmured. "Back to that again."

"We can't ignore it," Dr. Coulter said firmly. "We know Aiken had...different...sexual preferences. That world is a murky one, full of psychotic and obsessive behaviour."

"Almost like the homelife of your own dear department," Underhill said.

She fixed him with a cold eye. "You *are* a silly young man," she said. "And I'd forgive you nothing, were it not for two of your poems."

"I think we should get a back—" Stryker began.

"Which two?" Underhill asked, leaning forward with the first sign of real interest he'd shown since entering the room. Jane Coulter just stared at him, then turned away. Underhill sank back, his lower lip stuck out like a sulky child's.

Their feet run to evil and they make haste to shed innocent blood, he thought. They do but flatter with their lips, and dissemble in their double hearts. They don't care who killed the old bastard, as long as nothing touches them. I hated him, last night. I must erase that hate from my soul now that he's dead, but I cannot. At a stroke of his tongue he hath broken my bones. Perhaps there is such a thing as retribution, after all. But I wish he'd *felt* that knife in his mouth. I wish he'd *known*. God forgive me. His hands ached as he clenched them beneath the table, invisible punishment for this invisible evil. See, he thought, see how I am shamed.

"This meeting," Stryker was continuing, doggedly. "Can anyone tell me what happened at this meeting?"

"My secretary is transcribing her notes at the moment," Stark said. Sure enough, beyond the door, they could hear the steady rhythmic tap of a typewriter. "It was really rather a dull meeting."

"Except for the argument," Heskell said eagerly. "That wasn't dull."

"Hardly an argument, merely a difference of opinion about the use of the photocopier," Stark said wearily.

"Underhill threatened to punch Aiken," Heskell said with some triumph. He'd obviously been waiting for an opportunity to announce this.

"I didn't threaten to punch him," Underhill said rather loudly. "I only said I wished he'd pick on someone his own size so *they* could punch him."

"We're giving the lieutenant a very unbalanced view of the affair," said Frank Heath in his soft but penetrating voice. As he hadn't spoken much up to now, his entry into the conversation had something of a stopping quality. As it had before, Stryker remembered. He took another look at the big Negro. A handsome man, broad in the chest and shoulders, sitting with easy grace. An ex-athlete? "Most of us spend most of our time being quite ordinary people, Lieutenant, aside from our pretensions to scholarship."

"Some of us *have* scholarship," Fowler snapped.

"And some have scholarship thrust upon them," Wayland murmured.

"The point is," Heath went on calmly, "that after the business portion of the meeting, we behaved like perfectly normal, respectable citizens. We ate our sandwiches, we drank our sherry, and we talked about things like Christmas, children, dogs and cats, mortgages . . . and the price of hamburgers."

"Did any of you speak specifically to Professor Adamson?" Stryker asked.

"Of course. We all did," Stark said impatiently. "It was very casual, very friendly. We moved around. It was *supposed* to be friendly."

"Can any of you remember what Adamson said? I'm looking for a lead here. Did he mention what he planned to do after the meeting?" He looked around, but they all shook their heads. "Did he mention any names?" Again the heads shook in negation. "How about what he'd done during his vacation?"

"You make it sound like an assignment," Wayland commented. "What I Did on My Vacation, by—"

"He went to Greece," Kate said.

"Oh?"

Kate sat up impatiently and looked around at the others. "Look," she said. "He's going to keep us sitting here until he gets what he wants. Aren't you?" she asked Stryker.

"Oh, I are. Indeed I are," he agreed cheerfully.

"Well, then—let's get the thing over with. Frankly, I've got better things to do with my last Saturday before term begins than sitting around here showing off to the police."

"Ah, me," Stryker said. "Pearls before swine, of course."

She flashed him an irritated glance. Behind that smiling face, he was sitting and watching them, willing them to say the wrong thing. Didn't they *see* that? He'd *already* seen far too much in her opinion. They had to stick to facts, nothing else.

"After Dan poured the drinks, I was talking to you, Edward, and Frank. Isn't that right?"

"I believe so, my dear," Pinchman agreed amiably. There was warmth in his voice and Stryker could see he was fond of the girl. They all seemed to be—as if she were the awkward duckling they knew would become a swan one day. He could also see the old man looked tired, and was probably in pain from his amputated legs and the cold weather and the shock and strain. Stryker remembered that same tight numbness in his grandmother's face when her arthritis was very bad.

"That's right," Heath said in his gentle voice. "We were talking about vacations in general. Jane had been to France, I'd been to Italy, and Aiken came up and said he'd been prowling in Greece."

"Prowling?" Stryker asked.

Kate's eyes met Stryker's, but she looked past him to the previous night. Aiken had looked, as always, like the aging tenor in a touring light-opera company-dressed impeccably, his hair combed carefully over the small bald spot, his hands gesticulating gracefully, always assuming the spotlight was on him. He'd circled like a lynx around a flight of broken birds, attacking first one, then another. She had only been the first.

"He said he'd been prowling around Greece—he called it looking for Toys in the Attic! He said he'd visited Athens, Delphi, Thermopylae and so on. Frank asked if he'd had much sun and he made one of his usual cryptic remarks. Something like 'not much sun, but I saw the light near Delphi and solved the riddle of a Grecian sphinx'—whatever that meant."

"Didn't you ask what it meant?"

"Of course not—he *wanted* us to ask. It was a trap, as usual, and I was damned if I was going to be sophomoric enough to fall into it so he could deliver the punch line. I said something about nobody ever mistaking *him* for a sphinx and he turned on me. Toward me, I mean." She paused. "No—*on* me. Aiken had this theatrical quality of stillness. It was rather like guns swinging around to bear on me."

"And did he fire?"

"No."

"Blank cartridge?"

"Diversionary action," Pete Rocheleau said. "I backed into her and spilled the sherry."

"The Task of Amontillado—protecting the innocent," Richard said. "Nicely done, Pete."

"Yes," Kate agreed. "By the time we'd finished mopping it up, Aiken had moved on to his next . . . target."

"And who was that?" Stryker looked around.

"I think it was myself," Stark said.

"No, it was I," Jane Coulter said. "I was telling Arthur about an obscure biblical reference I'd tracked down—"

"I was there, too," Wayland put in.

"And what did Adamson say?"

Wayland sat up suddenly. "He said, 'Which of you is going to kill me?' So we all drew lots, and guess who—"

"He said nothing in particular," Jane Coulter said. "He simply listened for a moment, then said something about greener pastures, and moved on."

"And what would he have meant by that?"

"I haven't the vaguest idea," Jane said.

"You have to know what he was like," Kate said desperately.

"Which is exactly what I'm trying to find out," Stryker agreed. "Tell me."

She tried. "There we all were, trying to be pleasant, because we *like* one another, you know... and Aiken kept drifting around trying to turn it into the last act of *Hamlet*. He kept stabbing around, looking for..." She paused to consider. "It was as if he was looking for a fight. As if he had some secret he was bursting to tell, but nobody was asking him the right questions." She looked around. "I guess that sounds kind of melodramatic... but it's the best I can do. Sorry."

"That's fine," Stryker said. "Thank you. Anyone else?"

"I've been thinking," Wayland said slowly.

"Well, for goodness' sake," Heskell said. "How does it *feel* after all these years?"

"Fine," Wayland said absently. He looked down the table at Stryker, who was surprised to see the belligerence gone from his eyes. His statement was correct—he *had* been thinking. "It must have been some addict," Wayland said earnestly. "After all, the campus is surrounded by some of the worst slums in the city, right? And while I'm all for supporting the economically underprivileged, there's no doubt it's a cesspit out there. Particularly as far as drugs are concerned. I've been working on the local drug-abuse programme and I *know*, believe me. It's coming from the slums into the campus. There are a lot worse pressures than money—and if one of Aiken's students had a drug problem, well—they're at an emotional time of life, usually rebelling against authority. Perhaps one of them—maybe after taking some hallucinogenic—went for Aiken as a symbol. Maybe he wants to cut *all* our tongues out."

"My God, you can't be serious!" Fowler said, going white.

Wayland shrugged. "There are plenty of them around, believe me. I work with them, and they scare the hell out of *me* sometimes. They're not like *we* used to be. They shoot presidents—why not professors?"

"Aiken wasn't shot," Fowler said pedantically.

"I get the point, Mr. Wayland," Stryker said. "But just as one swallow doesn't make a summer..."

"One murder doesn't make a psycho," Kate said quietly. "But he *does* have a point, doesn't he?"

"He does," Stryker agreed.

"And while you're here wasting time talking about a stupid meeting, he could be *out* there..." Heskell said somewhat hysterically. "Planning another murder. One of us."

Stryker turned to his sergeant. "Tos, how many men will we have working on this killing?"

Toscarelli considered. "Yourself and I..." Some of the professors flinched visibly. "Plus Pinsky and Neilson, full time. Maybe a few more part time if you need them. Then the uniformed division, of course, as many as we can get, and the forensic people, and the people in Records..."

"As many as a hundred, would you say?"

"Oh, easy. Sure."

"And what will they be doing?"

Toscarelli tilted his head on one side and pursed up his mouth. "Forensic, they'll be doing the postmortem and all that stuff, fingerprints if any, examining the fluff and stuff found at the scene. The other detectives will be checking out Adamson's friends and family, all his students last year, and things like that. Then they'll fill in his movements over the past week, month, year..." He paused. "You want me to go on?"

"No, that's enough." Stryker looked down the table. "We have a lot of killings in the city. Like in most cities. I'm sorry to say that some of them receive less attention than others. But when a respectable citizen gets killed in inexplicable circumstances, I can assure you the investigation is massive. Once the papers get hold of this—"

"Oh, my God," Fowler gasped. "The newspapers, television... I'd forgotten all about that. Dan... the *publicity*."

"I know," Stark said. His face was grim. "I've already talked to the dean about it."

"Pictures in the paper, *names*..." Fowler went on.

"Indeed," Stark said drily. "Did you really think it was going to be a private funeral, Arthur?"

"I...didn't..." Fowler sank back, gaping.

"Quite," Jane Coulter said. "Quite."

"That's why I thought you all would prefer to talk to me first," Stryker continued. "I didn't want you to have to face—"

"Aiken's dead," Kate suddenly announced in a stricken voice. "Aiken was *murdered*."

"Indeed he was," Stryker agreed gently. While talking to the others, he'd been keeping an eye on her. Watching the change take place, watching the truth sink in. As it was slowly sinking in for the rest of them. First the annoyance at being dragged down here, the resentment at being suspected, the defensiveness most people felt at being questioned—it had all been going on under the conversation. It was what he had wanted to see, the reason he'd wanted them all together like this—he wanted to know who they were, and know how they were with one another. He'd learned a lot. He had a lot still to learn.

Kate looked at the others, at her own hands, looked again at Stryker. "It's *terrible*. He was stabbed, mutilated."

"Yes." His voice was even.

"*We're* terrible," she went on. "Sitting here bickering and bitching at one another, being obstructive and smart-ass and...in this room, here . . . all of us . . . is it always like this? Are people *always* like this?" she demanded, appalled.

Stryker smiled. It was a gentle, forgiving, kindly smile.

"Only those with something to hide," he said.

EIGHT

TOSCARELLI LOOKED down his list.

"So start," directed Stryker, leaning back in the chair and rubbing his eyes, then his ear, then his elbow, and finally his knees.

Toscarelli settled back. "So Underhill went home to his wife and kids, said his prayers and went to bed, right?"

"Right."

"Rocheleau went home, to an anniversary party, where everybody could see him all night, especially his mother-in-law, who will hate having to admit to it, wanting nothing more of her life than to land some crap on him." Toscarelli looked up, but Stryker's eyes were closed, so he went on. "Dr. Coulter went next, along with Trevorne and Wayland. She went on to *another* meeting—she must be a glutton for punishment—at the Dupont Hotel. It's only a couple of blocks away, so she walked, stayed until eleven-thirty, had them call her a taxi..."

"Jane Coulter, you are a taxi," murmured Stryker.

"...which took her to the faculty parking lot. He waited until she was safe in her car, which she asked him to do, and then followed her out on Gratiot for about a mile, which she didn't ask him to do but it was on his way home. Trevorne and Wayland went on to dinner, then back to her place afterward." Again he looked at Stryker, but apart from a scowl that drew his regular features into an ill-tempered knot, he hadn't moved. "Heskell went next, met his fiancée downtown, had dinner, went to a late movie, then back to his place. I bet she's ugly and rich."

"Or ugly with influential contacts," Stryker muttered. Neither of them had taken much to Heskell.

"Heath and Grey-Jenner went out together, then parted. She went home to her lonely bed, and..."

"Beautiful woman, for her age," Stryker observed. "Beautiful and sad."

"So?"

Stryker shrugged. "Just noticed, that's all."

"Glad to hear you're still alive in there," Toscarelli growled. He turned over a page. "Heath went home to see his invalid mother, but then went out jogging, alone. Left about ten, he says, didn't look at the clock when he came in. You buy that?"

Stryker shrugged again. "Ex-athlete, bound to want to keep in shape."

"Maybe he used it as an excuse to visit someone."

"Such as Adamson?"

"I had more in mind something female," Toscarelli said. "He didn't strike me as a locker-room-lover type."

"Didn't strike *me* as the living-with-mummy type either," Stryker countered. "I think we should look into Mr. Heath a little more."

"Oh, great," Toscarelli said. "They'll say we're picking on him because he's black."

Stryker smiled to himself. "I think we should look into them *all* a little more. Go on."

"Right. Let's see. Stark and Fowler next . . . no, Stark's secretary, Karen Lasterman, next. Another one living with mummy—but engaged, she says. Saving up for a house. I didn't know people did that any more."

"Some people do."

"Anyway, Stark and Fowler, they left together and went downtown like they do every Friday, to Stark's club, for a game of handball and a steak, but Fowler develops a headache, so they come back early and go home to their wives about eleven."

"You make it sound as if they keep a harem."

"They go home to a wife, one each, I meant. This place is getting to you."

"Yeah. That's all?"

"And Pinchman last. He worked on at his desk until he felt cold, and then left about nine-thirty, he says. He also says Adamson was still in *his* office, on the telephone, and that's that."

"Friendly bunch, aren't they?" Stryker said.

"What do you mean?"

"Heath and Grey-Jenner have a drink together, Stark and Fowler play handball together, Wayland and Trevorne sleep together . . ."

"You didn't like that much, did you?"

"Shocking breach of morals," Stryker said, sitting up. "She's the last?"

"You know damn well she is," Toscarelli said. "You made sure she would be. Now, why did you do that? I ask myself."

"Ask yourself, not me," Stryker said. "I'm busy. Wheel her in, please, and while you're out there you might as well get Pinsky to organise getting all these alibis checked out. It has to be done." He stared at the door as it closed behind Toscarelli. "It all *has* to be done," he muttered to himself, and stared down at his tight, white knuckles as they interlocked, and clenched.

CHRIS UNDERHILL emerged from Grantham hall, dodged the crowd standing by the entrance, and turned into the wind. He wished it could blow through his brain the way it was blowing through the leafless trees. "For I have sown the wind, so I shall reap the whirlwind." He trudged on until he slipped on some ice and had to grab the edge of a splintered wooden fence to stay upright. He looked around and found he had wandered into Junktown. The empty eyes of condemned buildings looked back blankly over the vacant lots where snow barely covered the litter. Against a lamppost on the farther corner, a black in a leather jacket lounged, smoked, and watched him with an air of assessment. Down the road, an old woman shuffled along the narrow ice-free path in the centre of the broken pavement, her arms stretched down by heavy shopping bags. A dog barked in the distance, a thin sharp snap of sound. Underhill shivered. He'd come too far, didn't know where he was. He looked back, and above the rickety houses saw the clean white curve of the Science Building, oddly flat against the grey sky. Aware of the black watching him, he started back, the unpredictable wind thrusting at his shoulders and spine. He managed a wry smile. "Woe to him that is alone when he falleth," he whispered to himself.

"FRANK."

The big Negro turned at the whisper, and after glancing back up the hall, went into the office opposite his own and closed the door.

"My God...this is terrible," Lucy Grey-Jenner's eyes were wide and her mouth trembled. "What did you *say*?"

Heath leaned against the door, his hands behind him. "I said that we went down in the elevator together, walked to the parking lot together and then went our separate ways. What did *you* say?"

"The same. Oh, thank God . . . the same."

"Well, it was obvious." His massive calm reassured her.

"You don't think . . . I mean . . . will they question it?"

"Why should they?"

Lucy went to the window and looked down at the Mall, all white with snow. A few students in bright winter coats crisscrossed it, drawn to the university even between terms. It was the centre of their lives, with or without lessons. They shouted and waved at one another, meeting and pausing in small knots. Many of them looked up at Grantham Hall, pointing to the English Department. Lucy knew she couldn't be seen, but she automatically stepped back from the window.

"What if one of the others overheard you talking to Aiken last night?" she asked in a tense, low voice. "What if one of them heard you threaten to tell her?"

"I wouldn't mind that," Heath said. "What worried me is whether any of them heard *me* say I'd wring his goddamn neck if he did."

THE REPORTERS, disgruntled by a brief and uninformative statement made by Stark, lay in wait for the next member of the Grantham University English faculty to step from the elevator. It was Mark Heskell.

He glanced around at the men with their notebooks, smiled, and blinked repeatedly as the flashbulbs went off in his face. "I'm sorry, I have nothing to say . . ."

They clamoured and pleaded, and he hesitated.

"Well, of course, it's a terrible thing . . . for him to have been stabbed and mutilated in that way. Society has a lot to answer for when—I beg your pardon? No, really, I can't tell you any more . . . Please let me through. Surely the police will have released the details through the usual channels?" He looked around at the reporters. Reporters who would still be around when this was over, who might move up to be editors one day. He took a breath and conveyed the impression of reluctant kindness. "My name is Heskell. No, I have no idea who might have done this, except that it must have been a fiend of some kind. Who else could cut out a man's tongue, except some psychotic madman? It's frightening to think that he's at large at this very minute, perhaps watching another one of us. I shall *certainly* demand police protection."

When Heskell had finally walked away, the reporters looked at one another and grinned. January was a slow news time, a flat time. What better than this, a loony killer who cuts people's tongues out? Last man to a telephone booth is a loser . . .

NINE

KATE HADN'T BEEN in Dan's office more than three or four times in the past year, and she'd forgotten how small it was. Smaller, even, than her own—but so luxuriously furnished that the lack of size seemed somehow prestigious. It was in the inner core of the building, connected directly to the conference room and the large departmental office. Tucked away, it had always seemed a retreat, a private sanctum, protected from the traffic of the halls.

Invaded now, by Stryker, the room had become lopsided. Although seated behind the desk, he was somehow the room's centre. He needed a shave and the lines of his face were blurred by tiredness, she thought. Still the blue eyes sparkled, and he seemed in imminent danger of exploding in all directions at once. She seated herself gingerly on the edge of the leather chair that faced the desk, ready to run if he broke free.

She smiled at him, but he didn't smile back.

Oh, well.

The door beside her opened and Sergeant Toscarelli came in. He settled himself beside the desk and produced the notebook he'd used before. For such a big man he had an amazing ability to gradually disappear into his own stillness.

"Tell me about last night," Stryker suggested, not even glancing at Toscarelli, his eyes only for her.

"About the meeting, you mean?"

"No, after the meeting."

"Richard and I went out for dinner. We went downtown at Chow's. Afterward we walked around a bit and then—"

"It was cold last night."

"Yes, it was."

"Weren't you cold, 'walking around'?"

"Not at first. Richard wanted to clear his head before driving."

"Oh, very commendable." Stryker's voice was sarcastic. "And then? When his head was clear?"

"Then . . . we went back to my place, for coffee."

"Your place, not his."

"Richard lives at the Delta Theta house—it's not very private."

"Isn't he a little *old* to be a fraternity man?"

"He was a Delta Theta when he attended Grantham. Now he's their resident faculty adviser. He likes living there—it keeps him in touch with what the kids are thinking. He does a *lot* of work with students, outside class. The attic of the house has been converted to an apartment. It's close to campus and easy for him. He doesn't like possessions or fuss." She heard herself babbling, and forced her mouth shut. She wished he'd look away from her once in a while.

"He apparently likes *some* possessions."

She frowned. "I don't understand."

"Neither do I, yet." He looked away, finally, but only for a moment. "I *do* understand you used to be engaged to Wayland."

"Oh, well . . . yes. Years ago. College romance."

"What happened?"

She sighed and gave a careless shrug. "We grew up. I don't see it has anything to do with this."

"Bear with me," Stryker said. "Do you often go out with Wayland now? As you did last night?"

"From time to time. We're still good friends, we have a lot in common."

"Old friends? Or *more* than old friends?"

"Old friends, that's all." Through the window beyond Stryker's head she could see the tops of the trees in the inner courtyard. They moved fitfully, silently, their branches crossing and recrossing. The grey sky was reflected in the curved windows of the Science Building. The small office was warm, and she felt momentarily stifled. "Nothing more."

"But you shared sentimental memories."

"Yes, of course we do."

Stryker reached into his jacket pocket and brought out a pair of spectacles. He clapped them on his nose, peered down at his notes, then looked up at her over the rims. "In fact, according to Mr. Wayland, yesterday was by way of being an anniversary for you. Is that true?"

"Anniversary?" Kate was puzzled. What on earth had Richard said? They'd been watched in the conference room, there had been no opportunity to talk privately. But just before coming in to make his statement, he'd leaned over, kissed her on the forehead, and said something about having to tell the whole truth. And he'd called her darling, something he hadn't done in years. He'd said it rather loudly, too, as if for the benefit of the blank-faced police-man by the window.

"That's what he said." Stryker was obviously waiting for an explanation or comment of some kind, and she had the feeling he knew she was floundering.

"Oh, well, that was probably his joke. We have all kinds of anniversaries—he makes them up when he feels like it. The First Time We Ate Asparagus Together. The First Time We Went to a Concert Together. The First Time We Climbed a Tree Together. It's just a silly thing." She smiled to herself. "Richard is—"

"How about the first time you ever screwed together?" Stryker asked with every appearance of lively interest. "You celebrate that, do you?"

"*What?*" She felt as if he'd slapped her.

"You heard me." He gave a mocking leer. "Wayland says you did, last night."

"Does he?" she stalled.

"He says you spent the night doing that. Did you?"

She felt her face getting hot, and hated her treacherous complexion. "He stayed very late," she said, her mind racing. How late had he *said* he'd stayed? What time should she say? "Very late."

"You slept together?" Stryker kept his eyes down now, his hands propping his head as if it were too heavy for him. "You were in bed together all night?"

"We were together," she said, and realized she was twisting her watchband around her wrist, an old, bad habit. She tucked her hands beside her. "What we did or didn't do is hardly relevant or any of your damn business." What was it about Stryker? she kept asking herself. Why couldn't she keep it light and natural with him? From the first moment she'd seen him, some memory had nagged her, something about his harsh-edged voice, his way of moving, of speaking. She was already making a poor job of this interview because of the way he made her feel—wary, defensive, *angry*. What *was* it? "But if it gives you a cheap thrill, good luck to you, Lieutenant."

"Sorry if I disappoint you, Miss Trevorne." He looked up, challenging her. A break in the clouds let a thin shaft of sunlight into the room, momentarily turning the big lenses of his glasses into a blank mask, and Kate's heart fell like a stone through fifteen years of dismay. She stared at his face, the blankness of the glasses, the shadow of his hand across his forehead, and she remembered.

Oh, God, the smug, smiling, laughing bastard—she remembered him now. She *remembered*.

He was still talking. "I get the impression that you don't think much of the police. Or am I wrong?"

"No, you're not wrong." Her throat was so tight she was surprised to hear sound coming from it.

"Oh?" The sun blinked out and his eyes were visible again, surrounded by the glasses. Bright sparkling blue, dangerous. "Anything you'd care to tell us about?" He added a friendly, dangerous smile.

"No."

"Unpaid parking tickets? Come on, 'fess up, Miss Trevorne."

This archness was worse than his menace. "Don't be silly." (Did *he* remember? Oh, Lord—did he?) "Nothing like that."

Stryker, apparently, was feeling impish. He leaned forward, grinning. "Bathtub gin."

"No."

"Daddy on the Ten Most Wanted list?"

"Oh, for goodness' sake, no. (Was he doing this *because* he remembered? Was it going to be as bad as that?)

"Let me see—you tried to join the force but your feet were too small?"

"No."

"Too big?"

"No!"

"Did Richard Wayland screw you last night?"

"No!" She heard it too late. "Yes." She'd been looking down, everywhere, anywhere. Now she looked at him. He wasn't laughing. He wasn't smiling. And he wasn't amused. He was waiting.

"We were together until very, very late."

"What time did he leave?"

"I didn't notice the clock." She took a deep breath. "There's no clock in my bedroom." That was true enough.

"Then, how do you know it was very, very late?" He looked at her hands, busy again at her wrist. "Did you look at your watch?"

"I . . . I'd taken it off."

"I see."

"It was very late." She'd have to pick a time.

"Tell me about Aiken Adamson."

Wrong-footed, she glared at him. Did he want her to name a time or not? Did he believe her or not? "*He* wasn't with us."

He smiled and leaned back in his chair, removing the glasses. "That's right—he was here, having his tongue cut out. There was just you and Mr. Wayland, alone together, in a room with no clocks. Time, as it were, stood still. Romance. Birds singing. Orchestras playing. Were there any birds singing, Miss Trevorne?"

"What?" She stared at him. Was he mad?

"When Mr. Wayland left you—were any birds singing?"

"No. What on earth—"

"What time was dawn this morning, Sergeant Toscarelli?"

Toscarelli shifted in his chair, considering this question. A gust of wind touched the window, the blank branches beyond twisting and cringing. Somewhere, far away, a door banged. "About seven, I guess."

"Which means the little birds started up around six-thirty. So Mr. Wayland left *before* six-thirty. Well, well, we're getting somewhere at last. Did you see him to the door?"

"No."

Stryker looked *terribly* disappointed. "What a shame. Still, it *was* before six-thirty. Unfortunately, we just don't know how *much* before six-thirty it was."

"Didn't *he* say what time he left?"

"Alas, no." Stryker's face was a parody of regret. "*He* didn't look at his watch either. My, that must have been a truly wonderful evening." He smiled, blinked and sighed. "Why did you hate Aiken Adamson?"

She leaned back in her chair and made herself relax. "You're very good at that, aren't you?"

"At what?"

"The fancy foot-work, the quick change of angle, the Shark at the Top of the Stairs." She could smile too. "Unfortunately it becomes a little repetitious. One is . . . ready."

"Ah." The parody of regret changed to one of deep chagrin. "Make a note of that, Sergeant Toscarelli. One is becoming predictable. One is no longer impressive. One is *well* on the way to becoming a bore. Did your boyfriends kill Adamson, Miss Trevorne? Did you?"

"Maybe we did it together."

"As you seem to do so many things! Work. Sleep. Lie."

"I haven't lied."

"You haven't told the truth, either. You and Mr. Wayland have both made very heavy work out of what should have been nothing at all. Now, why is that, I ask myself? Why are you making such a *fuss*? Why didn't you just say you had dinner, came home, made love, parted? Why be coy about it? It's no big deal. Everybody's doin' it, doin' it, doin' it.''

"But not everybody *talks* about it, Lieutenant Stryker."

"Ooops—there go my big flat feet all over her delicate sensibilities. What a *clod* I am!"

Kate was totally nonplussed by Stryker's behaviour. He was crazy. He wasn't like any of the policemen in books, or on television or in the movies. In the conference room he'd seemed normal, but here—he looked crazy, he acted crazy, he *was* crazy.

"You *do* remember, don't you?" she finally asked.

"Remember what?" His eyes flickered momentarily.

"Me."

"Should I? Have we met before?" His eyes were steady now.

"Not really. It doesn't matter. Is that all you want to ask me? Is there anything else?"

"Oh, *scads*." He swivelled Dan's chair to face the window, only the top of his head visible.

"You went to school here, with Wayland?"

"That's right."

"Were you ever a student of Adamson's?"

(Could it be he didn't remember? That was almost worse.) "Yes—I had several classes with him as an undergraduate."

"Get good marks from him?"

"Straight A's."

"My goodness. And to a *girl*, too. I bet that hurt him."

"Aiken wasn't like that."

"Did Wayland have classes with him?"

Careful, Kate, she told herself. "Yes. Greek mythology. We both had it. That's where we met."

"Ah. So no doubt you celebrate *that* every year too, along with the rest of the things like Spinach, and Mozart, and Roller Skating?"

"And Screwing. Don't forget Screwing," she said sweetly. "Oh, yes, we celebrate that. Fireworks and everything."

Stryker whirled his chair around and brought his hands down hard on Dan's desk, making her jump. "Time!" he shouted at the top of his voice. He turned to Toscarelli. "What do you make the score?"

Toscarelli didn't bat an eye. "About even."

Stryker nodded. "Me, too." He turned back to her. "Thank you, Miss Trevorne. We'll have a statement typed up for you to sign on Monday." He waved. "Byeeeee."

"That's all?" But she was talking to the back of Dan's chair again. Uncertain, she looked at Toscarelli, stood up, hesitated, then went out. She closed the door very, very carefully, lest she break something fragile within.

After a moment, Stryker spoke. "Did I scare her?"

"I don't know," Tos admitted, putting down his notebook. "You sure as hell scared me."

Stryker looked at him out of the corner of his eye. "Thought I was cracking up, hey?"

"Maybe." Tos was being cautious.

"I made a mess of it," Stryker admitted to the trees beyond the glass. "I should have let you do it."

"Maybe." Toscarelli didn't want to hear this. He started writing in his notebook again.

Stryker's voice was harsh in self-condemnation. He turned the swivel chair back, put his elbows on the desk and his face into the small darkness of his palms. "She's lying, Tos. And Wayland is lying. Maybe some of the others, too. But they don't seem to be lying about anything that *matters*. I was wrong—I thought I would understand them, but I don't. They're not reacting like other people. They're all so ready to tell me how they hated Adamson's guts, how they'll dance on his goddamned grave. As far as I can tell, *everybody* dunnit."

"This isn't the Orient Express," Tos muttered.

"So Miss Trevorne would probably say."

Tos looked at him. "What was that about remembering her?"

"I haven't the faintest idea."

"Okay." Toscarelli's voice was distant.

The murder was only hours old, but Tos knew the signs. Stryker would get wound tighter and tighter into the case until it was all he breathed or slept or ate. And it would eat at *him*, in return. Before he'd been ill, he'd had the stamina to stand up to his own method. Now . . . Tos wasn't so sure.

Stryker ran his fingers through his curly hair, rubbed his face, pulled his ear. "Jesus," he muttered to himself.

It was a prayer.

TEN

KATE HURRIED toward her office, the sound of her steps echoing back from the walls of the narrow corridor. As she approached Aiken's closed and sealed door, she gave an involuntary shiver. The floor in front of it was slightly paler where it had been cleaned.

She felt cold. Aiken's blood had run there, and inside the office Aiken's body had lain, horribly murdered.

Somebody had been unable to stand it any more.

Had it been Richard?

Don't be ridiculous, she told herself, and pushed past the door, practically running now. Her mind ran on too.

Aiken had died "between eleven and one." Richard had left before midnight, and he'd lied to the police about it. Instinctively, protectively, she had lied too. But she was a bad liar, had always been. She'd made it worse, because she sensed Stryker had *known* it was a lie.

Richard *couldn't* have done it.

And yet, he'd been so angry last night. It wasn't the meal he'd had to walk off, but his rage at Aiken's constant, endless sniping.

She fumbled her key out of her handbag and got it into the lock, stepping across the sill with a grateful sigh of relief.

"Did you tell him?"

She gave a little scream as Richard's voice cut into her.

His blond hair was down over his forehead, and his coat was spangled with melting flakes of snow. He was leaning against her worktable, his arms folded across his chest, long eyes unreadable in the shadows.

"My God, you scared me!" Kate gasped. She dropped her handbag onto the desk and went over to him. "Did I tell him what?"

"The time I left?"

"No. I said I didn't know what time it was, but that it was very late. What on *earth* made you say you'd stayed the night?"

His familiar crooked grin turned her heart over. He took hold of her upper arms to draw her close. "Because I *wanted* to stay all night, as you damn well know, and because I wanted to make it clear that you were *my* girl. Also, I find being accused of fornication infinitely preferable to being accused of homicide, don't you?''

"Why did you want to make it clear I'm 'your girl'? What does that matter?''

"Maybe it was because of the way he kept looking at you. Or the way you were looking at him?''

She pulled away. "Don't be ridiculous. Why should I look at him in any special way? Or he at me?''

"You tell me.''

"You're imagining things. Oh, God. I wish we were somewhere else. That I'd never come back—''

"If you hadn't come back, I'd have never found you again,'' came the reply she wanted to hear. He pulled her back to him. "And that *would* have been a crime.''

"So is murder.''

"Not when it's Aiken's murder. *That's* deliverance.''

"You said you wanted to murder him, last night.''

He pulled back slightly and smiled. "So did you.''

"Maybe somebody was listening.''

His face darkened momentarily, then brightened again with his big, quick smile. "Come on. We've got nothing to worry about. I didn't kill him, and you didn't kill him, and since we were together nobody can say otherwise, can they?''

"Is that why you lied about last night?''

"Isn't that why *you* lied about last night?'' he countered.

"I didn't lie . . . exactly . . .''

He chuckled. "Look, what difference does it make? Why should the police waste time on us? After I left you, I drove around for a while, and then I went back to the fraternity house, but I can't prove that. Nobody was awake when I came in, as far as I knew. Now, the police would love that, wouldn't they, especially with . . . everything else?''

"There is no 'everything else.' It's past, it meant nothing. We were children, we knew nothing about it.''

He let his arms drop from around her and turned to look out at the few icy flakes of snow that were whirling over the Mall. "Whereas we know everything about everything now, don't we? All-wise and terribly sophisticated are we, Freud is mother's milk to us, anything goes—''

"Oh, for goodness' sake, forget it!" Kate said, irritated by his morose self-absorption. They'd been over it so many, *many* times. "It's a dead issue."

He turned and grinned at her. "As is Aiken, of course."

"Exactly."

He gave himself a little shake. "I guess you're right. Nobody knows but us chickens, and us chickens, we're saying nuthin'. Right?"

"Right."

"That's my *girl*."

"Now that we've dealt with last night, what about tonight?" She wanted to blot out what was happening, something that she could look forward to again. "Coming over?"

"No, hon, I can't. I *told* you—the meeting."

"Oh, yes, of course." There were so many meetings. She picked up the little carving he'd given her—the three monkeys with their paws over ears, eyes, mouth. Hear no, see no, speak no evil.

"Look, if it doesn't go on too late—I'll call you."

"Fine. I'll just be lying around eating chocolates and reading dirty books. You know me." She put the carving down hard.

He looked at her oddly, but gave her a quick kiss on the nose before going to the door, where he paused. "I hope I do, Katie. I really hope I do." He seemed worried by her apparent anger. "It's the Liaison Committee, and I have to go back to the house and change..." he pleaded in explanation.

"Fine. Good-bye, Richard."

"Katie..."

"Oh, go on, you big dope. Do your thing." She made it a joke. Relieved, he grinned and went out, with a wave.

Kate went over to stare out at the Mall, where the snow flurries danced and whirled, making the air twinkle but leaving no trace of their passage. Ice in the wind.

Her hands were cold, and she grasped the radiator briefly to warm them.

On her desk the telephone waited.

LIZ OLSON was, like Richard Wayland, a friend from Kate's undergraduate years. They'd attended high school together as well. Liz had stayed on at Grantham to take her doctorate, had done a year's sabbatical in France, and was back at Grantham when Kate had returned, bruised and rueful, from New York. It was she who had finally persuaded Kate to stay.

She was a tall, Junoesque woman, with wide blue eyes and thick golden hair that fell around her shoulders in the kind of natural waves other women spent a fortune to achieve. She never entered a room, she sailed into it, like a galleon. She did so now, sweeping into the shadows of the Tacoma and squinting nearsightedly until she located Kate in a rear booth. She was wearing a long red cape and high black boots, with a fur hat set back on her head. Several men turned to look, but she didn't notice them. She never noticed them.

Liz was only looking for Mr. Tallbar.

Since she was six foot in her stocking feet, the first thing she usually learned about a man was whether or not he had dandruff. This prospect, she claimed, had soured her soul. If so, it didn't show.

Now, settling herself opposite Kate in a swirl of red wool that nearly cleared the table of eating implements, she stripped off her gloves and took a deep breath, part relief, part anticipation. "Well?"

"I hardly know where to begin—" Kate said.

"Oh, God, don't start *out* with a cliché," Liz said in exasperation. "By all means descend to them gradually, but an opener like that one is definitely an underachiever."

Kate met the blue glare and drew strength from it. Nothing ever fazed Liz—she'd heard it all. Better men and women than Kate had poured their troubles on her lap, and she had very high standards. She knew Kate too well to indulge her in any way. Such lack of compromise was a kind of shelter. Kate could say what she liked, as long as she said it well. She gave Liz a brief outline of what had happened, start to finish.

Liz leaned back, slightly mollified, waited as the waiter awarded them each another martini, and then pronounced.

"Did you kill him?"

"Oh, for goodness' sake—"

"Oh, hell—I know. It's just that I'm never likely to have a chance like this again. So few of my friends go in for homicide."

"Listen, this is—"

"Serious?" Liz raised an eyebrow. "No, it isn't. Keep telling yourself it isn't. Keep it light, Kate. It's the only way you'll get through in one piece." She lit a cigarette and regarded her friend thoughtfully. "I know what you're like, remember? Everything a drama, everything the beginning and end of the world. Did Richard kill him?"

"No."

"Sure?"

"Of course I'm sure."

"He left before midnight."

"How did you know that?"

"I saw him go. He charged down the stairs and out the door like a mad buffalo and then roared away like his ass was on fire. What did you put in his coffee—kerosene?"

"He went home."

"So he *says*."

"Liz—" Kate said exasperatedly.

"Oh, all right, all right. Tell me about this policeman. Is he tall?"

"Is that the only thing you ever want to know about a man?"

"No, but it's always the first thing."

"He's about five-ten, I guess."

"Oh." Liz was only momentarily daunted. "Well, never mind. What is it about him that has you so twitchy?"

There was no use pretending to Liz. Kate leaned forward slightly and whispered. "He's the one."

Liz's eyes widened and she leaned forward too, her voice hushed and reverent. "Not . . . The One? Not really *The One*?"

Kate started to giggle. "Stop it."

Liz leaned back and took a long drag on her cigarette and smiled. "Well, for crying out loud, what do you *expect* me to say? You want to explain the dramatic pronouncement or—" She stopped suddenly. "Oh, my God, you don't mean *that* one? The one from the sit-in?"

Kate nodded. "He's *now* a lieutenant of detectives in Homicide. His name is Jack Stryker."

"Does he remember you?"

"I don't know. He acted pretty oddly, but . . . I don't know. I didn't recognize him myself, at first. Not until he put his glasses on."

"He wears *glasses*? God, how the mighty have fallen."

"Well, only for reading," Kate said. "When the light hit them, they were a bit like a helmet visor . . . and I remembered. He kept making me angry, but until then I didn't realize why."

"Angry? Don't you mean horny?"

"No. He's not . . . he's older, Liz."

"Aren't we all?"

"Yes, but . . . oh, he's *different* now. Tired and—"

"Oh, Kate, I'll bet he's still gorgeous. Isn't he?"

"Well . . ."

"Jesus wept." Liz was suddenly burdened by the knowledge of what lay ahead, added to the burden of all that had gone before. She stared at Kate with some pity and not a little delight.

It had been during the sit-ins of the mid '60s. Richard Wayland, student activist and potential nominee for the draft, had led a sit-in in the Department of English protesting the university's policy of making student records available to the government for the purpose of establishing preferment for the draft. Kate, adoring girlfriend of Richard Wayland, had gone along with it, swept up in the excitement of the emotional and somewhat ill-defined "cause." She, too, had joined the chanting, laughing and partially hysterical crowd—until the police had arrived. Then everything had changed. She had been terrified by the line of uniformed men advancing into the building, and had fled. One of them had followed, and cornered her in an empty upstairs office.

There he had proceeded to turn her over his knee and spank the living daylights out of her. Then he stood her up, kissed her hard on the mouth, and left her, returning to his colleagues, who were busy arresting everyone else.

Kate hadn't been arrested.

Humiliated, embarrassed, and most of all, filled with guilt at having panicked and deserted Richard and the others, she had cowered in the office until darkness had fallen. Then she had crept out and slunk home. She had told no one of her experience—except, of course, her best friend, Liz Olson.

She hadn't seen the cop's face, because he had been wearing those mirrored goggles so beloved of motorcycle patrols. She could remember nothing of him except his hand on her bare flesh, his mouth, and his laugh as he'd left her. He'd said only one thing. "Go home and play with your dolls, babe, this is no game for little girls."

At the time it had happened, Liz always more worldly-wise than Kate, had seen the funny side of it. She still did. That, she had crowed, was the ultimate in fantasy "rape." Come on, admit it, you enjoyed it. Kate, filled with rage and shame, had hotly denied any such thing. She said she only wanted to forget it.

But she hadn't.

Sometimes even now, in her dreams, the powerful, swaggering figure of the phantom cop would reappear to chase, capture and assault her. Sometimes she would wake up afraid, sometimes roused. Seeing Stryker again, in reality, had confused the issue even more in her mind. Now she had a *real* reason to be afraid of him.

Looking at her friend now, Liz recognized conflict. "So tell me," she said patiently.

Kate struggled with the unwieldy agitation that filled her—it was rather like trying to fold a balloon full of water. "All that was years ago. A lot has happened to me since then. I've grown up."

"That's *your* opinion," Liz said acidly.

"Well, dammit, I have. Maybe if I'd met him again under different circumstances . . . but to have him here investigating Aiken's *murder*. It's just embarrassing. And he's different too. He's got grey in his hair just as I do, and he's not a spectre, he's a man doing a job . . ."

"And he still scares the hell out of you."

"Yes."

"And you love it."

"No, of course I don't. Yes, I do. Oh, God, I don't know. It just adds another problem to the ones we already have. Don't you see, Liz? It gives an absolutely *ridiculous* dimension to all this. It's bad enough to be suspected of murder . . ."

"But he's seen you bare-assed and scared," Liz finished with great relish. "Oh, Kate . . . *why* couldn't he be taller?"

"I don't know. I wish he was, then you'd take him off my hands," Kate said distractedly. "There are other things that make it more complicated—things you don't know and I can't tell you, but they all have to do with the past, with *that time*, when we were all so damned passionate and idealistic, and now we're middle-aged and worn down and even part of the Establishment ourselves . . ."

"Isn't it hell?" Liz commiserated, her eyes dancing.

"You're not taking this seriously," Kate objected.

"Nope. And neither should you. I *told* you," Liz said.

Kate looked at her for a long time, and, to her horror, the tears came to her eyes and overflowed. "Liz . . . what if Richard *did* kill Aiken? What if I lied to Stryker and it turns out that Richard . . . that Richard . . ."

"Which worries you most?"

"How can you *ask* that?" Kate cried. Several heads turned and she snatched up a napkin to furtively dab her face.

"Just wanted to keep things clear," Liz said in a practical voice. "Look, the Richard you're talking about, the only Richard you ever *see*, as far as I can tell, is *not* the same Richard to whom you were engaged. He served in Nam, didn't he? That's changed him. Before, he was just weak. Now he's a mess."

"You don't like him. You *never* liked him."

"Oh, I *like* him all right, but I've never trusted him. Not since he dropped you flat on your little ass at the age of eighteen."

"He had problems."

"We all had problems. *He* apparently still has them. You can't go on protecting him, Kate. This Stryker has gotten older, you've gotten older, and Richard has gotten older." Liz leaned back and smiled briefly. "*I* haven't gotten older, of course," she said in a wry tone. "The point is, sweetie, that as you just said, this is murder. I admit, Aiken probably had it coming, but not just from Richard. From a cast of thousands. Let's be clear: if Richard is innocent, he has nothing to fear. And—"

"Do you really believe that?" Kate interrupted. "Do you *really* believe in truth justice and the American Way? That innocent people are never put in jail, that guilty people never go free? Come *on*?"

"So blame it on my youth," Liz shrugged. "I just find it hard to get away from the feeling one should tell the truth, that's all. Unless someone asks your weight or age, of course."

"Honourable exceptions."

"Exactly. If Richard is innocent, fine, then your lie was silly but harmless. On the other hand, if he's guilty, how are you going to live with yourself? If this Stryker is a good cop, don't you think he's going to catch up with Richard in the end? And where would that leave you?" She put out her cigarette and picked up the menu. "I was wrong. You *should* be serious, about this part of it anyway. Forget the past, forget everything except that Aiken was murdered."

"*Not* by Richard Wayland."

"If you really believe that, why didn't you tell the police the truth about last night?"

"Because it was Stryker, don't you see? Because he made me angry and upset and—"

But Liz was shaking her head. "That's only your rationalization, Kate. *I'm* not Stryker. Tell *me*. Did Richard leave you before midnight?"

"You know he did."

"And did he have a reason to kill Aiken?" When Kate didn't answer, Liz sighed. "Apparently he did, whatever it was—equally obviously, he could have done it. What's that you teach— Means, Motive and Opportunity? He had them all, Kate."

"But—"

Liz waved her menu. "Eat first, buts afterward. Your trouble is an empty head on top of an empty stomach. Tell the man what you want."

Kate stared up at the waiter.

He had a notebook just like Sergeant Toscarelli's.

ELEVEN

AFTER GETTING the interviews out of the way, Stryker again turned to the problem of the missing briefcase. It nagged at him. He'd never seen a college professor without a briefcase. They clung to them as if they were homes from home, which they probably were for men who constantly had to move from one classroom to the next. He got out the envelope that contained the personal effects found on the body, spilling them out onto the desk blotter.

After two or three minutes staring, he spoke. "Aha!"

Toscarelli jumped. He'd been tidying up his shorthand notes of the interviews, and Stryker's loud ejaculation had startled him.

Stryker reached out and picked up Adamson's keys. "His car. It's probably in his car."

"What is?"

"His briefcase. There wasn't one in the office, and that just didn't add up."

"So that's what the thief was after, the briefcase. Big deal!"

Stryker frowned at him. "There wasn't any thief."

"Boy, you sure are stubborn, aren't you?" Toscarelli grinned. "But what if the briefcase isn't in his car, will you accept *then* that there might have been a thief, after all?"

"I *might*," Stryker conceded. "But what would a thief want with some old sandwiches and a bunch of papers—"

"What makes you think that's what he kept in his briefcase?"

"It's what I keep in mine," Stryker smiled. "Well, what the hell do you know? He drove a Mercedes."

"You're kidding. On a teacher's salary?"

"Key ring is believing," Stryker said, holding up the leather tag. "Now, if you were a Mercedes belonging to a professor, where would you be?"

"If he left it on the street, I'd be in a hot-body shop by now," Toscarelli said. "On the other hand, if he parked it in a garage somewheres—"

"Let's ask Stark," Stryker said, getting to his feet.

"What's all the fuss about his car?"

"Not the car, the briefcase," Stryker said. "It's got to *be* someplace. If not in his office, then maybe in his car."

"And maybe in some garbage can, where the killer dumped it after taking out whatever he was after."

Stryker paused by the door. "Okay, have it your way. Which shall we try first—all the garbage cans within a five-mile radius, or his car?"

THE SNOW was coming down a little more heavily, and the thick clouds were already bringing dusk, though it wasn't yet three o'clock. The streetlights had come on, and crystals glittered randomly from the heaps of old and new snow beneath them. There were only a few cars in the faculty parking lot.

A sweep of Toscarelli's gloved hand over the hood of the third one revealed the gleaming metallic silver-grey finish of Adamson's Mercedes, as described by Stark. In the distance the whine of engines in low gear told them the salt trucks hadn't gotten this far out yet. The atmosphere was muted by the snow, single sounds pierced it, a bell from a church, a voice, a dog's bark, a car horn. But, for the most part, Stryker and Toscarelli felt isolated and somehow bandaged by the snow-covered bushes that surrounded the lot and the blank loom of the rear aspect of the Science Building.

Stryker pulled off a glove, fished the car keys out of the envelope. He carefully opened the door on the driver's side, and slid in behind the wheel. It was dark in the shrouded car, the mantle of snow curtaining the windows. A quick glance over the back of the seat and he had the briefcase.

It was brown tooled Mexican leather, very lived-in. Unlike Adamson's own meticulous appearance (before the killer's perforations had spoiled it) the case was an old and battered family retainer. It looked stuffed full to splitting with every bit of paper he'd ever owned. Handing the case out to Toscarelli, who was shifting from one frozen foot to the other, Stryker did a quick once-over and under, using only his gloved hand. Forensics would scrape it clean later.

The back seat was bare. The rear shelf held only a screen-scraper and a can of aerosol de-icer. The glove compartment turned up maps, a gas-company credit card and a parking-lot card, an empty leather-covered flask, a small notebook containing details of car servicing, and a hard-porn homosexual picture paperback from Denmark.

The driver's seat was pushed forward, for Adamson had been shorter then Stryker. As he felt around beneath it to give himself more leg room, he touched something soft. He pulled it out and found himself holding a mitten. Red leather on the underside, brown fur on the back. He stepped out and used his flashlight to look under both seats. No—only the one mitten. He struggled out of the car and stood up. "That's about it. The briefcase mystery is solved, anyway."

"My feet are frozen," Toscarelli said glumly. "No mystery about that."

"OH LORD," Kate said, stopping so short that Liz ran straight into her back. "There he is."

Liz squinted, seeing no more than two blurred figures at the far end of the faculty parking lot. "There who is?"

"Stryker. In the leather coat."

Liz squinted again, then fished in her handbag and produced her glasses. She looked through them without putting them on. "Who's his friend?" she asked in an odd voice.

"Oh, that's Sergeant Toscarelli. His partner."

"He's *huge*," Liz breathed reverently. "Come on." She grabbed Kate's arm and propelled her from behind the bushes toward the two men, flinging snow-covered branches wildly aside. Kate held back, but she was no match for a woman possessed.

"No—Liz—what are you doing?"

"I'm taking you over there so you can tell him what time Richard Wayland left you last night."

Kate stopped—or tried to. "I won't."

"Then I will—after all, I saw him myself, didn't I? I'm an eyewitness. They'll want to examine my testimony, of course. *Especially* Sergeant Toscarelli, I hope." She plunged on. After a moment, Kate slowly and reluctantly followed.

Toscarelli, sensing movement, turned. "Holy Mother," he murmured.

Stryker turned too, and saw the red-caped figure swooping toward them, blonde hair flying in the wind, eyes sparkling. "A Valkyrie" he announced, and then saw Kate Trevorne slipping and sliding in the wake of the big, striding blonde, who was closing in fast.

"Lieutenant Stryker? I'm Liz Olson. I live with Kate," Liz announced. "She's been silly and she has something to tell you."

Stryker raised an eyebrow and looked around Liz's shoulder at Kate, who couldn't seem to make up her mind whether to go red with embarrassment or white with anger. "Oh?" he asked quietly.

"Yes," Liz said firmly, "You see, Richard Wayland didn't spend the night with her at all."

"He didn't?" Stryker sounded unsurprised.

"No."

"I see."

"He left at ten minutes to midnight," Liz said inexorably, glancing uneasily at Kate's mouth, which kept opening and closing like an indecisive letter box.

"And where did he go?"

"How would I know?" Liz demanded, startled.

"I just thought you might," Stryker said, his face blank but his eyes momentarily alive as he glanced at Kate, then away. She looked so miserable, it seemed unfair to stare. "And you say you live with Miss Trevorne?"

Liz's high dudgeon was waning, and she was beginning to regret the impulse that had carried her forward. Her first impression of Stryker was not at all what she had expected. For a start, he was too real, too solid. After years of hearing about Kate's Mystery Man, it was unnerving to realise he had ears and shoes and everything. She was also unprepared for the sensation of barely suppressed anger that he gave out. She began to see why Kate had reacted as she had. She, herself, began to babble. Beside Stryker, Toscarelli seemed mesmerized by her, and clutched Adamson's briefcase to his chest like a bulletproof vest. "I live downstairs, Kate lives upstairs," Liz said quickly. "She called down the laundry chute and I—"

"Laundry chute?" Stryker asked quietly.

Kate was engaged in assessing the height of the Science Building. It looked like developing into a lifelong obsession. She spoke in a tight voice, without turning her head. "My house is divided into two apartments. There is a laundry chute that goes down to the basement. We keep bells by the chute. If we know the other one is alone and we have something to say, we open the door and ring the bell, and the other one comes, and we talk, or I go down or Liz comes up. I don't know what time Richard left, I didn't *look* at the *clock*."

"Well, I *did*," Liz said, "seeing as he slammed the door so hard it made my television blink. I thought Kate might like to have a chat, and she did, so she came down and we drank coffee and talked until about three this morning," Liz said flatly. "And that's that." She turned to Kate and sighed. "I know you're angry with me, but it's stupid to lie to the police. This is murder, and they need all the help they can get."

"Amen," murmured Toscarelli, and was rewarded by a blinding smile from Liz that nearly made him drop the briefcase. His feet were no longer cold.

Liz was still looking at Kate. "When you feel like forgiving me—if you ever do—my laundry chute is always open," she said. When Kate didn't answer, she sighed again in resignation. "I did it for you, sweetie, since you wouldn't do it for yourself."

Kate turned, looked at her and then glanced at Sergeant Toscarelli. "Oh, really?" she asked coldly.

"Thank you, Miss Olson," Stryker said. "I'm sure Miss Trevorne realizes you've given her a solid alibi, she'll feel much better—"

"I'm glad everyone knows how I'm going to feel, it saves *me* so much trouble, doesn't it?" Kate flared. She flounced off, got into her car, slammed the door and, after a few sputtering attempts, drove off with a skid that nearly took the rear light off the Mercedes.

"Ooops," Toscarelli said. He grinned at Liz. "You did the right thing, coming forward."

"Oh, I know I did," Liz said sadly. "And don't think I feel all virtuous about it, because I don't. She's her own worst enemy, sometimes."

Toscarelli's eyes slid sideways and lit on Stryker, who had taken a few steps away from them and was staring after Kate's car. "Some people are like that," he agreed. He settled the briefcase more comfortably on one hip. "You a teacher too?"

"Yes, French."

"No kidding." They regarded each other with pleasure.

"Come on, Tos," Stryker said, turning back to them with a determined air. "Let's get that stuff down to headquarters. Thanks again, Miss Olson. If we need a statement later on, we'll be in touch."

"Don't you want my address and phone number?" Liz asked.

"Sure. You get it, Tos." He nodded, gave a flicker of a smile, and moved away, his hands jammed in his pockets and his head down.

Toscarelli shifted the briefcase, got out his notebook, and took down Liz's phone number. The address he knew—same as Kate Trevorne's. "French, hey? I took Spanish at school, myself."

"Spanish is a very nice language," Liz said approvingly.

"Not like French, though."

"There *are* some differences."

"Yeah, I guess." They stood facing one another, smiling.

"Come *on*, Tos," came Stryker's voice from beyond the bushes.

"Right. Well . . . see you." Tos nodded and moved off.

"Especially if I see you first," Liz whispered to herself. Then the smile left her face and she went to her own car, to follow Kate home.

"WELL, WHAT DO YOU THINK?" Toscarelli asked as they drove downtown.

"About what?"

"About that Olson woman and her alibi for Trevorne. You think she made it up, or what?" Toscarelli spoke like a man doing duty as devil's advocate and hating every minute of it.

"No, I think it's probably the truth."

Toscarelli grinned in relief. "Me, too."

"It leaves Wayland wide open."

"Why should she lie for him?"

"Because she's afraid he did it, of course," Stryker said, his chin stuck on his chest as he slouched down in the seat and glared out at the snowbound traffic.

"Why? Because she knows something we don't?"

"Uh-huh."

"You'll get it out of her," Toscarelli said confidently. He moved around a stranded bus, cutting in front of a florist's van that couldn't make up its mind whether to go or stay.

"Sure. If there's no other way," Stryker said.

Toscarelli took a moment to give him a look. "What's that supposed to mean?" he asked.

Stryker just shrugged and sank a little deeper into his seat and his thoughts.

TWELVE

THE SECURITY GUARD usually ate his dinner in the student union, but the cafeteria wasn't open out of term time, and he had to make do with a local cafe that was twice the price and half as good. He resented this, feeling the university had somehow let him down. On the way in, he picked up an evening paper and settled himself to read over his meal.

There wasn't much detail.

But when he got to the part about Adamson's tongue being cut out he nearly choked on his fried potatoes. He'd missed that. He'd seen the argument, and the stabbing, and the frantic search, and the robbery, but he'd missed the tongue business.

Out of sight, below the window level, of course.

This left him feeling slightly cheated.

He sat back and stared at his empty plate, his eyes out of focus as he tried to decide how he was going to go about this.

Suddenly he smiled.

Well, dammit, why not?

Of course, he'd have to take it carefully.

Because two murders cost no more than one.

But he was no fool, not him.

He worked at a university, didn't he?

THIRTEEN

STRYKER ENVIED PLUMBERS.

He envied electricians, insurance men, computer programmers, stock-market experts, bricklayers and secretaries.

None of *them* had to work on Sundays.

Even thieves, pimps and killers could put their feet up on Sunday if they chose to—drink a little beer, watch a little pro ball on the box, read a book, scratch their balls or just sleep the hours away.

Not cops.

They'd spent most of the early part of Sunday checking out the alibis of Adamson's fellow academics, as a matter of routine. Later that afternoon, they had an appointment to view the home of the deceased.

Adamson's estate was handled by Benning, Stewart & Tate. Although dead, Adamson was still accorded the rights and privileges of any citizen unsuspected of a crime. His home was his castle. They could get a court order, or they could just break in on "suspicion" and take the consequences.

But the best way was usually the simplest.

Ask nicely.

Someone from Benning, Stewart & Tate was going to meet them at the house after lunch. Meanwhile Stryker had been writing up his initial report on the previous day's activities, talking the captain around to letting him stay on the case, and building up his strength while the others ran the errands. Mostly he was just going around in circles, like his goddamned chair. When they brought Wayland in for further questioning, it was almost a relief.

"I resent this," Wayland said loudly. Nobody paid the least attention to this protest, including Stryker, who merely guided the other man into the interview room and closed the door. After a night's sleep, he felt more able to ignore Wayland's mouth, but only just. He wasn't certain how long he could go on ignoring it.

"Nobody forced you to come down."

"Nobody *forced*? Crap. They came to the fraternity house and *loomed* over me in front of all the boys. They obviously meant business." Wayland settled himself in a chair and resentfully watched Stryker opening a file.

"I've been given some new information concerning your alleged timetable on Friday night," Stryker said evenly. "I have a witness who saw you leave Miss Trevorne's home *before* midnight. Would you care to amend your statement?"

"Who saw me?"

"Would you care to amend your statement?"

"Did Kate tell you?" Wayland demanded. "What a load of crap! She *never*!"

"Not Miss Trevorne. A disinterested witness."

"Someone passing? How could they know—" Wayland paused, slumped back in the chair, and regarded Stryker with deep suspicion as his mind worked over the possibilities. "Liz Olson," he finally announced in a bitter voice. "Wasn't it? Disinterested, my ass."

"Would you care to amend your statement?" Stryker repeated politely.

Wayland considered this. "No, I damn well wouldn't."

"I would strongly advise you to tell us the truth, Mr. Wayland, because—"

"Because you'll arrest me if I don't?" Wayland sneered. "You can't do that. I remember my statement, I remember what I said. I said I didn't *know* what time I left Kate's, and I still don't know, because I didn't look at my goddamn watch."

Stryker sighed, tapped a pencil on the table, looked up at the ceiling. "You said—you claimed—to have 'spent the night' with Miss Trevorne. We commonly accepted that to mean a major portion of both night and the following morn—"

"You can commonly accept what you damn well like. I didn't come down here to argue semantics with some high school dropout."

Stryker made a sound of disappointment. "Oh, come now, Mr. Wayland, that's a bit strong, isn't it? If it really worries you, I can easily have a transcript of both my university and police-college grades sent to you just *anytime*. I studied semantics with Professor Culpepper and I assure you I know what is commonly meant by SPENDING THE GODDAMN NIGHT!"

"It doesn't worry me, but it obviously worries you," Wayland said annoyingly. "I'm just *dazzled* by your qualifications, all right?"

Stryker closed his eyes, counted to eleven, and smiled. "Do you care to amend your statement, Mr. Wayland? Alternatively, I could interview all the boys down at the fraternity house—I'm sure at least one of them might be able to remember when you came in Friday night—*if* you came in."

"Don't you dare," Wayland said, paling.

"Not a matter of dare, a matter of routine," Stryker said. "There's a good deal of routine going on now, even as we sit here and chat. Detectives Pinsky and Neilson are currently going over old records, checking out class lists, interviewing waiters and cabdrivers—oh, all *kinds* of people. You'd be surprised what people overhear and see. You don't think we take everyone's *word* for things, do you, Mr. Wayland? We're just the most *suspicious* people you ever *met*. Care to change your statement?"

"To what?"

"To the truth. It usually serves."

Again, the long look of reflection. Wayland, dressed in jeans, shirt and pullover, regarded his polished loafers and the dark interval of his socks below the bottom of his jeans. His long body was slouched in the chair, his legs outstretched. In the harsh light of the interview room, Stryker could see that the carefully perpetuated image of handsome graduate student was beginning to show signs of wear. Little lines had begun to appear around Wayland's eyes and mouth. There was a slight scatter of grey in the sideburns, a surfacing of broken veins at the tip of the nose, a sag under the chin line.

"I don't want to change anything," Wayland said finally.

"Why not? What the hell are you so afraid of?" Stryker wanted to know. He *sincerely* wanted to know. "Don't you see what you're doing with all this bullshit? If you'd told a simple story, I'd probably have missed it. But now I've got to start looking hard at you, Mr. Wayland. At you, around you, and behind you. I'm going to get *very* nosy. Now, isn't that a shame? Especially if it's such a waste of time?"

"I don't give a damn how you wear your ass out," Wayland said.

"Maybe not. But I could hang yours out to dry."

"Is that a threat?"

"Good heavens, *no!*" Stryker widened his eyes. "I'm not the threatening type—I'm the stubborn type. I just keep going until I get there. And I'll definitely get there, believe me."

"Good luck to you," Wayland said with a smile. He sat up. "If there's nothing else, I'll be on my way, then."

"I'll arrange to have you driven back."

"No, thanks."

As Wayland reached the door, Stryker spoke again, in a conversational tone. "How far do you think I'll have to go back to find out what's worrying you, Mr. Wayland? Five years? Ten? Fifteen? Or will Miss Trevorne tell me, eventually? She's not a natural liar. She may be fond of you, but she can't keep it up forever, you know. It's not in her, she feels uncomfortable with lies and secrets."

"You do one thing to harass or upset her, and so help me—"

"My, my . . . *such* chivalry," Stryker said mockingly.

Wayland, white-faced, turned on his heel and went out.

Neilson, standing aside to let him pass, raised an eyebrow at Stryker and came on in, shutting the door carefully behind him. He was carrying a computer printout. Stryker, glad of any distraction to calm his anger, asked him what it was.

"Well, it's funny. You know the address Heath gave us, where he lives with his mother?"

"Yeah."

"Well, it's her place, not his. He's got another address, which he didn't think worth telling us about."

"Maybe he just owns it and rents it out."

Neilson shook his head. "No, I just now checked it out. The janitor says he lives there, all right, although he's 'away' a lot. He seems to think Heath is some kind of travelling salesman or something. I rang the bell—it's a pretty fancy apartment—but there was nobody home. The doorman says—"

"There's a doorman?"

"It's that kind of a place," Neilson said. He sat on the edge of the table and lit a cigarette. "He says Heath is probably out to church or running. He runs a lot when he's at home. I asked if he was around now, and the guy said he's usually around on the weekends, so I said was he around last night, and he said yeah, and I said was he around Friday night, and he says yeah." Neilson drew in a lungful of smoke and let it trail out slowly. "He said both Heath *and* his wife were there on Friday night."

"Heath told us he was divorced," Stryker said, sitting up.

"Uh-huh." Neilson's eyes glittered. "He did."

Stryker stood up. "Let's go."

PINSKY WAS RECITING from his little black book.

"The taxi driver, we located him, he confirms picking up Dr. Coulter at the hotel and taking her to the faculty parking lot at eleven-fifty. He watched her get into her car and he followed her as far as Jefferson, where he turned off and she went on out Pickard toward the Hills. That's the one." He turned over a page. "Heskell's fiancée confirms they were together." He leaned forward slightly. "I think maybe we should put some pressure on, there. She sounded angry about it, like she was saying they were together against her better judgement, you know? It was just a feeling I got."

Tos and Stryker exchanged a glance. Pinsky's "feelings" were generally reliable, if a little vague.

"Okay, do it," Stryker agreed. "Anything else."

"Fowler okay, Stark okay, confirmed by their wives for what it's worth, but they seemed straight. Rocheleau okay—his wife is worth a detour for, but that mother-in-law, Jesus, he was right. She would have *loved* to land him in it. Pinchman and Grey-Jenner still unconfirmed, Underhill . . ." he paused. "Now, there's something funny *there*."

"Well?" Stryker and Toscarelli both said together when Pinsky didn't continue.

"It's . . ."

"Just a feeling?" Neilson asked.

Pinsky nodded. "According to a neighbour, Underhill came home around seven-thirty, parked his car in his drive, went in and didn't come out. But the neighbour's wife says she heard the Underhill car start up and drive away around midnight. He does that quite a lot, apparently, and it gets her goat, because the driveway is right under their bedroom. The neighbour's bedroom, that is."

"Right, we've got the picture."

"So anyway, the guy, the *husband*, says the car was still there in the morning, and she dreamt it. So they had an argument about it."

"Terrific," Neilson said. "And?"

Pinsky shrugged. "She says it went, he says it stayed. Take your pick. She also says the Underhills don't get along so good, arguing a lot and so on. But that Underhill is absolutely *crazy* about his kids, and 'puts up with it,' to keep the family together. She says he's a saint."

"Puts up with what?" Tos asked.

" 'Goings on' is how she put it," Pinsky grinned. "She obviously doesn't like Mrs. Underhill much, so you can consider the source. I figure Mrs. Underhill is pretty good-looking, and the neighbour—"

"Here we are," Neilson said. "This is it."

It was one of the newer condominiums in an area being "reclaimed" and developed as part of the urban renewal and "Renaissance" of the city. To the right, the view was river and the wooded far bank, ahead the skyscrapers of the downtown area— and to the left, the grimy shreds and tatters of Junktown. There was a doorman cum security man on the door, and he nodded at Neilson.

"Is he in?" Neilson asked. "Has he come back?"

"Yeah—about twenty minutes ago," the doorman said, looking at the others. "I didn't say nuthin', like you said."

Stryker, Pinsky and Toscarelli suddenly became interested in architecture as Neilson paid off his informant. "*She's* in too," the doorman threw in for free as they went in through the glass doors. "Come in about ten minutes ago."

"What do you reckon a place like this costs?" Pinsky asked in the lift, which was panelled in black walnut and trimmed in brass.

"More than the four of us make in a year," Neilson said. "The janitor says when it was built the apartments were going for a hundred thou, but a lot of them have changed hands since then, with the price going up each time. He reckons the last one went for nearly three."

"Hundred thousand?" Pinsky gasped.

"Hundred thousand."

"Jesus," Toscarelli breathed. "He must be into something on the side."

"I think you could safely say that," Neilson grinned.

They all looked at him, but he just kept on grinning and led them down the hall. "This is it," he said and rang the bell. There was a long wait, and then the door swung back, revealing Professor Lucy Grey-Jenner wearing a velvet robe that had been hastily thrown over nothing else.

Neilson looked at Stryker, Pinsky, Toscarelli and "Mrs. Frank Heath." "Sur*prise*!" he murmured with great satisfaction.

"Four years now," Heath growled. His massive presence in the room was like a storm front building up. "And if it weren't for my mother, we would have made it public long ago. She's an old stubborn woman, and me marrying a white would just about kill her." He looked away abruptly. "Not that she's got much longer, anyway. But there's no reason to spoil her last months when it isn't necessary. Lucy understands."

Professor Grey-Jenner had reappeared, dressed in a skirt and sweater that revealed the still-young lines of her slim body. Nervously she lit a cigarette and sought reassurance from Heath, but his eyes were on the far horizon. His big hands were clenched by his sides, and he was making a great effort to control his anger. Even Toscarelli felt intimidated by his powerful outline against the window.

"Did Adamson know about your relationship?" Stryker asked.

Heath stood very still, then shuddered briefly from head to toe. Neilson and Pinsky stepped back involuntarily when he turned around, and Toscarelli stepped forward. Stryker did not move. "Yes. He reminded me of it during the meeting. He said he thought it would be a real step forward in race relations if we made our love public. He thought it would be *wonderful*." The scorn in his voice tore the words to shreds. He looked Stryker in the eye. "He said that. *Wonderful*."

Short of apologising for the existence of his entire race, Stryker could think of no adequate response. The one thing that was beginning to bother him most about this case was why nobody had killed Adamson *sooner*.

"People on campus would understand," Lucy said wistfully. "There would be no question of children, I'm too old to have children now. Frank already has three beautiful children by his first wife. All we have is each other, there'd be no trouble there, you see, it's just Mother Heath . . ."

They could see how much it tore at her, and Heath reached out to touch her arm gently. "She's a strong woman," he said, meaning his mother. "My old man left when I was born, and there were four others besides me, all hungry, all needing. She did what she could for us, she was stubborn and crazy and she did it *all* for us. Everything was for us. I've got a brother who's a doctor, another a lawyer, sisters both teachers like me. I was lucky. I got an athletic scholarship to USC. Got a taste for campus life—"

Tos snapped his fingers suddenly. "You played for the Packers," he said in some awe.

Heath nodded. "Until I busted both knees," he said wryly.

"He was also Phi Beta Kappa," Lucy said quietly.

"Yeah," Heath said. "That and fifty cents will buy me a cup of coffee anywhere." He amended that. "Anywhere up North, that is."

"But why don't you just...get married secretly?" Neilson asked.

"That would be cheating," Lucy said in a thin voice. "She never cheated him. He's paying her back."

Heath looked at her. "*You're* doing the paying," he said, and pulled her to him, held her close. He looked at the others over the top of her head, and his eyes hardened. "I suppose you think it's crazy."

"No," Stryker said. "But I bet it's damn tiring, running back and forth between the two of them."

Heath looked at him in some surprise, and then, slowly, began to chuckle. "Damned women."

"Ain't it the truth?" Pinsky said. "I got four daughters myself."

"Jesus," Heath said sympathetically.

"So you were here together all Friday night?" Stryker asked.

They both nodded. "I came directly here," Lucy said. "Frank went home, made sure his mother was settled, then came out for his run. She sleeps a lot, you see, and has no clock in her room. As long as he's there when she wakes up in the morning, she's happy."

"But what—" Toscarelli began, stopped, looked around and started again. "What if she needs something?"

"The nurse is there."

"Nurse?" Stryker asked. "You didn't mention any nurse when you made your statement."

Heath shrugged. "I didn't figure you'd check."

"We *always* check," Stryker said severely. "She'd have said you went out."

"I *told* you I went out—jogging," Heath reminded them. "Came in around 4 A.M., and the nurse was asleep, or I hope she was, anyway. She's none too young herself, come to that. I can be real quiet when I want to be. Wild kid with a boss-man momma and four kick-ass brothers and sisters learns to be *real* quiet about sneaking home, believe *me*."

"How THE HELL can he *afford* a place like that?" Pinsky wanted to know when they were back in the car.

"You heard him—three years pro football. Don't you remember him with the Packers?"

"I don't get much time for football," Pinsky said morosely. "They're always watching soaps and crap like that."

"He probably invested his money—check it out, will you, Neilson?"

"I already did, as far as I could on Sunday," Neilson said. "She's got some money too—and they both earn good salaries with no other expenses but themselves."

"Heath has his mother."

Neilson snorted. "According to my sources, she can pay her own way. Mr. Heath's mama was one of the busiest madams in town, once upon a time. That house she lives in a mile or so from here had quite a reputation. She was called Mama Jubilee, I think."

Tos swerved the car slightly. "Jeez, even *I* heard of *her*. Blacks only, and she meant it, I remember that."

"She was really fussy," Neilson agreed.

"Apparently still is," Stryker said.

"Blacks think we walk funny," Pinsky mused reflectively. "Among other things."

"Well, that sets up *their* alibi, anyway," Tos said.

Stryker shook his head. "If Grey-Jenner is willing to live as his mistress in secret, it's hardly going to strain her to lie for him, is it? A jogger at midnight is pretty anonymous, especially if he wears one of those tracksuits with a hood. It's only two miles to the campus if you cut through the alleys. He's a big man, and I think he's an angry man, but he keeps a tight rein on it. He's under pressure. Suppose Adamson found out about the two of them—said he'd talk. What do you suppose someone like Heath might do to him?"

"You're not crossing them off?"

"I *had* crossed them off. Now I'm putting them back on." He looked at his watch. "Let's get something to eat, then head for the Hills. We can drop in on Professor Coulter on the way. I want to return her mitten."

FOURTEEN

PROFESSOR COULTER'S HOME was a small New England-style red-brick house set behind a long tidy garden, its shrubbery round-shouldered with snow. The front path had been cleared, and at the side they caught sight of a shovel being wielded rhythmically by a short, stocky man in a hunting cap and dungarees. Leaving Pinsky and Neilson arguing about Heath in the car, Toscarelli and Stryker rang the bell. It was answered by a roundabout little person reminiscent of Binnie Barnes, all ruffles and flutters.

"You must be Mrs. Feather," Stryker said, removing his cap politely. Something about the house or the woman herself made it seem the right thing to do in this year of 1935. "I'm Lieutenant Stryker. Is Professor Coulter in?"

"Oh, my—please—come in," whispered Mrs. Feather. "She's *working*, you see." This was apparently something akin to direct conversation with God and all his archangels. "But if it's *very* important—" She gazed at him and saw that it was. "I'll tell her. Just a moment." She turned and started down the hall, then glanced back and gave a tremulous smile. "The mat . . ."

They dutifully wiped their wet shoes on the mat and, after a moment, Mrs. Feather scurried back and said that "Jane" would receive them. She led them to a room at the rear of the house, book-lined and made cozy by a real fire. What they took at first to be a fur rug in front of it moved suddenly and revealed itself to be a huge dog. It stood up and looked into Stryker's eyes.

"It's all right, O'Bannion. Friends," said Professor Coulter from her desk, and the dog returned to its position by the fire. She put down some papers she'd been checking and smiled at them. "Irish wolfhound. Supposed to be bred to be the companion of kings. I often wonder what he makes of being reduced to looking after two old girls like Milly and me. Have you come to arrest me?"

"Not just yet," Stryker smiled. "I really—"

"What a pity," she interrupted, getting up and coming over to them. "I've always wanted to be arrested at home. I was arrested in Syria, once, for taking photographs. They were merely of a

Hittite grave, but I neglected to notice the military airfield behind it. I was held in protective custody in Crete during a local uprising. And spent two days, once, in a Tunisian prison—most unpleasant—but never at home. It would have been interesting to compare procedures."

"I'm sure if you put your mind to it you could manage a small crime," Stryker grinned. "But I've only come by to ask you about your mittens."

"Mittens?" She asked in an astonished voice. *"Mittens?"* Even O'Bannion raised his massive head in some surprise and fixed Stryker with a quizzical look.

"Well, one mitten actually."

O'Bannion put his head down again, bored.

Mrs. Feather appeared in the doorway, bearing an enormous silver tea service and a plate of biscuits on a tray. "I thought...tea...I thought perhaps...the cold...afternoon..."

"Yes, yes, Milly...very kind," Jane Coulter said, indicating the low table beside the fireplace. "Sit down, gentlemen, please. Let us be civilized."

They sat gingerly on the fragile sofa while she placed herself opposite and poured out the tea. Mrs. Feather, after proffering plates, napkins, etc., sat down on a small, distant chair and picked up some petit point. Her large eyes watched them as her needle flicked in and out, in and out. Stryker looked around. It was a remarkable room. Every available surface was covered with *things*. Photographs in little silver frames, statues, rocks large and small, icons, photographs in big silver frames, brassware, carvings, dolls, pots—objects of every conceivable description. It was the room of a magpie—cluttered, claustrophobic, but fascinating. It occurred to him that merely the dusting of them must have kept little Mrs. Feather on the verge of exhaustion.

"Now, about this mitten," Jane Coulter said briskly when the cups had been distributed. In Tos's hand the fine china looked like something from a doll's tea set.

"Yes." With difficulty, Stryker put down his cup and produced the fur-backed mitten he'd retrieved from Adamson's car. "This one..."

"That's Kate Trevorne's," Professor Coulter said. "Not mine."

Stryker stared at her in surprise. "But I saw one like it fall from your pocket on Saturday morning, in the conference room."

"Indeed, so you did, but not *exactly* like it." She turned to Mrs. Feather. "Milly, fetch me my mittens from my coat pocket, will you?'' She smiled at them and sipped her tea until her companion reappeared bearing the mittens. Jane Coulter took them from her, and Mrs. Feather retreated to her chair and her embroidery. "There, you see? Mine have brown leather palms, Kate's have red. Ergo, that is probably one of Kate's—or someone else's—but *not* one of mine. Where did you find it?''

"In—" Tos began.

"The faculty parking lot," Stryker finished.

"I see. Well, *I* find it extraordinary that you'd come all this way just to return my mitten. Very kind.''

"Actually, we were on our way to Professor Adamson's house.''

"Oh, I see. So it wasn't a special trip, after all.'' She seemed faintly disappointed.

"He lived not far from you," Stryker observed. "Were you friends?''

Her eyebrows went up. "Friends? Aiken and I? Impossible. He had no friends on the faculty, as you must have gathered by now. He was popular enough with the students, he made it his business to be, for he required adulation. But as to his relationship with us, well—" She leaned forward. "We were rivals, you see.''

"Rivals? You mean for tenure and so on?''

"Oh, no, nothing like that. We both had full professorships and tenure and, at any rate, were rapidly approaching retirement. No, I meant academic rivals, Lieutenant. We live for two things in our profession: the possibility of encountering and encouraging a promising student, and the fight for stature in our chosen fields of expertise. To maintain that stature, we must *publish*, as often as possible. Books, articles, and so on. I, myself, have managed to keep my head well up, I'm not shy to say it. I've worked hard, and I deserve it.'' Her smile softened what might have sounded like arrogance.

"You're brilliant, Jane," murmured Mrs. Feather. "You always were.''

"No, I'm a *worker*," Dr. Coulter said, half turning on the sofa to correct the point. "Brilliance is not enough, Milly. But Aiken thought it was, you see." She turned back to the men. "That was his fault, his abiding fault, in fact. He thought that if you did something well, or cleverly, it hid the fact that it was claptrap. He was shallow, surface glitter only. The man never *delved* for anything in his life. He lived off others.''

"You mean he took other people's work''

Dr. Coulter looked alarmed, as if perhaps she'd gone too far. "I didn't say *that*," she said. "But he . . . took advantage."

"Of who?"

"Whom," she said absently, putting down her cup. "I prefer not to name names, of course, mostly because I can't remember them. But, over the years, I think he dipped into more than one student's research and turned it to his own advantage."

"Hardly a crime."

She looked slightly disappointed in him. "Not in your terms, perhaps, but certainly in ours. I'm not saying he wasn't clever, but that he thought cleverness was enough. Indeed, that it was *all*. It isn't."

"Did he steal work from you?"

"From *me*?" She was astounded. "He wouldn't have *dared*. And anyway, our fields were entirely separate. No, I found him unpleasant but manageable. He preferred weaker targets. If you measure friendship by concern, then Aiken was not my friend. Had he been in trouble I wouldn't have lifted a finger to help him. To his credit, I suppose, I'd have to admit that he'd have been astounded if I had ever done so."

"Don't say that, Jane. You are the kindest of women," came Mrs. Feather's dutiful whisper from her corner.

"Thank you, Milly." Professor Coulter accepted the tribute graciously but gave the two policemen a wry, amused look. "Nevertheless, I felt no kindness toward Aiken, and I will not pretend to have done so. He could be amusing occasionally, of course. He was a *witty* man."

"If you were asked to name his murderer, who would spring to mind?" Stryker asked.

She looked at him a long time, without speaking, then sighed heavily. "I can see your difficulty, Lieutenant. Instead of one or two suspects, you've got a plethora. Most people, if pressed, would rather let Aiken's murderer get away than be instrumental in convicting a friend. A lot of people would even find it excusable that a friend could be driven beyond endurance to that final, terrible act."

"But that doesn't *make* it excusable," Tos said. "Killing is wrong."

"But surely you've killed in the line of duty?" Dr. Coulter said, raising an eyebrow. "Do you consider that wrong?"

"Yes, I do," Tos said evenly. "We all do. It's always a last resort."

"Perhaps Aiken's killer found it a last resort too."

"Maybe. But I don't expect he sleeps easy on it, any more than we do," Stryker said, standing up. "Thank you for the tea, ladies. I'm sorry to have barged in like this."

"I wish I could have been more help to you," Jane Coulter said, then added. "Oh, dear."

"What is it, ma'am?"

"Well, I just realized, about Kate's mitten. You don't connect it with Aiken's murder, do you? I'd hate to think I'd led you to think that *she* was—"

"It's all right, don't worry about it," Stryker reassured her. "We only found it and thought it was yours, that's all."

"Shall I return it to her?"

"No, I'll do that," Stryker said.

"Because I'm certain Kate . . . I mean, she would *never* . . ." For once, Jane Coulter seemed out of countenance.

In front of the fireplace, O'Bannion stirred, pricking up his ears at the sound of her voice, its change in tone. Slowly, he began to rise.

"Don't give it another thought," Tos said quickly.

"Ah. You're very kind," she said. O'Bannion subsided, but instead of closing his eyes he kept them open and fixed unwinkingly on the two men now edging toward the door. "I wish you luck in finding Aiken's killer."

"Yes, ma'am. I expect we'll need it," Tos said with a very, very big smile and a last, furtive glance at the dog.

"What'sa matter," Neilson asked when they returned to the car. "Did she get away from you?"

"Very funny," Tos growled. "She's just a nice little old lady, don't be so fast with your mouth."

"*Sooorree,*" said Neilson, giving Pinsky a look.

"She reminds me of the people who milk rattlesnakes," Stryker said unexpectedly, and they all looked at him in surprise. "She called Adamson 'manageable'—but everyone else either hated him or was afraid of him or both. Not her. He didn't worry her one damn bit."

"With a dog like that, why should she worry about anyone?" Tos asked. "She probably didn't have any reason to be scared of him."

"Or maybe she had a reason *not* to be scared," Stryker said.

"Same thing," Tos said dismissively, starting the engine.

Neilson looked at Stryker thoughtfully. "No, it isn't."

Stryker looked at his watch. "We're late," he said. "I hope the lawyer hasn't given up on us."

ADAMSON HAD LIVED in Lakeside Hills, on a meticulously cleared curving road from which only occasional glimpses of sprawling ranch-styles or upright mock-Georgian outlines were possible through the trees or at the far end of gravelled drives.

In the city, filthy slush spattered the drifted, thrown or shoveled snow—but out here all remained deep and crisp and even. It was a land of banker kings and advertising-agency princes, and an unlikely setting for a college professor.

When they finally located the mailbox bearing Adamson's name, they found a car had preceded them up the drive. A two-tone grey Rolls was waiting before the closed garage doors. Pinsky drew up beside it and stopped the engine of their own sedan, which barked and hiccoughed before finally accepting defeat. A small, dapper man got out of the Rolls. "Lieutenant Stryker? I'm Roger Stewart." He extended a perfectly manicured hand, sans glove. "I live nearby, so I got elected for duty." Stewart's clasp was warm and strong, as befitted a senior partner of one of the city's most prestigious law firms, but surprising in one of his light stature. Handball, Stryker guessed. Uptown Athletic. At least twice a week.

"I expected a junior clerk to be stuck with this."

"Would have been," Stewart agreed with a brief smile. "But Adamson was an old and valued client—and, as I say, I live nearby. Do you have his keys?"

Last rites, Stryker thought, and produced them. They went across the wide patio of the mock-Colonial house, their city shoes squeaking in the powdering of snow that had blown under the overhanging roof. The sky was pale, and the air was much colder out here. Their breath hung in the stillness. A few birds made their contribution, and a bush beside the entrance gave a tentative creak and rustle in a momentary current of air. Otherwise the key in the lock was the loudest sound around.

As the door swung open, stale warm air came out to envelop them, bearing the smell of good furniture and good polish, but nothing remotely human. No cooking odours, no soap recently lathered in the shower, no cigarettes, no aftershave, no sweat.

Nobody home.

Stewart went in and they followed, stamping the snow from their shoes onto the black and white tiles of the entrance hall. "I think

Professor Adamson had a daily housekeeper during the week, but no one living in. No living family, either.''

They moved to the archway that opened onto the sitting room. No doubt about it, Stryker thought—this had been a rich man's house. The walls were a pale robin's-egg blue, the carpet a dark bronze and overlaid with oriental rugs. Much of the furniture was custom-made, the rest antiques. Stryker, whose parents had been antique dealers before their joint and premature death on a buying trip to Europe, touched an inlaid tabouret and thought of them. They'd left him little but a few pieces of furniture, memories, and a knowledge he'd never been aware of acquiring as he grew up, so gently had it permeated his mind. It was there with him now, in his eyes and fingertips, and he knew something was wrong. College professors just *don't* have this kind of money.

The smaller paintings on the walls were delicate and lovely in their way—but overshadowed by the four large modern oils that hung, one to each wall. All by the same artist, and painted by a hand of true power. Stryker didn't have to know much about modern art to know that. What was equally obvious was that they had all been painted for this room and no other. The colours toned with their surroundings, the proportions were exactly right—and the subjects would have made them unsalable to the general public. The subjects were men, their activities detailed precisely, the erotic intention totally clear.

"Good God," murmured Stewart as Neilson snickered and muttered something to Pinsky, who shifted from one foot to the other and began examining the rugs. Stryker silenced Neilson with a glance, then looked at Stewart. The little man was obviously embarrassed. "I had no idea...that is to say, one *guessed* but..." He cleared his throat, regained his calm. When he spoke again, there was a wry, humorous edge to his voice. "No doubt his neighbours waited in vain for an invitation to tea."

Stryker grinned. "You didn't know him well?"

Stewart shook his head. "No, I'm glad to say, I did not. We've handled his account for years, of course, but it was not a social relationship. My wife would love this."

"Your *wife*?" Toscarelli exclaimed, deeply shocked.

Stewart smiled. "She's a psychiatrist." He unbuttoned his coat and looked around. "Well, where do you want to begin, Lieutenant? And what, exactly, are you hoping to find?"

"Anything that might give us a lead to his killer," Stryker said. "For example, where did he get his money?"

"Oh, that's easily answered," Stewart said. "He inherited it."

Stryker stared at him, having expected anything but that. "But— I was told he was illegitimate. Brought up in an orphanage."

"So he was. But the man who fathered him eventually acknowledged the relationship in his will. He had no other living child to leave his money to, so Adamson got it all. I've always thought it was in the nature of a guilt payment. The old man had never acknowledged Adamson in his lifetime. It came as a complete shock to Aiken when we got in touch with him. He'd had a difficult and rather unpleasant time of it until the age of twenty or so, and I think it had made him very bitter. At first he even considered rejecting the inheritance—until he learned the full amount."

"If there were no other children . . ."

"Oh, there *had* been other children, but they had died before the father. Rather tragically, in their teens. A boating accident. Wife went a little crazy, killed herself a few months later."

Something stirred in the back of Stryker's mind. "You don't mean Adamson was . . . Ezra Craddick's son?"

Stewart looked at him and his mouth twitched, as if it wanted to smile. "I said no such thing, Lieutenant, you jumped to that conclusion on your own."

Stryker considered this. Ezra Craddick had been a local millionaire who'd hit big with some early automotive patents and parlayed the income into a fortune with shrewd investments. He'd been a pillar of local Catholic society, a man known for his great rectitude and high moral standards.

"Why didn't Adamson change his name when he found out?"

"It was a condition of the will that he did not, and that the relationship was, as far as possible, kept secret."

"His mother?"

"Had died when he was a year old. Syphilis, contracted in a professional capacity. The support of her—patron—ended with her death, and the boy was placed in public care."

"Until inheriting a fortune in his twenties," Stryker said. "No wonder he was bitter. But instead of going wild with his inheritance, he became a professor of English. Why?"

Stewart raised his hands and shrugged. "He *did* raise a little discreet hell for a few years. Then he settled down. I believe he said he'd found frivolity and idleness boring. I don't think he was fitted for any other occupation, temperamentally. He certainly had no business sense whatsoever—we've handled all his investments for him since he inherited.''

And done well out of it, no doubt, Stryker thought without rancour. Stewart seemed pretty straight. For a lawyer. "What happens to the money now? Who inherits?"

"Quite a few people, as a matter of fact. He was by way of being a will freak. Always cutting people out and putting others in. It hasn't been through probate, but as there are no surviving relatives, I thought there would be no objection to my providing you with a list of cui bono." He reached into his inside pocket and drew out a folded paper. "This is the current—the *final* list. Frankly, I have no way of knowing what criteria he used in choosing them. Nor do I know whether he told them about it or not. He was a secretive man. But he might have—he was the sort who liked to manipulate people."

"So we've been told," Stryker said, taking the paper and opening it. As his eyes went down the list, he became very still.

There were about twenty names on the list—with a note beside each indicating the amount he or she was to receive. Among the names that were not known to him were some that were—including one that he'd seen a few hours earlier. Richard Wayland was to inherit fifty thousand dollars.

Frank Heath, Chris Underhill, Kate Trevorne and Lucy Grey-Jenner were to get ten thousand each.

"Is this all his estate?" Stryker asked. The bequests listed added up to nearly half a million.

"Oh, no, not at all," Stewart said. "The balance goes to various things. Orphanages, hospitals, the university. I've brought you a copy of the will, too. It's a very—" He hesitated as he drew it out of his inside pocket. "It's a very *personal* document. Not at all the usual thing. Some of the comments in it are *very* odd indeed, a few virtually slander. I tried many times to get him to alter some of the passages, but he was adamant. I always hoped he would mellow in time—but there wasn't *enough* time, unfortunately."

"How large is the estate?"

"Oh, once all the assets are realized, I should say somewhere in the region of three million," Stewart estimated. "He never used the capital, really, lived on the interest for the most part. It simply *grew*—like Topsy." He grinned suddenly.

"I can see why you took the trouble to come yourself," Stryker said.

"Indeed," Stewart nodded, taking no offence. For all his dapper elegance he seemed a very practical man. "The firm has and shall do nicely out of it. My problem will be to administer the will without offending anyone. With his being murdered like this, the press will be sniffing around like hounds. Especially when they find out how wealthy he really was. Aiken has even managed to be awkward in death—how like him!"

"Fifty thousand is a damn good motivator for murder," Neilson said, peering over Stryker's shoulder.

"So is ten," Pinsky observed. "Ten isn't bad."

"That's why I thought you should see it," Stewart murmured.

"Look at this," Toscarelli said. He had taken the will from Stewart and begun to scan it. He held it out to Stryker, pointing with a huge finger.

"I see Dan Stark is in the will too, but you didn't list him," Stryker said to Stewart. "A hundred thousand—is that right?"

Stewart shook his head. "He's not a *direct* beneficiary, he doesn't inherit himself, but on behalf of the English Department of the university. A Special Fund to be used at his discretion for the improvement of the department. He *did* know about that, because Aiken had discussed it with him and we'd exchanged several letters on the subject. Stark could either use it to establish scholarships or lure good teaching talent—whichever seemed appropriate. It was conditional on Stark being chairman—any change there and the money reverted to the estate."

"Pinchman, too," Toscarelli said, moving his finger down.

"Edgar Pinchman, yes—but again, not directly benefiting. Most extraordinary, that. An endowment on Pinchman's behalf to the *Cattlemen's* Association to pay the medical expenses of any member injured sufficiently to require amputation."

"You're kidding," Neilson said.

"No, I am not. Aiken seemed to find it very amusing. Said Pinchman didn't need the money himself—had plenty. That's what I meant about his will. If you look farther down you'll see there's a bequest to a certain Mary Jeske for the 'purchase of medical equipment.' I happen to know—"

"She runs a whorehouse down on Clary Street," Pinsky said in his slow, ruminative way. "Kinky stuff."

"So I hear," Stewart said drily. "Then there's the Maud Fineman Scholarship, to be established at the Horticultural College for the benefit of 'promising young male gardeners.' You see what I mean about its being a personal document. There are dozens of bequests like that—all open to a number of interpretations. Mostly small, but all—rather unpleasant."

"Legal?"

"Oh, yes, entirely legal. I drew the document myself." Stewart made a face. "God help me when it comes to administering it. He specified a public reading—" He made a despairing noise and shook himself. "Well, where do you want to begin?"

Stryker, bemused by these revelations of Adamson's twisted personality, deployed his men. They went systematically through the sitting room and the library, looking for address books, diaries, letters—anything that would give them leads into the private life which Adamson had kept so scrupulously separate from his professional one.

They found letters, all right, and a sheaf of poems written to someone called "Apollo Emergent" that made even Stewart blush.

Pinsky found the card file. A catalogue of "friends" (or conquests), describing each as to appearance, performance, and duration of relationship. Most seemed to have been "paid off" with gifts or money after a night or a week; very few lasted longer. The file went back for about five years—presumably he culled it annually. Four seemed to have meant something to him—and all four of these names were among the direct beneficiaries of his will. One was the artist who had painted the pictures in the living room. None were connected with the university.

"It's incredible," Stewart murmured, shaking his head. "How could he have had the time for it all? The *energy*? He taught full time, he published articles regularly..."

"He never had to take his wife shopping or change any diapers," Pinsky observed. "Or take out the garbage, even."

"Let's try the bedroom,"; Stryker suggested.

All the beautiful things in Adamson's home could not ameliorate the atmosphere which was building up as they turned over papers and photographs revealing his private obsessions. Stryker felt almost sick to his stomach. He'd worked for Vice for a while on his way up, and was supposedly immune to such things. He was enthusiastically heterosexual himself, but counted several homosexuals among his acquaintances and one as a good friend. None of them were anything like Adamson had been. In all his experience, he couldn't recall having encountered such a person. Underlying everything Adamson had been, done or said was a feeling of resentment and hate that was sour, bitter and frightening.

He found himself feeling almost glad the man was dead.

That's very unprofessional, he told himself. Stop it.

The bedroom was, in its way, the worst of all. It was a monument to Adamson's ego. It was difficult to imagine him doing anything as mundane as sleeping there, or suffering from the flu, or belching or scratching. The ceiling was mirrored, as were portions of each wall. Louvered mahogany doors accounted for the rest of the wall space. These slid back silently to reveal, in turn, closets, an entertainment centre with video cassettes neatly labelled and racked, a bar with refrigerator, and the entrance to a luxurious bathroom that connected with another, smaller and more austere, guest bathroom.

The only furniture in the room was the king-sized bed, overlaid with a fur spread in shades of red-brown.

As Neilson and Pinsky went gingerly through clothing and drawers, Stryker looked around, wondering what was missing. Then it hit him—no windows. He went to the mirrors at the head of the bed and examined them closely. After a moment, he found an indentation and swung one panel back to reveal a window beside the bed, uncurtained and dusty. If this mirror swung back, did the others?

They did.

And behind the sixth one, he found the safe.

Stewart, catching sight of it, straightened up. "Ah," he said. "I *wondered* where that was."

Stryker looked at the steel door. "Do you have the combination, by any chance?"

"Not by chance—Aiken gave me the combination for just such an event. He kept what he called 'loose change' in it. I'll need you to witness any cash for audit purposes." He sighed and turned the knob, referring to a small notebook he'd produced. "I find all this very distasteful. I suppose you're used to it." As he swung the door open, he turned. "I didn't mean that in a derogatory way, I meant—"

"I know what you meant," Stryker said quietly.

Stewart flushed slightly and opened the safe. It contained two small grey steel boxes and a green-backed looseleaf notebook. The boxes were not locked and contained various pieces of gold jewellery (male) and about two thousand dollars in cash. While the others were counting and listing the cash, Stryker picked up the notebook.

After a moment, he dropped it, turned away, and went into the bathroom to wash his face with cold water. When he returned, he found Stewart had picked it up and was looking at it, his face rather pale.

"I think this should be burnt, immediately," he said in a thin voice. "No question, it should be destroyed."

"I'm afraid that's impossible," Stryker said. "It could be evidence."

"It *is* evidence," Stewart said. "Evidence that Adamson was a vicious monster." He put the book down. Neilson, curious, stared at it, then at the two of them.

"What's so terrible?" he asked.

"Try it," Stryker said.

Neilson picked up the book and began to leaf through it. Stryker watched his face, the tough young smart-ass of a streetwise cop, newly into plain clothes, all ambition and lip. Maybe he and Stewart were wrong, maybe they were middle-aged and overreacting. Then Neilson looked up and he knew he was right.

Looked at coldly, word for word, what was in the book *wasn't* so terrible. Merely the jottings of a gossip magpie. Notes about the failings of Adamson's fellow human beings. Sometimes letters or photos were attached to the relevant page—along with notes about the victim's reactions when Adamson revealed to them what he knew. For Adamson *had* been a blackmailer.

Not for money.

But for fun.

Stryker remembered Kate Trevorne's comment about Adamson "turning his guns on you." In the tight, backhanded writing of the green notebook, Adamson repeatedly wrote with venomous relish of the "trembling lips" or "pale face" of his "targets." How cleverly he had dropped this hint or that, letting his victim (and *only* his victim) know that he was privy to his or her secrets. And not the big, dark secrets, either. That would have been too easy, too ordinary, too much like crime for a connoisseur.

The sources of Adamson's glee were the petty shameful secrets that revealed so much about a victim's inner life. Page after page of it, gloated over, savoured—and used. Stryker could almost imagine Adamson's voice. He thought it would have been a high, light voice, as thin and sharp as a hypodermic needle filled with acid.

"...bloated Maud Fineman and her hothouse roses. They aren't the only thing that young gardener of hers gets up in that greenhouse of hers—although how he can manage it with that two-legged Pekinese I'll never know. Perhaps he's nearsighted—or very, very desperate for money...

"...Dr. Kuchinsky's little 'operations' at Mary Jeske's. Did he take a *Hypocritic* Oath instead of the one that says he's supposed to ease pain? I'm told the girls cry for hours, but he never leaves a scar. What *skill*..."

"...Councilman Griggs and his 'private' toilet. Ought to be private, with that peephole through to the Ladies' Room so he can watch *all* their little movements..."

"...doesn't anyone wonder *why* Abernathy buys so much chocolate sauce? Or where he puts it, so the dog can lick it off?...

"...I've heard of bodies buried in the garden, but Nancy is running out of places to hide those rum bottles...and all in memory of that sailor..."

"...only got the money back in time. Church funds were never meant for horses, were they? Or is it all God's creatures? I must ask him next week, after the service..."

"The names will have to be checked out," Stryker said, feeling suddenly weary. "We'll be as discreet as we can, but we have to know if they had alibis. They all must have hated his guts."

"Talk about grinding the faces of the poor..." Neilson murmured, and put the book down.

There was silence in the room, and then Stewart spoke, his back to them, his voice reflective. "My wife had a theory about him, you know."

"Oh?" Stryker asked, hoping for some objectivity.

"Yes," Stewart said. "According to her, he was a compulsive victim, a monstrous egotist and yet a self-hater, in search of an executioner."

Stryker nodded. "Then, I guess we could say Aiken Adamson was a successful man," he said, and reluctantly began to copy names from the green book. "We now have a suspect list of about two hundred. We really appreciate that, don't we, boys?"

"We *really* appreciate that," echoed Toscarelli, Pinsky and Neilson.

FIFTEEN

NORMAL MONDAY MORNINGS are bad enough, Kate thought.

This Monday morning is the pits.

They'd had the weekend to brood. The smiles they exchanged as they wandered in were brief and unconvincing. One by one, they went to their pigeonholes and discovered a directive from Dan—if approached by press, students or other faculty, they were to say nothing, admit nothing, discuss nothing concerning the murder of Aiken Adamson. Otherwise business as usual.

Fat chance, Kate thought. Even here, in the supposedly safe cloister of their own departmental office, the tension was painfully evident. No small talk at all. Someone, opening a letter, hissed like a snake in anger or dismay. Another cursed softly over some bill, a third crumpled things into balls one after another and tossed them into the wastebasket. Kate surveyed her own meagre harvest: an overdue notice from the university library, an offer to buy reference books at a third off, a long-overdue paper from a student, a note from another begging her to make space in a Monday-Wednesday class, and a notification of a conference in California she had neither the time nor the money to attend. Looking up, she tried to smile but it was not returned.

Mark Heskell was frowning at Dan's note, Jane Coulter was stuffing things into her briefcase, Pete Rocheleau was folding up a letter on blue paper, and Arthur Fowler was tearing another into pieces. As he went past her to drop the resultant confetti into the basket, she saw he'd put on mismatching socks. Arthur? He *must* be upset.

Mark Heskell, going out the door, bumped into a distracted Chris Underhill, who didn't even bother to snarl.

Frank Heath and Lucy Grey-Jenner stood to one side, both engrossed in their mail, looking for all the world like an old married couple, with their heads tilted the same way, their bodies in sympathetic proximity. And Edward Pinchman, sinking into a chair, muttering to himself angrily.

Kate, looking at them all, saw they were suddenly strangers, and felt isolated and peculiar. She supposed they viewed her the same way.

Uneasy at her own altered perceptions of colleagues and friends, she left the main office and walked to her own. Richard was before her, unlocking his door, across the hall. He looked up at the sound of her step. His own unopened mail was clutched in his hand along with the handle of his briefcase.

"My God, where have you *been*?" Kate demanded. "I kept phoning you all day yesterday—didn't they give you the message?"

"I was out."

She stared at him. He seemed suddenly a stranger too. He put his briefcase down, very deliberately, and turned to stare at her. His eyes told her he was not only a stranger, but an enemy. When he spoke, his voice was dangerously calm.

"I'd like you to give a message to your good buddy Liz Olson, she of the ever-open mouth, but I don't think you'd like carrying it. Just thank her for her 'help,' will you?"

"Richard, you don't understand—"

"Oh, but I do, that's just it. She has nothing to do with this department, and any alibi she gives you is far stronger than any *I* might provide. Very sensible of you to make the switch. The fact that it leaves me with my ass hanging out—"

"It wasn't my idea," Kate said hotly. "I tried to stop her—"

"I'll *bet* you did. Just like you tried to stop your precious policeman from dragging me out of the fraternity house in front of most of the kids and transporting me to the police station like some criminal? He put me through the wringer, all right, the bastard."

"He didn't—"

"Oh, yes, he did."

"You shouldn't have lied, Richard. Having no alibi is almost better than having a tight one. Most people don't have alibis at all for any given time—"

"But *you* do, don't you, sweetheart? Thanks to Liz. You'd almost think you'd realized you'd need one, wouldn't you? So much for me trying to protect you—"

"You were protecting yourself, too," she flared.

He went pale. "I see. Well, thank you for that, Kate. There's nothing like the trust and confidence of friends to see you through, is there?" He picked up his briefcase, went into his office and slammed the door.

Instantly she felt her own anger ebb, and the old habit of forgiving and protecting him tugged at her. She hesitated, wondering whether to cross the miles that lay between them, took a step—and then jumped as the nine o'clock bell rang.

No time.

So he thought she'd betrayed him. Left him standing alone without an alibi, without a friend, when he'd lied so glibly for her? Well, she hadn't *asked* him to lie, had she?

And he *had* left before midnight.

Appalled, she listened to her own silent accusations. So this was what murder did to people. Aiken Adamson was dead—and his poison lived on after him. No good would be interred with his bones.

TWO CLASSES LATER, she went to collect the reading lists she'd left to be photocopied. As she entered the departmental office, she was astonished to see the four secretaries spring apart like guilty schoolgirls. Three of them hurried to their desks and began typing furiously. Karen Lasterman came over to the reception desk.

"Can I help you, Kate?" Karen had been departmental secretary when Kate had been both student and student assistant to Dan Stark, and had yet to begin calling her "Miss Trevorne." Karen was a tall, slim blonde girl who'd come straight to the department from secretarial school, and she was fiercely loyal to it and everyone in it.

"My reading lists ready?"

"Sure." She retrieved them from the copier.

"Thanks." Kate lingered, perversely. "How's . . . everything?"

Karen's mouth grew grim. "Well, a couple of the girls were cornered by reporters but managed to get away. Mostly it's been the gawpers that have caused trouble."

"Gawpers?"

Karen made a face. "You know—sight seers. We've had more kids up here making more damn stupid requests about classes and schedules than we have enrolled in classes this term. I finally had to call Security and ask them to put someone on the stairs and elevators to stop them unless they had legitimate business up here. A bunch of ghouls, if you ask me." She leaned forward slightly. "Even a few stray faculty members from other departments."

"I suppose it's inevitable," Kate murmured.

Karen shrugged. "I really thought that Lieutenant Stryker would have solved it all over the weekend, but no. He was on the phone to Dan first thing this morning, wanting to make appointments and asking me for everyone's class schedules."

"Whatever for?"

"I suppose he wants to talk to everyone again."

"Oh, God."

Karen looked surprised. "I think he's kind of cute."

"I don't think he's kind of anything but necessary—and I wish he weren't."

"Even if it meant having Adamson alive again?"

"Even that." As she went out, she heard the birdlike chittering of the secretaries begin again, higher and faster than before. She supposed they were happy, in their way. Murder was much more interesting than who was dating whom these days.

She came around the corner, propelled by rising indignation, to discover someone standing in front of Aiken Adamson's office door. It was a young girl carrying a large brown envelope. She turned as Kate approached, startled and somehow guilty. Kate assumed this must be one of the "gawpers," caught in the act.

"What do you want, there?" she asked, perhaps a little more officiously than she'd intended, for the girl flushed.

"I read . . . about him dying," she faltered, her knuckles whitening on the envelope. She could have been a student, but lacked the arrogance.

"And?" Kate asked sternly.

"Well, I had this for him and now I don't know what to *do* with it."

"What is it?"

"Something I was typing up for him. I took a long time because Jimmy got sick again, so I was working over the whole weekend and then this morning I saw the papers and I probably won't get paid now, and I need the money so much—" The words came faster and faster, as if a plug had been pulled. Tears threatened to follow.

"Oh, I'm sorry, I didn't mean to bark at you," Kate said, feeling small and mean. "Look, you did this for Aiken, is that it?"

The girl nodded. "I've had it for *weeks*, and when he called me on Friday afternoon he was so *angry*, so I worked all weekend—"

"Okay, okay...look, come on to my office and tell me all about it. I'll see you get paid."

"Oh, will you?" The sun came out from behind the clouds. "Soon?"

"If I can. Why didn't you just take the thing down to the office?"

The girl blushed. "He told me that he should have given it to one of *them* to type, but he didn't want anyone to know about the book in case they stole his ideas. He wanted to surprise everyone, he said."

More likely, he didn't want to pay the going rate, Kate thought, and when she asked the girl what her fee was, her suspicion was confirmed. How typical of Aiken to get some poor kid to type his measly manuscript on the cheap and then browbeat her into the bargain. "You need the money now, do you?" she asked.

"Yes. Jimmy being off work and all, and the pills the doctor prescribed cost so *much*—"

"Okay, don't worry. I'll give you a cheque myself, and get it back from Aiken's estate, all right?" Kate wrote out the cheque. After all, the girl wasn't a sensation-seeker, Kate had scared her half to death, and she *did* look a little threadbare.

"Oh, that's wonderful," the girl said, swelling with gratitude until she looked almost well fed. "And I'll give you a receipt, all right?"

"Fine." Kate took the bit of paper, glanced at it and stuffed it into her purse.

"Gee, I don't know how to thank you, Miss Trevorne."

"No need. I hope your Jimmy is better soon."

Kate smiled the girl out, then turned to look at the fat brown envelope resting on the corner of her desk. Another of Aiken's clever, clever articles? Or that thing on the erotic aspects of mythology he'd been threatening to bring out for the past fifteen years? No—the girl hadn't been embarrassed when she handed it over, just very relieved. On impulse, Kate opened the envelope and peeped inside, squinting to read the title upside down. "Four" something "Cavalry"? A study of Custer's Last Stand, perhaps?

The eleven o'clock bell went, leaving her no more time for snooping or conjecture. She'd have to read it later. Quickly she shoved Aiken's manuscript into the bottom drawer of her desk and fled down the hall. Students were traditionally expected to wait fifteen minutes for a full professor, but for a lowly instructor like herself, only five.

SHE COULD SEE it in their eyes.

What was the point of talking about crime fiction when a real-life murder had been committed over their very heads? The lecture room in which Kate's History and Development of the Crime Novel took place was on the third floor of Grantham Hall, more or less directly below Aiken Adamson's office.

They kept glancing up, as if expecting blood to drip through the ceiling onto their nice new notebooks.

"Now, you'll probably have done *Crime and Punishment* and *Les Misérables* in your other classes, and that's why I haven't put them on the required-reading list. But we will be referring to them in the first six weeks of class, in which we'll be covering the roots of modern crime fiction, so if you haven't read them it might be a good idea to do so. *Crime and Punishment* is, of course, a classic examination of the psychological effect of guilt, and *Les Misérables* of pursuit and persecution, on the murderer, and how the police use these effects to their advantage. In both books we have examples of the character of the Relentless Police Officer. In those earlier works this character was seen as heroic. Nowadays it is more often used to personify bigotry, a closed mind and a bully. I leave you to judge which is closer to the truth."

This gentle gibe always produced a ripple of laughter. This morning's was more uneasy than amused. Had she put more bitterness than usual into her voice or had it sounded to them as it sounded, suddenly, to her—a cheap shot? She glanced up at the rows of students and found her eyes instantly locked with Stryker's. He had taken a seat near the back and she hadn't noticed him in the sea of faces—until now.

He was not amused.

Stricken, Kate went back to her lecture notes, skipping the rest of the page about "cops." More cheap shots for laughs—why had she thought them so amusing before now?

"In addition to studying the crime novel as literature and as entertainment, I also propose to investigate structures and to compare methods not only of the detectives, but of the writers themselves. We'll examine their individual ways of achieving their aim—which is to keep the reader mystified until approximately five pages from the end. That is the so-called 'ideal contract' between writer and reader—the former fairly supplies the clues, and the latter agrees to suspend disbelief while trying to solve the puzzle. The reader does not *want* to solve the crime ten pages from the *beginning*, he *wants* to be mystified and dazzled—that is the entertainment he has paid for. But he would also like the opportunity to *try*. Indeed, in the Ellery Queen novels, Dannay and Lee actually inserted a challenge to the reader before the ultimate revelations, informing them that all the clues had been supplied and they should be able to do what Ellery was about to do—name the killer.

"True—in a well-constructed mystery novel the clues *are* supplied. But we must remember that this is a game, a treasure hunt, a crossword puzzle. All is not what it seems. To provide clues, most authors use what I have come to call the Mock Turtle Approach—Multiplication, Pretension, Distraction, and Derision . . ."

Somehow she got to the end. All through the lecture she could feel Stryker's eyes on her. His steady regard unnerved her so that, to her at least, everything she said had a double meaning. Or worse, no meaning at all.

The bell finally went, and the room echoed with shuffling feet, slamming books, chirpy conversations or moans about the unexpected demands of a course some had thought an "easy credit." In about two minutes the room had emptied, save for Kate and the man in the back row. "Very interesting," he said without moving.

"I'm glad you thought so," she said, gathering her papers together and jamming them into her briefcase.

"I'm glad to see you've included Charlie Chan on your reading list," Stryker said, indicating the photocopied sheet lying on the desk in front of him. "How they ever managed to build six superb books into two dozen lousy movies I'll never know."

"All right, I'm impressed," Kate conceded. "Did you merely come to scoff, or will you remain to prey?"

"You have a free period now."

"So I do. Are you going to usurp it to put me through the wringer, as you did Richard Wayland?"

"I didn't put him through the wringer," Stryker protested mildly.

"You dragged him downtown . . ."

"We asked him to come down, yes . . ."

"And questioned him . . ."

"That happens to be my job."

"So they said at Nuremberg."

He raised an eyebrow. "Look, think what you like of me personally. I can't stop you. But since you weren't present at the interview I had with Wayland, I would respectfully suggest that any impression you may have received concerning the way it was conducted must necessarily be biased."

She picked up her briefcase and started for the door. "You sound like a lawyer."

He stood up as he considered this. "Guilty. Of sounding like a lawyer, that is. *Not* of harassing Wayland. Any aggression displayed was his, not mine." He paused. "Sorry, I *did* raise my voice once. That's all. If he told you I did anything more, he must be very afraid of me. Why would he be afraid of me, do you suppose?"

She went out into the hall and he followed close behind her. "He doesn't have an alibi and he didn't like Aiken," she said.

"About half the population of this city are in the same position," Stryker commented. "*You're* the one who's unique, with your alibi. *I* don't have an alibi for the relevant time either. And from what I'm learning about the man, I'd guess that if I'd known him I might have been tempted to bump him off, myself."

"Well, then—" She was walking very fast down the hall and he was keeping pace, keeping close.

"Being a son-of-a-bitch doesn't deprive Adamson of the right to society's vengeance for his murder. I'm paid to investigate cases of homicide. God judges the dead, the courts judge the living. I'm neither." He scowled at her as they neared the far doors. "Where the hell are you going, anyway?"

"To the union to get a sandwich."

"You haven't got a coat on."

"I'll run." She was, nearly.

He reached into his jacket pocket and produced a mitten. "Maybe this would help keep you warm.

She glanced at it, stared at it, stopped. "Is it yours?" he asked.

"I do have a pair *like* that," she conceded reluctantly. She knew it was hers, she could see the place on the thumb where her briefcase habitually rubbed. "Where did you get it?"

"I found this under the front seat of Adamson's car." The second bell had rung and the hall had cleared of students. His voice was soft, and the silence that followed his statement was a question in itself.

She put down her briefcase and took the mitten to examine it. "I might have dropped it last Wednesday," she admitted slowly. "Aiken drove several of us downtown to see an exhibit."

"Nice of him."

"Oh, he didn't intend to do it. But my car wouldn't start and Jane's was blocked in. We were standing in the parking lot deciding what to do when Aiken came along and was more or less shamed into offering." Was it her imagination or did he seem relieved? "Do you want this back for evidence or anything?"

"No, you can keep it." He watched her rubbing at a dark stain near the thumb. "Chocolate sauce," he volunteered, and regretted it, as her eyes met his.

"You had it *analyzed*?"

"Yes." He regretted having to admit that, too.

"My goodness!" Her eyes widened. "I guess you'll have to charge me with being drunk in charge of an ice-cream sundae."

"And a hot dog with mustard. Index finger area, halfway down."

She found the mark—a very tiny mark—and looked at him with a martyred expression. "Then, I guess it had better be sloppy eating. Do you give any time off for subsequent use of napkin?"

"No—we're tightening up on that."

Their eyes met again, held for a moment, and then Stryker bent down to pick up her briefcase. He offered the coat he'd had over his arm. "If we're going over to the union, you'd better use this."

"No, thank you, I'll be fine."

He spoke through clenched teeth. "Take the goddamn coat—we don't allow time off for pneumonia, either. I'm hungry, you're hungry, we'll go, we'll eat. All right?"

"Is this an official interview?"

He pushed open the door and a blast of icy air flapped the coat like a cape as she put it over her shoulders. "No—for official interviews, *I* wear the coat and *you* hide behind the briefcase. Move it, will you? I'm freezing my ass off, here."

The union cafeteria was already filling up. They found a small table in a corner and settled down. He noted with approval that they both had taken the tuna-fish sandwiches. "They really do them right, there, don't they? Egg, onion—the works."

She regarded him cautiously as he bit enthusiastically into one of the union's undoubtedly superior tuna-fish sandwiches. He was dressed more neatly than he had been on Saturday—he could have passed for a graduate student in his blue shirt and black-and-white herringbone sports coat. He wore a tie, his shoes were highly polished, he'd shaved—all very presentable.

"What do you want from me, Lieutenant?" she asked.

He finished chewing, took a swallow of coffee, leaned back. "I need a spy," he said.

"A *spy*?" Startled, she could only go on staring at him.

"Right. I need to know what goes on in your department over the next few days. *I* can't hang around, and some undercover guy dressed up as a student would stick out because students don't hang around up there either. No—I need a spy."

"And naturally you thought of me, seeing as I'm so obviously disloyal, sneaky, backbiting and two-faced."

"Seeing as you have an alibi which I *think* is solid, and also because you seem the kind of person who might be interested in justice. At least I was frank—I could have called it something else."

"You think my being a spy would have something to do with *justice*?"

"If it helps me catch a killer, yes." He leaned forward and put his elbows on the table. "What's the matter—old-fashioned concepts bother you? Or is it just not your problem?"

"I didn't say that."

"Yes, you did. Your face, your tone, everything. Look, I'm trained to smell out killers, and I tell you that there is something rotten in that holier-than-me ivory-tower department of yours. I'm not giving up on other possibilities—no way—but I'm certainly not going to discount my instinctive feelings about your little crowd of cronies simply because you all use big words. Big deal! Big words buyeth not *this* man's awe."

"Why don't you ask Dan? He has an alibi, doesn't he?"

"Nope—he's too defensive about his 'little flock.' All the older ones are like that. I'm asking *you*. I want *your* help."

"But *why*?" She leaned back, took a deep breath, and said it. "Is it because of that day you didn't arrest me with the others?" His face stayed blank, but something in his eyes flickered. She leaned forward, nudging her coffee cup perilously close to the edge. "It is, isn't it? You think I 'owe you one,' don't you?" He still didn't say anything. "Oh, you smug *bastard*!" she burst out, startling them both. Her coffee cup started to go over, and his hand shot out to catch it.

"Take it easy, Kate—"

"*Kate?* How dare you—"

"Are you okay, Miss Trevorne?" It was Jody Longman, tray in hand, looming large with concern next to their table. "You want to come over and sit with us?" He nodded toward another table, where several of Richard's fraternity charges sat. They were all watching, and Kate felt herself blushing furiously, knowing that the least plea from her could lead to a nasty scene—they'd love any excuse to take out Stryker, or any other cop.

"No, thanks, Jody. I'm fine, really."

He eyed Stryker. He was a big boy—they were all big boys at the other table. "We all like Miss Trevorne here, you know?"

"I don't blame you," Stryker said calmly. "I like her too."

"Yeah, well—"

"It's all right, Jody, really. I was just angry about something silly, that's all. You go eat your lunch—you haven't got much time before your next class, have you?" she asked desperately, not knowing his schedule. Eventually, after another eye-to-eye battle with an amused Stryker, Jody moved off.

After a moment, Stryker spoke. "It *was* silly, you know. I was hoping you'd forgotten it."

"I'll bet you were," she said in a low, tight voice. "I've *never* forgotten it. You and all those other cops, my god, you swarmed into the old department as if we had an atomic bomb in there, swinging your sticks and yelling. It was terrifying, just terrifying . . ."

"Is that why you ran?"

She looked away. She could still feel the way her heart had pounded. It was pounding now. The sound of his boots clattering up the stairs behind her, down the hall, the way she'd been cornered in that empty room, nearly gibbering with terror. She knew he was not tall, but he'd seemed huge then. Even when she'd realised he was young, the helmet and dark glasses had made him seem like some dark and evil knight, so menacing. If she could have seen his eyes then, as she could see them now . . .

"That wasn't me, you know," he said softly. "That was a kid about three months out of the Academy. It was my first demo and *I* was terrified too. You figured you had a cause, you all felt noble and wonderful, right? Me, I was scared out of my socks that I'd mess up. So much noise, so much smart-ass *hatred* coming at us. I was scared of you all, scared of hurting you, if you want the truth, but even more scared that my fellow officers would *see* how scared I was. When you lit out it was a relief—you gave me a chance to run away too. We got to that classroom, I thought maybe we'd talk about it, I could use my 'social skills' and all that crap—but then, when you spat at me—"

"I didn't," she protested, aghast.

"The hell you didn't. On me *and* my badge. I'd just gone through two years of hell to earn that uniform, and it meant a lot to me. What you and your pseudo-intellectual buddies were protesting about actually had my sympathy—but when you did *that*, something in me snapped. Okay, I'm sorry, but I could have killed you I was so angry. Instead . . ." He stopped.

The memory that lay between them shimmered and flamed momentarily. They both remembered his hand on her bare flesh. The sound of it, the heat of the impact, echoed silently, and they looked anywhere, everywhere but at each other. They should have laughed, of course. Under any other circumstances they *would* have laughed, because it was only a long-ago incident, kind of wild and kind of exciting, and they were grown up now.

Weren't they?

The noise and the chatter and the laughter of the students washed around them, blurred into no sound at all but made a kind of cocoon, isolating them. "You could have reported me, got me thrown off the force, you know that?"

"Yes, I know that." She, too, spoke quietly. She remembered spitting now. Remembered how he'd gone rigid, his tentative half smile had been wiped away as he'd wiped the spit from his uniform and then moved toward her . . .

"Did you know it then?"

"Yes." (But she'd also known she deserved that spanking.)

"Okay. Then, I guess I owe *you* one."

Now that it was out in the open she felt strangely empty—as if she'd given something saved from her childhood to a total stranger. It was gone forever, whatever it was. "We're even," she told him.

"Then, help me." He leaned forward now, she could feel his warmth on her face, their hands were close on the table. "The things you were protesting about then must have meant something to you—you must have cared about 'fairness' and 'justice.'"

"I cared about Richard, that's all. My convictions were rather secondhand, even then. As I've gotten older I've learned to pick and choose my 'beliefs,' in order to survive."

"I know what you mean," he said. "I haven't got many of those old shiny ideals left, myself. I'll tell you, they were heavy to carry around all the time—hence the chronic backache of middle age. One of the few I've got left is doing the best I can at my job. Corny, but I'm stuck with it. I'm trained to catch killers so people with or without ideals can sleep nights, you know? Maybe not every night, but most nights."

"But don't you see? I'm *not* trained," Kate said, seizing on this. "The only detective training *I've* had has come from books, fiction. What if I told you something that was irrelevant and you drew the wrong conclusion from it? I don't want that on my conscience?''

"Neither do I. As it happens, I'm pretty cautious about jumping to conclusions."

"Oh, really? I've heard they call you 'Jumping Jack,'" she said with a half smile. "You jumped to the one about Aiken Adamson being murdered by one of us in the department."

"No, I didn't." He smiled too. "I just sort of sidled up to it and gave it a nudge, that's all. Anyway, don't think of it as telling on someone, think of it as trying to clear everyone else. Don't you want it over with? I do."

She narrowed her eyes and looked at him, the Innocence Kid, the Man in the White Hat, the Good Guy. Was he being honest with her? Well, she'd do him the same favour. "I don't want to be part of it."

The mask slipped, and for a moment she saw the face she remembered, bleak and angry. His face changed so quickly, he was such a sudden man. "I see," he said in a dead voice. "Let the dirty cop do the dirty cop's job, is that it? You people who don't want to get 'involved' make me sick. Involved means 'caring.' Are you so frozen up in yourself that you don't *care* if people die before their time? Have their life ripped out of them as if they were animals who didn't deserve to breathe? That's what a killer does, you know. He *decides* who will be sacrificed so that he can survive. Don't you think that's disgusting? Don't you think that's *wrong*?''

His anger had left her and moved to the killer. He was telling her why he went on, what drove him, what burned in him and made him look so tired. She couldn't believe all cops felt that way, but if even a few did, then all her old protests and outrages had been misdirected. The trouble was, these days every direction looked wrong to her, somehow. Nothing was clean, all right. Was that what "maturity" meant? Accepting that?

"I'm not as strong as you are," she said.

"Strong? Jesus, don't you think I'm *still* scared?" he demanded. "It's not strength—it's more like running faster and faster so you don't fall down, that's all. I need your help, Kate, I'm begging for it."

"I . . . can't give it."

He looked at her for a long time, then looked down at the lapel of his jacket, and brushed something invisible from it. "That's twice," he said, and walked out.

SIXTEEN

STRYKER'S ANGER and resentment carried him through the maelstrom of students and all the way up the English Department. Oh, Stryker, he told himself, you stupid, horny bastard. Aren't you getting paid back now? He didn't know why he was so surprised at her reaction. He couldn't expect other people to compromise themselves and/or betray their friends for an abstract concept like justice. Maybe that was why he'd become such a cynic—because he always *did* expect it, and was always disappointed.

He'd so desperately wanted her to be different.

That was something which might have come from that rookie of fifteen years ago—not the old, mean cop he'd become. Rookies have dreams of fair maids—old cops have horns.

Oh, what the hell, he ordered himself, get on with the job. He stiff-armed the glass door to the main office and spoke to the secretaries in general. "Does anyone know where Professor Pinchman is? I had an appointment with him, but he's not in."

Karen Lasterman came over. "Oh, I'm sorry. I should have put a note on his door and I forgot. He went home about two hours ago—he wasn't feeling very well."

"Oh? Nothing serious, I hope."

"No, I don't think so. His health is kind of up and down, you see. He had a lot of pain from his legs but he refuses to give in until it gets the better of him, and then he's *furious*." There was unmistakable fondness in her voice as she described the old man's stubborn struggle to keep going. "We usually have to *force* him to take time off."

"Did you have to force him this morning?"

She frowned. "No, not really. He looked pretty bad. I offered to call him a taxi, but he said someone was driving him home."

"That's the Madison Hotel, on Hamilton?"

"Yes, that's right."

"Okay." He thought a moment. "Anyone else free right now?"

She leaned back and consulted a schedule taped to the wall beside the reception desk. "Frank Heath will be free at three o'clock, and so will Mr. Underhill. Everyone else had classes right through from—'' The bell in the hall rang stridently. "From *now*. Monday is our busiest day. Tomorrow would be a lot better."

"Tomorrow and tomorrow and tomorrow," said Stryker.

"Pardon?"

"Nothing. Thanks." He went out feeling all dressed up with nowhere to go. He could have come the heavy cop and dragged one of them out of class, but there was no point. He glanced at his watch. He was due at the postmortem at three, and the Madison Hotel was on the way. Maybe he'd look in on Pinchman. Why not? Hassling a cripple seemed to be Kate Trevorne's concept of a cop's favourite pastime—who was to argue with a member of the public?

He found a parking place and walked back to the hotel. The thing that had bothered him about Pinchman's story was his comment about 'feeling cold' around nine. Was that because of his disability? The heating wasn't turned off until eleven. He might be lying about how late he'd stayed—or his watch might have stopped. If he *had* been there later he might have noticed something or someone. It was worth a minute, anyway.

The Madison was an old hotel, still very shabby on the outside, but surprisingly modern within. There was still a desk, but it was no longer manned. Stryker rang a bell marked SERVICE and after a moment a man appeared, napkin in hand, surrounded by the aroma of vegetable soup—some of which had come along for the ride on his chin. "Yeah?"

"Pinchman?"

"2D—at the back."

"Is he in?"

"Came in a couple of hours ago."

"Alone?"

The man's narrow eyes narrowed more. "Young guy with him."

"What did he look like, this 'young guy'?"

The man shrugged—it was all of vast disinterest to him. "Like a young guy, what else? Tall, had a beard, like that. Who are you, anyway? Cop?"

"Cop," Stryker agreed, and walked toward the lifts. As the doors slid closed, he turned and met the now avid stare of the manager, wiping his chin with his napkin.

Pinchman's escort could have been Wayland, or Underhill, or a student, Stryker thought. When the lift doors slid back, he saw further evidence of money spent on the hotel's conversion. He supposed the rough exterior had been preserved as a kind of camouflage, blending it into the rather run-down neighbourhood that was slowly being taken over by the university. He wondered if this hotel would eventually fall, like the rest, to parking lots and blank-faced, characterless buildings like Grantham Hall. He hoped not. The plaster work on the ceilings was beautifully intricate, and the old light fittings had been preserved and restored. The carpet was thick and muffled his steps. Someone had taken a lot of trouble over this place, and he hoped they were willing to take a lot of trouble to prevent its loss.

He was so absorbed in the décor that he was almost at the door of 2D before he smelled the gas.

It was a thick old door and had some tight new locks. After five or ten kicks, Stryker ran back down the hall and banged on the door of 2A. To the questioning and suspicious face that eventually presented itself through the crack, he barked an order for an ambulance and the police, in that order. He had to produce his identification before agreement was reached. The three wasted minutes built up in him a store of frustration.

He went back to the door and kicked it in on the fourth try.

An invisible tide of gas poured out and enveloped him. As he reeled back he caught sight of the manager approaching, his annoyance visible the length of the hall.

"I'm going in," Stryker shouted. "Watch for the ambulance."

Pulling up his scarf he ran in, not daring to turn on a light. A faulty switch could provide just enough spark to blow half the hotel clear into the next street. Groping in the dim light, he staggered through the obstacle course of unfamiliar furniture to the windows, and threw them open one by one. Cold wind blew in, and snow started to settle on the carpet as he went to a door on his left. Bedroom. Empty. Door opposite? Kitchen? Yes.

He was feeling the gas now.

The stink was in his nose and throat, his brain singing and his stomach bitter. There—a dark shape huddled before the open door of an old gas oven, and from within a steady hiss. Cursing and choking, Stryker turned all the knobs until the hissing stopped, then tried the one window. Stuck.

He picked up a saucepan sitting on top of the cooker. Glass, pan, water and peeled potatoes flew out and down onto a small garden below. The wind came in bringing snow. Fair trade, Stryker thought blearily—snow for potatoes—and he knew he was close to going under.

He grasped the slumped figure under the arms to drag it out through the living room to the hall. The old man was surprisingly light, but even so he fell twice with his burden. He was nearly to the door when the first uniformed cop appeared.

A few whiffs of oxygen cleared Stryker's head, but it took some time for his heart to settle down, and his lungs sulked painfully. The paramedic who'd arrived with the ambulance was using a respirator on Pinchman, whose face was losing the rosy flush of asphyxiation.

"Will he make it?" Stryker asked, leaning against the wall.

"He might," the paramedic said. "We can be real insistent about it when we want to be. Suicide, was it?"

"Head in the oven."

"Ah, the old ways are still the good ways," the paramedic said cynically. Five minutes later, they wheeled Pinchman away and Stryker went back into the apartment. The note was in the typewriter on the desk under the window:

I can't face living any more. I killed Aiken Adamson. I hope
        we don't meet in Hell. Edward Pinchman

Poor old bastard, Stryker thought.

He looked around the room. The smell of gas was nearly gone, and the room looked as if nothing had happened there. Nothing at all. He flicked the wall switch, and the lamps came on, pooling soft yellow light onto the worn wood and upholstery of the big old chairs. Pinchman's crutches leaned against one of them. His books lined the walls with a lifetime of reading, his pipe rested beside an empty coffee cup on a nearby table, his desk with its pile of blank typing paper looked ready for work.

Only the man was missing. Gone with an escort of sirens through the white world of the streets to the white world of the hospital. They'd try hard to bring him back, Stryker thought, but maybe we should have let him go. Maybe he was one of those who had really wanted to leave.

He sighed and turned toward the hall. Outside the broken door, a uniformed officer from the black-and-white that had answered the call stood waiting for his orders.

"Close the windows, get the door back up, and then seal it," Stryker said abruptly.

"You mean lock up?"

"I mean *seal* it. I'm coming back and I want everything exactly the way it is now."

The patrolman watched Stryker bouncing down the hall and scowled. What the hell? Locking up was one thing, officially sealing was another. He looked into the apartment. The old man had tried to kill himself, right? He'd written a note, stuck his head in the oven, turned on the gas. It was as plain as the nose on your face.

Wasn't it?

SEVENTEEN

THE OTHERS WERE waiting for him at the mortuary.

"Hey, it looks like *you're* in the right place," Neilson said, when he saw Stryker's disheveled clothing and white face. "They got a slab waiting for you."

"What happened?" Tos asked anxiously.

Neilson and Pinsky looked at one another. "Aww," Neilson said sympathetically. "Him doesn't *feel* good."

"Shame," Pinsky agreed.

"Knock it *off*, goddammit!" Stryker said half laughing. "I got a dose of gas, that's all. I'm *fine*."

"You don't look fine," Tos said severely.

"You look lousy," Neilson agreed.

"Lousy," Pinsky echoed. "*Really* bad."

Stryker looked up. "You don't look so hot yourself."

Pinsky instantly began to worry. "I feel okay," he said defensively. "What do you mean, I don't look good?"

"I didn't say you didn't look good, I said you didn't look so hot, which is hardly surprising as it's goddamn cold in here," Stryker said.

"Whadya mean, gas?" Neilson asked suddenly.

Stryker looked at him approvingly. "So, what do you know, somebody around here has ears." Neilson looked smug.

Quickly, he told them what had happened. "Has Bannerman started?"

"Yeah," Neilson said. "He said he has a waiting list, people are just dying to get on it."

"Oh, God," Pinsky moaned. "*I* was waiting for *that*."

They came into the long room in single file. The smell of formaldehyde didn't quite mask the throat-catching odour of decayed blood and death. Neilson went a little pale.

Ahead, at the far end of the room, Bannerman—almost obscured by his swaddling clothes of surgical smock, red rubber apron, cap, gloves and big rubber boots—turned at the sound of their hard heels on the tiled floor. "About time."

He turned back to the shape on the guttered metal table. Beside him was a trolley laid out with bistouries and scalpels, bone saws, surgical drills, containers for samples, and the rest of his paraphernalia.

The whine of the electric bone saw began again, and they saw that he had progressed to the head. His assistant delicately inserted the suction pipe to clear away the blood and other liquids.

Adamson's body lay naked and mutilated under the strong light. Neilson, after one quick and horrified look, concentrated on the face of Bannerman's assistant. He was startled to see she was a girl in her twenties, and quite pretty. She was intent on her grisly work, her face blank with concentration. Only the reddish curls escaping from under her cap and the long sweep of her eyelashes proclaimed the woman within. Neilson was both repelled and fascinated to find loveliness amid such gore. She seemed totally unmoved by the brutal laying open from throat to groin of an elderly man. Adamson's internal organs had already been removed and were in jars along the trolley, neatly labelled for later examination and tests.

"Damn," Bannerman said, and put down the bone saw to strip off a torn rubber glove. "Bone fragment." He washed his hands, powdered them, and thrust them into fresh gloves. As he came back past the foot of the table, he reached out and pinched one of the dead man's toes.

"Why do you do that?" Stryker asked, expecting some technical explanation.

"Do what?" Bannerman asked absently, retrieving the bone saw from where he'd laid it casually on Adamson's shoulder.

"Tweak his toe. I've seen you do it lots of times during a PM. Does it tell you about muscle tone or—"

Bannerman looked affronted. "What the hell are you talking about?"

"He's right," Pinsky put in. "You do it every time."

Bannerman stared at them, then at his assistant, who nodded solemnly, her eyes twinkling. "I didn't even realise I did it!" he said slowly. There was a silence, and then he cleared his throat in an embarrassed way. "I suppose it's a kind of... gesture of affection."

There was another silence.

"A what?" Stryker finally managed.

"A 'gesture of affection,' he said," Pinsky offered helpfully.

Bannerman eyed them warily, waiting for the attack. Stryker and Neilson both opened their mouths to speak, caught the assistant's eye, and thought better of it.

"That's nice," Stryker said in a strangled voice.

"I suppose you think it's funny," Bannerman said belligerently. "Did it ever occur to you—".

"Have you measured that dent in his head?" Stryker asked quickly. He liked Bannerman; he didn't want to hassle him.

"Just coming to it now," Bannerman growled, and flicked the bone saw into life again to resume cutting. "It was long and round in cross section—like a lead pipe, maybe."

"I suggest that Miss Scarlett did it in the library with the lead pipe," Neilson said to the assistant. She started to grin, then turned it off quickly. Neilson was enchanted to have even gotten through to her.

"Did it have to be heavy, this pipe? Have to be lead, for instance?"

"No. We've taken some skin scrapings…" Bannerman put aside the saw and eased his fingers into the opening in the skull. He pried at the brain, the grey-white mass slippery in its meningeal layers. "Ah—I suspected this when the bone started to fragment. Take a look."

Stryker edged forward gingerly. "That clot?"

Bannerman nodded. "The killer should have been content with the bash on the head. That's a huge subdural haematoma—it would have killed Adamson before morning if he'd been left alone. No need to stab him at all. Of course, that didn't show, so the killer couldn't have known. If he had, he might have gotten away with making it look like an accident. The edge of the desk was rounded and it was metal—if Adamson had slipped he could have hit his head on it and…"

"Maybe that's what happened," Neilson said.

"According to the reports, the desk was rolled steel with a plastic coating," the assistant said in a soft voice. "The scrapings from the scalp showed—"

"Aluminum," Stryker said. She looked at him in surprise.

"That's right."

"I've just come from the apartment of a man who is a double amputee and walks with aluminum crutches," Stryker told Bannerman. "Could he have hit Adamson and made a dent like that?"

Bannerman shrugged. "The kind of crutches that lock over the wrists and forearms?"

"That's right."

Bannerman thought about it. "Double amputee for how long? How old a man?"

"About sixty-five, but—"

"Been crippled for twenty years," Pinsky said. "I asked."

"So he's built up the muscles in his arms considerably," Bannerman mused. "Yes—as far as force is concerned, it's possible. The blow needn't have been all that hard, because Adamson's skull is on the thin side—hence the degree of trauma."

"But Pinchman would have fallen over if he'd swung a crutch off the ground," Neilson objected.

"Maybe," Bannerman agreed. "Unless he leaned against something."

"He could have leaned on the desk," Pinsky suggested.

"Why don't you take him in for questioning?" Bannerman said.

"Because he's already in the hospital," Stryker said. "He tried to gas himself."

"Did he leave a note?" Bannerman asked.

"Oh, yeah. Confessed to it."

"Well, there you are, then," Bannerman said, turning back to Adamson's body. "He knocked him out. Then—not realizing he'd die anyway—he finished him off with his own paper knife. Did he say why he'd done it? In the note?"

"Adamson was a vicious man with a vicious tongue."

"And disabilities can build up one hell of a frustration load," Bannerman said. "One word too many...you can see how it could happen. It would explain the frenzy of the attack and the difficulty in pulling the knife out of the breastbone. He'd have been kneeling or even sitting on the floor beside the body—"

"Yeah, I get the picture," Stryker agreed. "It fits."

"Well, then?"

Stryker shrugged. "Any other little revelations you can give me about him?" He nodded toward Adamson's hollow carcass.

"Not a lot," Bannerman said over his shoulder. "His heart was in good shape—he might have lived another twenty years." He sounded regretful, as if it had been his fault this one had gotten away.

"Okay, thanks." Stryker started for the door.

Over the clink of the instruments, Bannerman spoke again. "What about the insulin?"

Stryker froze in mid-step. Pinsky banged into him from behind, deflecting Neilson into the sharp corner of an empty metal table. Neilson swore under his breath and rubbed his hip.

Stryker turned slowly. "Insulin?" he asked thinly.

"Insulin," Bannerman repeated, barely suppressed joy in his voice. "Adamson was a diabetic. They found an injection kit and a box of insulin ampoules in his desk, presumably an emergency supply in case he had to work late, as he did on Friday. Something about the ampoules must have bothered somebody, because—"

"Me," Pinsky said.

Bannerman nodded. "Because they were put through for analysis."

"My dad's a diabetic," Pinsky went on. "He uses it. It didn't move right—in the bottles. Too thin."

"You didn't tell me this," Stryker said to Pinsky.

"I didn't *know*, I only asked for them to check, I didn't know for sure, did I?" Pinsky said defensively. "It was only a feeling I had."

"Ah," Tos said.

"Four of the ampoules contained tap water," Bannerman said, reaching for a container to take yet another sample from the ravaged carcass. "We did a blood check earlier today. It was dangerously hypoglycaemic. If this poor bastard hadn't been hit in the head and stabbed, he just *might* have died in a diabetic coma. Now—do you figure the substitution was made by the one who hit and stabbed him—or someone else altogether?"

"You bastard," Stryker said. "Why didn't you tell me this before?"

Bannerman's chuckle echoed off the tiled walls. "You didn't ask me."

When they got back to the station, Stryker put in a call to the hospital. Pinchman was still alive—but only because someone had noticed a residue on his tongue. Apparently not content with gas, he'd also given himself a big overdose of barbituates. He was in a coma. They didn't hold out much hope for him, but said he was tough. Maybe. Maybe.

Stryker put down the phone. "Tomorrow morning I want to go over Pinchman's place with a fine-tooth comb," he said to Tos.

"What for?" Neilson piped up from his desk.

"I don't know. Something."

"But—"

"Humour me, I'm in a delicate state," Stryker said wearily. "And before you say it, *I'll* say it. I'm going home to bed."

"About time," Tos said. "You want me to drive you?"

Stryker looked at him. "You're already driving me crazy, so why add to the effort? I'm fine, thanks."

They watched him go out of the room, then looked at one another. "How come he wants to go over Pinchman's place?" Neilson asked. "What's to find there?"

"He hates to let go before he knows it all," Tos said angrily. "He hangs on to a case like a fat woman hangs on to her last doughnut. Has to finish up every damn crumb on the plate."

"Hey, listen," Pinsky said suddenly. "He's whistling."

"Oh, shit," Toscarelli groaned.

"What does *that* mean?" Neilson asked.

"Trouble," Toscarelli said. "Probably for us."

It was still snowing, but lightly. The silence gave some grace to the city, and Stryker went through the back streets slowly, making the first tracks in some of them, hearing the groan of the snow as it packed beneath his tyres. The snow had drifted, softening the lines where edge met edge, and against every lampost, every mailbox, every building and curb, giving them each a soft, flowing outline.

He loved the city like this, hushed and briefly suspended in its headlong run to destruction, mantled with a transient beauty that hid all the dirt and slowed all the hate. In two miles he passed only four cars, and the drivers smiled as they edged past one another in the rutted, twinkling streets. The snow made them momentary partners in adversity, witnesses of that fleeting moment in time when nobody had spoiled anything. Yet.

He didn't have much chance at beauty, these days.

He tried not to think of anything except what he saw or felt, the whiteness and the shadows, the chill touch of an occasional flake from the open window against his cheek, an icy kiss from the night. In a bubble, he moved from place to place, taking an hour to drive what normally took ten minutes, crossing and recrossing his own tracks, breathing slowly, keeping very still.

Pretending.

He arrived home, parked the car, and went into the apartment. He looked at the freezer, thought about eating, decided against it, and went to bed. In the warm and comfortable dark, he relaxed his body and waited for sleep to come.

It did not.

EIGHTEEN

THE SUICIDE ATTEMPT of Edward Pinchman was the topic of conversation in the Security Office when the guard reported in before going over to the library. He listened, made the right sounds—surprise, dismay, regret, shock, sympathy—and inwardly cursed his own impatience. He should have realised the old guy was weak, being a cripple, and might take the easy way out, rather than pay up.

The security guard admitted to himself that he'd been a coward to try the easy one first. Well, wouldn't you? he asked the wind as he crossed the dark Mall. Wouldn't anybody?

Now he was left with the other one.

No cripple. No easy mark.

Tough. Dangerous. Smart.

And maybe crazy, too.

He had to be careful, he had to think about it.

He entered the stillness of the library, locked the door behind him, and began the long round, walking slowly. Whenever he came to windows that overlooked the Mall and Grantham Hall, opposite, he glanced up at the windows of the English Department, many of which were still lit.

There had to be a way.

He'd think it out while he watched the windows, later.

Maybe it would come to him.

NINETEEN

"Lord, I hope today is better than yesterday," Frank Heath muttered as he looked through his mail. "They kept staring at me, wondering if I was a murderer."

"I know what you mean," Pete Rocheleau nodded.

"Just glare back," suggested Underhill.

"Easy to say," Heath observed. "You've got mostly senior or graduate students. I have *three* freshman courses this term, and I am now prepared to mount a demonstration of sympathy for any animal in the zoo. We have become genus *Suspect*, species *killer*. Suddenly, we're *fascinating*—but for the wrong reasons."

"Well, *I'm* not prepared to face them unaided," Heskell said, producing a small bottle from his pocket and shaking out two green-and-black capsules. "It's either this or I leap up onto my desk and start screaming." He threw the capsules into his mouth and swallowed them back with a toss of his head.

"They won't change anything," Jane Coulter said disapprovingly. "The situation still exists."

"They'll change *me*," Heskell said dramatically. "The situation can do what it damn well pleases."

Dan Stark appeared in the doorway of the inner office. He looked haggard. "Ah, good—most of you are here," he said as Lucy Grey-Jenner and Arthur Fowler came in. "I'm sorry to have to tell you that, late yesterday afternoon, Edward Pinchman attempted to commit suicide. It will probably be in the papers if...he dies."

They gaped at him, their letters and papers in their hands, half in or half out of their coats, all held in suspended animation before the letter boxes.

"He's still alive?" Jane Coulter asked in a shocked whisper. "Can they save him?"

"Alive, yes—but I'm told the doctors don't hold out much hope," Stark said. "As you know, his health hasn't been good for some time..." His voice faltered slightly.

"He killed Aiken," Heskell said suddenly. "That's it, isn't it? *He* was the one."

"I don't know..." Dan said weakly.

"There was a note," Heskell said. "There must have been a *note*."

"I believe a note was found, yes..."

"Then, the conclusion is obvious," Heskell said triumphantly. "He killed Aiken, then, stricken with remorse, he killed himself. End of story."

"They sought to take him, but he escaped out of their hand," Underhill intoned.

"If and when I learn any more, I'll let you know, of course," Dan Stark said. He gave them a bleak, forlorn look and turned away.

"I can't believe it," Jane Coulter said, looking ill. "I can't take it in. Why? *Why* would Edward have killed Aiken?"

"Why would anyone?" Lucy Grey-Jenner asked. "Because Aiken was Aiken—who needed any more reason?"

"Edward was a good friend," Fowler said, visibly shaken by the news. "A good man. I can't believe it."

"Neither can I," Kate said angrily. "And I don't."

"Well, that's a waste of tranquillizers," Heskell said chirpily. "All's well that ends—and now back to the boring old routine."

This cheery announcement drew some shocked and scathing glances from the others, which he returned with jaunty boldness. "Well, no sense being hypocritical, is there?" he went on. "I mean, it's a shame about old Pinchman, but who are we to know what went on between them? Some old hatred, simmering away—"

"Don't be ridiculous," Kate said.

"Well, we all *wanted* to kill Aiken from time to time, admit it!" Heskell said defiantly. "Him and his posing and his bragging and his constant threats to stun us all with yet another rivetingly boring revelation—"

"Oh!" Kate said suddenly. They all stared at her. She went to the door of the inner office. "Dan? Can I have a minute?"

Stark, nearly to the door of his own office, turned and came back as she advanced across the secretaries' domain. "A girl came in yesterday with a manuscript she'd been typing for Aiken. She seemed pretty hard up, so I paid her for it. Can I get it back from his estate? I got a receipt."

"Oh, I'm sure that's quite straightforward—although you should have sent her to me," Stark said.

"Well, she was pretty confused and upset, and I had a class—so I just did the quickest thing, then forgot all about it. Sorry."

Stark smiled at her. "You *are* a soft touch, Katie. Anybody with a sad story and you're right there. What was the manuscript, anyway?"

"I don't know, I only peeked—" She stopped, for he was grinning at her. "Well," she said defensively. "You would have, too."

"I'm sure I would, and will," Stark agreed.

"Did you know if he was researching anything about the Greek Army?" Kate asked.

"The Greek Army? *Aiken?*" Dan was amazed. "Surely not."

"Well, I *was* looking at it upside down," Kate conceded. "It looked like 'Four something Cavalry'—but I could have been wrong." The nine o'clock bell sounded in the hall, and she raised her voice over the clamour. "Anyway, I'll give it to you later on, all right?"

"Fine, any time," Stark's voice was suddenly loud as the bell stopped. He started back to his office, then stopped. "Is Wayland ill, by the way?"

"Richard? Not that I know. Why?"

Stark shrugged. "I gather he missed all his classes yesterday afternoon. Thought you might know why."

"No idea. Maybe he *was* ill. Did you call the fraternity house?"

"Yes, last evening *and* this morning. No sign of him."

"You mean—literally?"

"I mean they told me he hadn't been in the house since yesterday morning and they haven't heard from him. Or so they say. They might be covering up for him.

"Covering what?" Kate asked.

Stark looked a little pink. "Oh, you know—"

Kate came back a few steps. "No, Dan, I don't know. Covering up what?"

His brows drew together and he seemed to be trying to make up his mind about something, when the second bell rang. He looked very relieved. "You'd better skedaddle or your class will have escaped."

"Oh, lord..." She ran to the door. "I'll ring the house after this period. They *must* know where he is."

KATE'S FIRST FREE period was at eleven. She rang the fraternity house as soon as she got back to the office and found that Richard still hadn't appeared. His mail remained in his pigeonhole and there had been no call from him.

"Is that Jody Longman?" she demanded when a voice informed her that Richard was nowhere in evidence.

"Y-yes . . ." came the tentative reply.

"This is Kate Trevorne."

"Oh, hi." Jody's voice warmed considerably. "I didn't know it was you, Ms. Trevorne. Don't *you* know where he is?"

"Would I be calling if I did?"

"Guess not. Sorry." His voice lowered to a whisper. "The police were here looking for him last night, too."

"Were they?"

"Yeah. We were having a party—we thought it was a bust. Everybody flushed their joints down the john and then they only wanted him. Blew the whole thing." He sounded grievously wounded. "It was the same one who was bothering you in the cafeteria."

"Lieutenant Stryker?"

"That's the one. Supposed to be really something."

"Oh, he's something all right—but we won't say what," Kate muttered.

"Mr. Trevorne—is it true? About Professor Pinchman, I mean? Being the one who killed old Adamson?"

"Where did you hear that?"

"Somebody said so," he mumbled evasively. "I don't believe it, myself. Do you?"

"No, I don't, Jody. Not one damn bit. See you." She put the phone down, glared at it, then picked it up again.

THERE WAS STILL a faint odour of gas hanging in the cold apartment. Damp patches under the windows showed where the snow had fallen and melted, and the flattened cardboard they'd put over the broken window in the kitchen was barely adequate to keep out the icy air. The day was bright and clear and sunlight lay cruelly on the worn patches of the plush sofa, the faded colours of the old Persian carpet, and the pair of aluminum crutches leaning forlornly against what might have been Pinchman's favourite reading chair in the far corner.

"Tag these as possible murder weapons, right?" Neilson asked, going toward them.

"Yeah, in a minute, in a minute," Stryker said, moving to the middle of the room.

"You gotta stand and stare first," Pinsky told Neilson.

"You what?" Neilson demanded, thinking Pinsky had slipped a gear or two since the previous night.

"Stand and stare," Toscarelli said patiently as Stryker pivoted slowly in the middle of the room. "Don't touch, don't pick up, move, or alter. Most of all, don't assume."

"I *went* to college," Neilson said sarcastically. "I *read* the books."

"Then, read the room," Stryker suggested.

Neilson, obviously thinking this a childish exercise, sighed pointedly and looked around him. "He sure liked cactuses," he said finally. "Look at all the ugly little bastards."

"Cacti," Stryker said pedantically. "What else?"

Neilson shrugged. "Jesus...oh, all right. Living room, two windows overlooking courtyard, usual furnishings, old carpet..."

"Old *Persian* carpet, worth maybe two thousand dollars," Stryker corrected him. "Go on."

"No kidding?" said Pinsky, moving his feet back and staring downward. "It doesn't *look* like much."

"What else?" Stryker asked Neilson.

Neilson shrugged. "A lot of books, desk, typewriter. He smoked a pipe yesterday—I suppose you're going to do something like Sherlock Holmes with the pipe ash?"

"I wouldn't know pipe ash from horsefeathers," Stryker said. "If you say he smoked yesterday, *I* believe you."

"Right. Okay." Neilson went over to look at the pipe in the ashtray, and the coffee cup beside it. "He drank coffee yesterday, too."

"I want the contents analyzed right away," Stryker said. "And also fingerprinted, so be careful."

Pinsky had been looking around, and now he fixed Stryker with a suspicious eye. "Because the note was typed, is that it?" he asked Stryker. "Because the signature was typed also."

"Maybe."

Pinsky grinned in satisfaction. He sat on the arm of the easy chair and nearly knocked over Pinchman's crutches. Grabbing at them, he almost went over, himself. Neilson snorted. He still wasn't used to Pinsky's habit of crashing into or over things and generally teetering on the fine line between vertical and horizontal at least nine times a day.

Neilson looked from Stryker to Toscarelli to Pinsky. "This is a game, right?" he asked uneasily. They were just standing there, looking around, like a bunch of goddamn lighthouses or something. "Twenty questions?"

Nobody said anything.

"Look, the guy left a note and put his head in the damned oven, right?" Neilson probed.

"That's how it looks," Stryker agreed neutrally.

Neilson's face screwed up. He glared at Toscarelli, who was looking into the kitchen on the far side of the room, at Stryker, who was over by the windows, at Pinsky, who was still holding the crutches and whistling through his teeth absently.

"Hey!" Neilson shouted.

Pinsky jumped. "What?" he demanded. "What, what?"

Neilson was pointing to the crutches and Pinsky dropped them as if they'd grown suddenly hot. "I still got my gloves on," Pinsky said self-righteously. "I didn't . . ."

Stryker and Toscarelli had turned. Neilson was so full of it he could hardly speak. His mouth felt stiff.

"The guy has two artificial legs, right?" Neilson said.

Stryker nodded, then started to smile.

"And wings, maybe?" Neilson added shyly.

"It's a good thirty feet from the chair to the oven in the kitchen," Stryker agreed.

"Aha!" said Pinsky.

THEY WERE STILL looking around the room when the voice came through the open doorway, sharp and angry. "I want to see the note he *supposedly* left."

They all turned. Kate Trevorne stood there. Her colour was high—she'd walked from the campus, and the icy hair had reddened her cheeks. Her curly hair looked like a bronze chrysanthemum, and her brown duffle coat hung open over a red pullover. Stryker thought she resembled a robin, beady-eyed and wary, edging her way into a strange garden.

"What the hell are you doing here?" he demanded.

"I called the police station and they told me you were here. I want to see the note Edward left. Is that it?"

"Don't touch it!" Stryker shouted as she marched across the room to where the note was still stuck in the typewriter.

"I'm not an *idiot*," she said over her shoulder. She stood, hands jammed in pockets, leaning over the typewriter. Then she straightened up. "Edward didn't type that."

"Oh?" His tone was skeptical.

"This is a manual typewriter," she said. "Edward and I share a guilty secret—we're both touch typists. It's considered very non-intellectual to be good with your hands, so we keep quiet about it. Touch typists develop bad habits, they also have weak and strong fingers. Whoever typed *this* did it one-fingered, the pressure is the same on every letter." She was very calm now.

Neilson, Pinsky and Toscarelli looked at one another and grinned. Stryker just watched her, and said nothing. She turned away and went into the kitchen—he followed and stood in the archway. Her eyes went over everything—broken window, cooker, sink, the litter of things on the drying rack—spoons, cereal bowl, frying pan, basting tube, wooden spatula, a potato peeler, dishes, glasses, cups. She picked up the basting tube and squeezed the rubber bulb a few times. Her hair fluffed up and down in its breeze. She used it to point to the wall above the cooker. "There's a pan missing," she announced.

"I threw it through the window to let the gas out," he said. "It was full of potatoes. It must still be down there."

She dropped the baster back into the rack and went over to the window to peer through the narrow gap between cardboard and frame. "It is," she said. "Also a lot of potatoes. *Peeled* potatoes." She turned and stared at him. "How come he peeled potatoes for dinner if he planned to kill himself?" Suddenly what he'd said struck her. "*You* broke the window? *You* found him?"

"He could have killed *himself*," Toscarelli called from the sitting room. "He's just getting over pneumonia, he should have waited for—"

"SHUT UP!" Stryker bellowed.

"Nothing wrong with *those* lungs," came Neilson's wry voice.

"How did you know there was a pan missing?" Stryker asked Kate in a normal tone.

"You saved his life."

"So far. How did you know about the pan?"

She shrugged. "I've been here lots of times, often cooked his dinner, especially when I first came back and started teaching. I was very rusty, and Edward gave me lots of coaching so I could make a good impression. He's a very special man. He would never kill himself. *Never*."

"Not even if he'd murdered someone?"

"Not even then."

"You don't argue about his being a killer, just a suicide."

"I don't *know* about his being a murderer, but I do know he's had plenty of reasons and plenty of opportunities to kill himself over the years, and never did it. He was in almost constant pain—the pills were always there." She looked at the gas cooker. "And he hated the smell of gas. I refuse to believe it was suicide!" Her voice broke.

Toscarelli came over and gave Stryker a dirty look.

"So does he. Don't let the little bastard stampede you."

Kate looked at Stryker. "You don't?"

"I believe he hit Adamson. I don't think he meant to kill him, and I don't think he tried to kill himself, either." He nodded toward the crutches. "Those were found leaning against that chair. *He* was found in the kitchen, head in the oven, thirty feet away."

"You mean somebody else was here? Somebody else tried to kill him? And made it *look* like suicide?"

"Isn't that what you came here to tell us?" Stryker asked. "You said he didn't try to kill himself, so what were you suggesting? Divine intervention? Martians?"

"And you think this was the same person who killed Aiken?"

He fixed her with a baleful eye. "I certainly hope so. I don't want to think we've got more than one killer running around knocking off the English faculty of Grantham University one by one."

"And you still think it's one of us?" Kate asked.

"I don't know. My guess is that Pinchman knocked Adamson down—for some unknown reason—and then left him not realising how seriously he'd hurt him. Then someone else came along, found Adamson lying there unconscious, and took advantage of the situation to finish him off with his own paper knife. If you think back to Saturday morning, you'll recall that Pinchman was pretty astounded when I said Adamson had been stabbed to death."

"Did Edward *know* who did it?"

"I think he might have guessed. Hence his attempted murder."

She took a deep breath. "Then, I *will* help you, if you still want me to. I didn't mind when Aiken got killed, I hated him. But I mind like *hell* about Edward."

Stryker glanced at the others warningly. "All right," he said cheerfully. "How about coming down to the hospital with me right now? Maybe you can get through to Pinchman—he certainly isn't responding to anyone else. Want to try?"

"Oh, yes . . . please."

"Right. You go down and get the elevator back up—I just want to give these guys a few jobs to keep them busy." She went out, and he went over to them. "I think it was Wayland who brought him home. I think *she* thinks so, too."

"She wants to help," Pinsky protested.

"Help who, exactly?" Stryker asked cynically. "Check with the fraternity house again. If he's still not there, I want an APB out on him stat. Also, I want all alibis checked again, this time for *both* yesterday afternoon and Friday night. That may close some bolt-holes and open up some others. We'll cover them all, in case Wayland can explain himself to my satisfaction."

"Do you think that's likely," Neilson asked.

Stryker's eyes were cold. "No," he said.

THE ROOM WAS in semidarkness. Edward Pinchman was lying on the high hospital bed, his normally ruddy cheeks pale and flat. All Kate could see from the door was the hawk line of his nose and his grey hair drifting across the pillow. The covers were drawn up under his chin, and he looked to her like one of those medieval saints carved atop a tomb, motionless, dead.

Then she noticed the shallow but steady rise and fall of his chest. She swallowed a twenty-nine pound lump in her throat and went slowly toward the bed. On the far side a young policeman was seated, pad and pencil in hand. Waiting to take down everything Edward said? To be used in evidence? She looked again at the sleeping face. Had she been wrong about the note? *Could* Edward have murdered Aiken? Written his good-bye. Taken barbituates—and then walked thirty feet without the aid of crutches?

Either she had to accept Edward was a murderer, or that someone *else* was a murderer—someone she knew, perhaps even someone she loved. The result of the conflict came without warning. One moment she was standing there quietly, the next gushing like a geyser. Hot tears overflowed. Desperately she looked around the room. There were vases and bouquets everywhere. "He hates cut flowers," she said wildly. "Please have them taken away. That's why he raised cacti, he said they were survivors, as he is . . ."

"All right," Stryker said softly.

"Flowers die," Kate went on. "All beautiful things die, he said. They age and wither..."

"Take it easy." Stryker's voice was strong and calm, something to hang onto.

As Kate rummaged in her purse for a tissue, she saw how the sheet dropped pathetically from Edward's knees, and supposed they had his "tin legs" in a closet somewhere, like left luggage. In coma the lines of age had disappeared from his face, and only the slack falling back of his flesh told his years. "Oh, God," she snuffled. "How cruel to hurt him even more..."

"Has he said anything, Calder?" Stryker asked.

"No, sir, nothing," the young policeman said wearily. It had obviously been a long night of waiting and listening to a man breathing. From behind her tissue, Kate glanced at Stryker. The boy had called him "sir," and it struck her that this man she resented and feared was someone who had won authority in the world not noted for easy promotion.

His glance was cool and impersonal. "Would you like to try to wake him?" he asked. "Sometimes a familiar voice can work wonders."

"I'll try," she said. She took a breath and spoke in as firm a tone as she could manage. Her "teacher's voice." "Edward? Edward? It's Kate. Wake up, please. Wake up and tell us what happened to you."

There was only silence in the room. No flicker, no movement. Nothing changed. He lay as he had lain before.

"Edward—it's Kate, dear. Wake up, please."

Still nothing. She looked at Stryker. "It isn't working."

"You give up too easily," he said mildly. "These things take time. Go on, try again."

After ten further minutes, a nurse came in and ostentatiously lifted Professor Pinchman's wrist, to take his pulse.

"I guess that's it," Kate said, turning away. She took a step toward the door and stopped, abruptly, as an eerie sound filled the room. It was Edward taking a deep and ragged breath. A hurricane couldn't have been louder, or so she thought. But when he spoke, in a perfectly normal tone, it was deafening.

"Cradle," he said. Quite clearly.

And again. "Cradle."

Kate turned, but for all the change in his outward appearance, he might never have made a sound.

"He did speak, didn't he?" Kate gasped. "It *was* he?"

"Calder?" Stryker asked, ignoring her.

"It sounded like 'cradle' to me, sir."

"Me, too." He turned to Kate, who was clutching the bed-clothes in the region of Pinchman's shoulder, watching his still face. "Try again," he commanded, and she did.

"Edward . . . wake up, please. Please, Edward."

"Try repeating 'cradle.'"

"Cradle. What do you mean, Edward? What cradle?"

"He's asleep," the nurse whispered. "His pulse has changed. You won't get a response now."

"Homoeostasis," Kate murmured.

The nurse looked sharply at her. "Yes, exactly."

"What the hell is homoeostasis?" Stryker exploded, his exasperation making his voice seem even harsher in the quiet of the room.

"The body is healing itself," Kate said. She nodded toward a small tag at the end of the bed. "Edward is Dr. Wilkie's patient. Good doctors, and he's one, let the body do as much of the healing as possible. Right?" She looked at the nurse, who nodded, almost smiling.

"So now you're a part-time doctor, too?" Stryker snapped. "Isn't teaching crime enough?"

"Look, I don't know what 'cradle' means either," Kate snapped back. "But I do happen to know Dr. Wilkie, and what other doctors say about him. My uncle is a doctor, two of my cousins are doctors, and—"

"All right, all right," Stryker muttered. He looked up, suddenly wary. "You got any cops in your family?"

"Not one." From her tone, it was an achievement.

"Thank God for that." He spoke to the young policeman. "Stick with it, Calder. It's not the most exciting assignment you'll ever have, but it's important."

Kate looked at Calder sympathetically. He probably could think of a million better things to do than sit hour after hour in a dark room with a sleeping patient and an elderly nurse with varicose veins. Not even anything to read. He probably prayed for a fist fight to break out in the hall. "Try reciting 'The Walrus and the Carpenter' from memory," she suggested. "That's what I always do when I'm trapped somewhere."

"You would," Stryker grunted, and opened the door for her. "Come on, I'll drive you back to school."

"You don't have to—I can get a cab."

"I *know* I don't have to," he snarled. "I happen to be headed that way, myself. All right?"

For some reason, the car had shrunk while standing in the parking lot. Kate, sitting in the passenger seat of the unmarked police car, felt stifled. Her heart pounded and thudded like a prisoner beating on the walls of a cell, and her throat was tight. The car moved through the slush in the streets with an adhesive sound, the windscreen wipers went whack-thunk at the splatters from the truck ahead of them, and she saw that Stryker was driving very carefully and correctly, the way a good policeman should. He wore his glasses. He used his turn signals when passing. He didn't even cut in on the expressway, not once. She kept waiting for him to scream or shout or curse, but he did nothing, said nothing.

All right, she thought, you win. "Do *you* know what cradle might mean?" she asked.

"Nope."

"Maybe it will be like 'Rosebud,' in *Citizen Kane*."

"Jesus, I hope not."

More silence, except for the windscreen wipers. "What do you want me to do?"

"About what?"

"About helping you?"

"Tell me about Pinchman. Did he get along with Adamson?"

"As well as anyone did."

"Did Adamson snipe away at him the way he did the rest of you?"

"Not really—I suppose because of Edward's disability. But he didn't like him, I know that. I think he was jealous, actually."

"Jealous? Adamson was jealous of Pinchman?"

"Oh, yes. Edward didn't have students following him around, the way they did Aiken, but everyone on the faculty *liked* him. He was so generous with his time—I loved the hours I spent with him, talking about everything under the sun and moon. He made me laugh so much. In spite of all his suffering, the world is a game to him. 'We're all marks in a big scam,' he used to say. 'The fun is trying to figure the play before the touch.'"

"That's con man's cant," Stryker said in surprise. "Did he always talk like that?"

"Oh, of course not. We both love slang—any kind. Another shared shame. I thought he was my special private discovery—until I found out that everyone on the faculty thought the same thing.

He has a knack of making you think you're the only person who really knows him. I don't think it's conscious—he just has that kind of charm. He..." She paused, fighting the tears. "He sort of lights up when he sees you. As if he'd been just sort of ticking over until you appeared."

"You sound half in love with him."

"So is everyone else."

"But not Adamson."

"No. Looking back, I suppose Aiken was like a naughty kid—when he couldn't get love, he went for attention, any way he could get it."

"And succeeded. Can you think of any reason why Pinchman would have been driven to striking Adamson with his walking stick?"

"No."

The sun off his glasses turned them into a mask, hiding him, making him strange and menacing. The car, too, unsettled her. It smelled of men and cigarettes and spilled coffee and something else she couldn't place until he raised a hand to lower the sun visor and his jacket opened.

"You're wearing a gun," she said involuntarily.

"I'm a cop on duty," he said. "I'm carrying a badge, too."

His hands on the wheel were competent and sure, but they were hands she didn't know. And she certainly didn't know where they'd *been*. "Have you ever killed anyone?"

He sighed. "Yes. Twice."

"I'm sorry. Is that what everyone asks?"

"More or less. What about secrets—any secrets Pinchman might have had—aside from slang and touch-typing?"

She couldn't take her eyes off the gun. And his hands. And his mouth, especially his mouth. He had to repeat the question, startling her out of the dark cave where she was hiding with her new-found discovery, terrified he would turn and see what had happened to her. She faced front, and clutched her handbag tightly. "As far as I know, Edward had only one secret, and it's hardly anything that would lead him to hit Aiken."

"Well?" Stryker asked impatiently when she didn't go on. "Come on, what was it? You said you wanted to help."

"I..." She was struggling. "You must promise not to tell anyone. He made me promise and I never have."

"I'm conducting a murder investigation, Miss Trevorne. If it's relevant..."

"It's not. It can't be. But it's the only thing I know about him he's ashamed of, and you mustn't tell him I told you."

"Oh, for crying out—"

"He writes books."

Fortunately they were stopped for a red light, otherwise he might have run into something. He gaped at her. "I would have thought that was something he'd be proud of, being a literary—" He paused. "Dirty books?"

"No." Her tone implied much worse.

"Well?" Why the hell was she sitting there like that, eyes straight ahead, cheeks flushed and mouth trembling? he wondered. She looked frightened, vulnerable, years younger. The way she had—

"He writes Westerns," she finally managed to say. "Edward Pinchman is really Jake Laredo, creator of Silver Whip, Zack Murray, and the Rainbow Kid."

HE HAD MANAGED to stop laughing by the time they reached the campus. Kate on the other hand, had grown more and more angry. He pulled up to the curb and cut the engine. "All right, I promise. I won't tell a soul unless I find it's relevant to the case."

"Thank you."

"It does explain one thing." He told her about the legacy in Adamson's will to the Cattlemen's Association. "Obviously Adamson knew about it."

"Not from me, he didn't."

"Okay, okay—no need to get so uptight. Personally, I think it's great. My son is a total fan of the Rainbow Kid."

She turned slightly. "You have a child?"

"My ex-wife has him. In California. I'm allowed to send him presents. On high days and holy days, I'm even allowed a brief phone call."

The sudden, unexpected bitterness in his voice cut into her. "Don't you ever see him?"

It was his turn to stare straight ahead. "It's better that I don't. Apparently it would traumatise him, and interfere with the benign influence of his stepfather, who is rich, influential, and an all-round good guy. Nothing dirty, like a cop."

"That's terrible."

He shrugged. "The world is full of terrible. Killing is terrible."

"That is killing. A kind of murder."

"Please don't bleed on the upholstery," he said shortly. "It leaves a stain." Through the closed windows, they could hear the bell from the tower of Oldfield Hall. "Don't you have a class now? You'd better get moving."

"Yes. Thank you." She opened the door. "If there's any change in Edward . . ."

"I'll let you know." He watched her get out and close the door, watched her come around the front of the car, the wind pushing the heavy duffle coat apart, moulding her sweater against her breasts. She clutched the coat shut. He rolled down the window. "And remember—you've promised to tell me if anything odd happens. I'm counting on you."

He started the engine and pulled away. She was three steps onto the Mall before she remembered. "Wait . . ."

But he was gone, the car caught up in the river of traffic, turning a far corner now, disappearing.

She'd meant to tell him about Aiken's manuscript, the one the girl had brought in. It probably wasn't important, just a bit of unfinished business, one of a million ends Dan would have to tie up, she supposed.

Oh, well.

It would give her an excuse to call Stryker later.

She paused momentarily, one foot lifted to mount a pile of slush. The hesitation put her off balance and caused her to come down squarely in the middle of it. Ice slithered into her boot. She stood there, staring at it.

An "excuse" to call him?

Oh, Kate, she thought. You bloody fool!

TWENTY

"MRS. UNDERHILL?"

"Yes."

"My name is Stryker." He showed her his badge and card. "I'm investigating the death of Professor Adamson. May I come in?"

She was a vivid woman, pale-skinned, with a shining cap of black hair and enormous blue eyes. Her clothes were bright and colourful, and she moved quickly, like a nervous colt. Her fingers were stained with nicotine, and there was a freshly lit cigarette in her hand. He had a feeling there usually was.

"Sit down, please," she directed when they'd reached the living room. It was also colourful, with a mixture of modern and antique furniture, the latter re-covered in primary colours. "Can I get you anything? Coffee? A drink? Or is it true, about being on duty?" Her voice was edgy, thin, too bright. Like the clothes. Like the room. He had the feeling that if he'd had a silver hammer, and knew where to tap her, she'd shatter into a million shards of crystal.

He wondered if she was always like this. If so, she was a strange partner for her poetic husband. Underhill would surely have been better suited by a quiet woman, tender, gentle, who gave him space? This woman gave only signals of fear and tension. Was it her nature, or was it the situation?

"Nothing, thank you. I'd like to talk to you about Friday night?" He spoke slowly, gently, trying to get her to relax. She kept looking at the clock, her watch, his watch upside down. Checking, comparing.

"Friday? But . . . I thought it was all settled. Professor Pinchman confessed."

"You know about that?" It hadn't been in the papers yet.

"Chris called me a little while ago."

"I see. Well, until we can talk to Professor Pinchman we still have to follow on with the original investigation. Just routine."

She laughed brightly, brightly. "You mean 'just routine, ma'am, just routine'—like on television? It must make it difficult for you, all those television cops. Stealing your best lines."

"The hardest part is seeing them solve everything in an hour. Sometimes it takes us weeks, months—even years."

"But you always get your man?"

"That's the Mounties. I wouldn't say our percentages are quite that high," he conceded with a smile, trying to make her let go of whatever it was she was clutching inside with a grip like death. He took out his notebook, and saw her nod to herself. Just like on television, he could almost hear her saying to herself. Just the same. "Now, your husband came home on Friday night around seven-thirty, and stayed in for the rest of the evening, is that right?"

"Oh, yes, that's quite right." She had put out the cigarette, and was now lighting another. "All evening."

"And all night?"

She frowned and waved the smoke away with a wide gesture, jangling the bracelets on her thin wrist. "I don't understand what you're getting at."

"The reason I ask is, we have a report that your car drove out around midnight that night, and returned sometime in the early hours."

"Nonsense."

"So your husband didn't go out?"

"No, of course not."

"And you?"

"What?" She was lighting another cigarette, oblivious to the one already spiraling smoke from the ashtray.

"Did you go out, at all? That night?"

"Why should I?"

"Perhaps to see someone? A friend?" He watched her. "A lover?"

"How dare you? I'm a happily married woman."

"Is anyone really happily married?" Stryker asked, leaning back and closing his notebook. "I mean, years go by, the same things over and over again, especially in bed. The same jokes, the same snores, the same back turned over too often. I've been there myself. *I* certainly wouldn't blame a person for reaching out."

"Well, I would." She got up suddenly and went to a cabinet in the corner.

"I admit Chris has changed quite a bit in the last year or so. It's just a phase, this religious thing of his, I'm sure that's all it is. He used to be so funny, so witty—now I'm afraid he's become a bit of a Puritan. Not very conducive to poetry.'' She was pouring out some whiskey into a crystal goblet. Her hand was shaking, and the cigarette wobbled into the air, sending out little jerks of smoke which drifted up to her eyes and made her blink. ''Although I suppose an argument *could* be made for Donne and Hopkins. Chris keeps trying it, anyway.'' Brightly, brightly.

''Isn't poetry supposed to be a little mystic?'' Stryker asked.

''Mystic, certainly, but 'born again' isn't exactly delicate, is it? Thump, thump, thump, they pound it down your throat. Even the children . . .'' She faltered, put the whiskey to her mouth quickly.

''I understand your husband is very fond of your children.''

''Oh, yes...to the point of suffocation.'' She inspected for dust here and there, moving around the room.

''You don't approve of that?''

She whirled on him. ''I don't see what all this had to do with murder, if you don't mind my saying so. Chris and I are fine. The children are fine. The dog is fine and the cat is even better. The goldfish . . .'' she made a gesture. *''Comme ci, comme ça.''*

''Are you friendly with with your neighbours, Mrs. Underhill?''

''My *neighbours*?'' It seemed he'd introduced a new species of lower lifeforms into the conversation. ''I don't even know their names. I'm not a neigbourly type, I have too much to do.''

''Particularly between midnight and three in the morning?''

''I told you—''

''You told me your husband didn't go out between midnight and three o'clock on Friday; but your car *did*. Did you loan it to someone, Mrs. Underhill? Was it stolen? Why didn't you report the theft if—''

''If you're basing all this on something my so-called neighbour said, you must be a pretty poor judge of character, Lieutenant. They're a pinch-faced bunch around here, all stiff necks and lace curtains . . .'' Again she lifted her drink.

''Do you know Mr. Heskell, Mrs. Underhill? Mr. Mark Heskell? He seemed to know *you* quite well.''

The glass fell.

And shattered.

HE FINALLY FOUND a parking space a good six blocks away, and he had to trudge back against the flow of traffic to the library. He went through the double glass doors and began trolling for Underhill. It seemed like half the English Department had decided to up sticks and repair to the library. Stark was in the Medical Department, Fowler in the Modern History section, Heath was crouching before the Philosophy shelves, and Coulter was on tiptoe trying to get down a volume from Near-Eastern Geography. Stryker paused to get it for her. She smiled benignly at him.

"And they say there's never a policeman around when you need one. Were you looking for me, Lieutenant?"

"No, Dr. Coulter—for Underhill. According to the schedule, he has a seminar here in a few minutes."

She nodded. "Upstairs, right at the back. There are small classrooms in each corner of the library to take overflow—mostly from the English Department. We all make use of them from time to time, primarily for seminars, as the atmosphere is more relaxed. I think he might be up there now."

"Thanks. Do you want any more books from the top while I'm handy?"

"No, thank you—this will do nicely." She hugged the tome to her chest and beetled off to a small study desk which was already top-heavy with books and papers.

He went up the central stairway and through to the rear stacks, situated behind a second set of swinging doors. This area was less opulent than the first, shelves crammed and closely spaced, the study desks smaller and in fours instead of pairs.

He found Underhill in a corner classroom, writing a list of assignments on the board. He spoke over his shoulder when Stryker opened the door. "You can start copying these...and put your first offering on the desk."

"I'm afraid I came empty-handed," Stryker said.

Underhill whirled, startled. "Oh. Sorry. Thought you were one of my students."

"I'd like to talk to you about last Friday night."

"Oh?" He turned back to the blackboard and continued to write. The chalk squeaked and he muttered under his breath.

"And yesterday afternoon. Did you, by any chance, take Professor Pinchman home during the morning?"

The chalk broke and fell at Underhill's feet. He bent to pick up the pieces, and when he straightened, his face was flushed. "Edward? No. I had classes most of the morning."

"Last Friday night, then. According to your statement, you went home and stayed there, right? With your wife and family?"

"That's right."

"All night?"

"Of course all night."

Stryker pulled out a chair and sat down. "What was the argument about, Underhill? Money? Sex? The kids? Or maybe your religious inclinations."

"What argument? What are you talking about?"

"The argument that sent your wife from the house, Mr. Underhill. From the house and straight to the arms of her lover." Underhill was gaping at him. "Did Adamson tell you about it at the party, Mr. Underhill? What everyone knew but you—that your wife was having an affair with Mark Heskell? Did you drive home in a rage and confront her, accuse her?"

Underhill moved backward and bumped into the desk, sat down on the edge of it, put his hands to his eyes. "All wickedness is but little to the wickedness of a woman," he said.

"Your wife isn't a wicked woman, Mr. Underhill, she just misses the man she married, that's all."

"She that is not with me is against me," Underhill said.

"Oh, stop it," Stryker said impatiently. "Frankly, I can see her point of view if you go around mouthing stuff like that all day."

"I don't," Underhill said, dropping his hand. "At least, I don't *mean* to—but there are so many apt observations in the Book one just—"

"Your wife left the house at midnight, taking your car. Did you follow her? Perhaps what woke the neighbours was *two* cars going out, not one."

"No, I didn't follow her."

"Why not?"

"Because I knew where she was going! Why should I follow her? He that toucheth pitch shall be defiled therewith. I wanted nothing more to do with her, God help me, I might have killed her if she hadn't left then. She knew that."

"Really? What about 'vengeance is mine, sayeth the Lord'?"

Underhill's lips pulled back in a wolfish grin. "The Lord never had an unfaithful wife."

"Kind of missed out there, did he?"

"Oh, God," Underhill moaned, turning away. "Why *Heskell*? That soulless blasphemer! That's what I couldn't understand. When Aiken told me, I thought he was making it up, it was so outrageous. But she *admitted* it. I have never known such pain...I swear to you...real physical pain. I couldn't speak, couldn't breathe...I just stared at her."

"He makes her laugh," Stryker said.

"Laugh?" He didn't seem to know the word.

Stryker consulted his notebook. "She left your house at just after eleven o'clock, she says. But she didn't arrive at Heskell's place until nearly twelve-thirty. That's an hour and a half unaccounted for. She says she drove around."

"Then, she drove around. Carole's not a very good liar when she's challenged. She panics, and it shows."

"Indeed. How about this for panic, Mr. Underhill? How about the possibility that she was enraged by Adamson's having exposed her affair to you, that she drove to the university and saw his office light on, that she went up there, killed him, and then went on to Heskell?"

Underhill's face went deathly pale. "That's totally impossible, there's absolutely *no* way—"

"Heskell says she was very upset when she arrived at his flat."

"Of *course* she was upset—but not because she'd killed someone. Because we'd had an argument and I'd threatened to divorce her and take the kids. She loves them—so do I. She was going to break it off, to end it. She promised me that, and I believed her."

"Or was it the other way around, perhaps?" Stryker pressed on. "She threatened to divorce *you* and take the kids away from *you*? According to her, you adore your daughters. She took off in your car, left you alone there. You brooded, worked yourself up. You were alone all night—no corroboration now. No alibi now. Did *you* take your wife's car, drive past the university on your way to Heskell's apartment and catch sight of Adamson's light still on? Did you go up there to confront him and end up killing him in a rage? How's that for a possible scenario?"

"Why should I do that? Better to kill Heskell, surely?" Underhill was shaking now, but there was no panic in his voice. "What good would it have done to kill Adamson?"

"Murder isn't always logical—he was killed by someone who was in a terrible rage, someone who resented or feared something he'd said, resented it enough to find some triumph in cutting out his tongue. Was it you, Underhill?"

"No."

"Was it your wife."

"No!"

There was a noise behind Stryker, and he turned to see several students standing in the open door. He silently cursed their intrusion and stood up. "We'll talk again," he told Underhill. "Don't leave the city." As he turned, Underhill spoke. His voice was still shaky.

"I never would have left them alone in the house."

"I beg your pardon?"

"My little girls. I would never have left them alone in the house. Not for *any* reason."

"Is that your alibi? Two little girls, sound asleep?"

"No." His voice was steadying. "That's my joy, Lieutenant. Alibis are *your* problem."

Stryker looked at him for a moment, then went to the door. The students stared sullenly at him, then reluctantly parted to let him pass. As he moved through he was jostled, roughly, and somebody muttered "Fascist pig bastard."

"At your service," Stryker agreed, and walked away.

TWENTY-ONE

"So UNDERHILL doesn't have an alibi for Friday night, after all?" Toscarelli asked, settling one hip on Stryker's desk and sipping at his paper cup of coffee.

"Nope. Nor does he really have one for yesterday afternoon—he had two classes before eleven, and a student conference, then nothing until one," Stryker said with a grimace. "*And* he has a beard. It *could* have been him who took Pinchman home. Say Underhill helped him out, got him home, then saw the possibility of pinning the killing on him by faking a confession and suicide."

"To save himself?"

"Or to save his wife," Stryker said. "Poor bastard."

"You feel sorry for him?"

"I feel sorry for *any* guy who finds out Heskell has been humping his wife," Stryker said sourly. "Jesus—*Heskell.*"

"That the one with the dimples?" Pinsky asked, from the next desk. He was polishing his shoes, trying to get rid of the salt stains that had built up as he walked to about a hundred doorways, checking alibis. "The one who shot his mouth off to the reporters on Saturday?"

"The same," Stryker nodded. "I mean—Carole Underhill is an attractive woman. Why she should go for that middle-aged *cherub*—" He hadn't the voice for his dismay.

"Instead of a doll like you?" Neilson asked.

"Instead of anybody," Stryker said. "Even *you.*"

"Ah—it was only because she hadn't *met* me yet," Neilson grinned. "No wonder she settled for Heskell—despair must have set in, waiting for me to come along, the man she'd love."

"Hah," Pinsky said to his shoes. "I told you Heskell's fiancée was lying. Now *he* doesn't have an alibi for Friday night either."

"Oh, he does," Neilson said. "Mrs. Underhill."

"Oh, yeah," Pinsky said after a moment.

"Not until twelve-thirty," Stryker pointed out. "His fiancée says she left him at eleven. I timed the distance between the Underhill place and Heskell's apartment. Twenty minutes at the most, maybe as little as fifteen late at night. Carole Underhill says she drove around, but maybe she went to Heskell first—and then they both went over and bumped off Adamson."

"How did they know he was there?" Pinsky grunted, putting one shoe on and pulling the other off.

"Maybe she saw the light on when she drove past—it's on the route she'd probably have taken."

"But she couldn't be sure he'd still be there when she went back—and anyway, it could have been the cleaners, couldn't it?" Neilson asked. "The lights, I mean?"

"Not at eleven-thirty."

"She could have gone straight up and done it, *then* gone to Heskell," Pinsky said definitely. After a moment, however, he went on. "Or maybe Heskell did it and she's lying about him being home when she got there. Maybe he came along after . . . maybe they're covering up for one another."

"Why should Heskell want to kill him?" Tos asked.

"Because everyone else wanted to," Pinsky said with a cheerful grin. "He's the type who likes to keep up with the crowd."

"What did Heskell actually say?" Tos asked Stryker.

Stryker thought back to his interview with Heskell. The careful curl drooping over the forehead, the wide tie and the long shirt collar that was his attempt to look like Lord Byron, the roll of fat on the back of his neck, the gravy stain on his lapel. "He tossed his head," he finally said. "He denied it, then admitted it, then bragged about it, then started bad-mouthing Underhill for not paying enough attention to his wife."

"Sweet guy," murmured Neilson.

"So where does that leave us?" Pinsky asked in a strained voice as he bent over to put his shoe back on.

"It leaves us at the end of the day, going home," Tos said wearily. "We can start all over again tomorrow after a good night's sleep."

Stryker ignored him. "Heskell's got ambitions, I'm told. He's very political, very active in university affairs. Some people feature him as president, eventually. *He* certainly thinks he will be. Now, if someone like Adamson got hold of some scandal about him, he could take care of Heskell's ambitions, all right. Especially if he made it very, very public. He still might be able to count on Carole Underhill keeping her mouth shut, maybe even Underhill himself—but *not* Adamson. There would be only one *sure* way to shut Adamson up."

"But Heskell has an alibi for yesterday when Pinchman was being set up—he had classes right through and he was at them, I checked. And he *doesn't* have a beard," Neilson said.

"I already said it could have been Underhill, covering up for his wife," Stryker reminded him.

"He might cover up for his wife, but not for Heskell," Pinsky said. "We can't eliminate any of them for sure, can we?"

"What about Wayland?" Stryker asked suddenly.

"Vanished into thin air," Toscarelli said. "But they'll bring him in eventually. We got a picture from the Records Office, and we've circulated it to the night guys. Leave it to them. Come on, I'll drop you off home."

Stryker appealed to Pinsky. "Will you get him off my back? Tell him I'm fine, I can drive myself."

"He's fine, he can drive himself," Pinsky repeated dutifully.

"You didn't tell him about the phone call," Neilson said.

Toscarelli scowled at him and shook his head, but Stryker had heard it, and stopped. "What phone call?"

"Goddamn you, Neilson," Toscarelli growled.

"What phone call?" Stryker asked, coming back.

"Your girl called, what's her name, Kate Trevorne," Toscarelli said casually, crumpling up his empty paper cup and tossing it into the wastebasket. "It was nothing."

"What did she say?"

"She said she'd call you back in the morning. See? Big deal. It was nothing." Toscarelli was getting into his coat.

"She didn't say what it was about?" Stryker persisted.

"Nope." Toscarelli struggled with his buttons. "Well . . . something about a manuscript of Adamson's. She *had* said it was nothing. That was her very word. 'It's nothing, I'll call him back in the morning,' she said."

Stryker rocked back and forth, heel to toe, and thought about this. A manuscript?

He looked at Toscarelli. "I don't know why you keep calling her my girl," he complained.

"She's just your type," Tos said. "A nice girl, steady, intelligent, a little shy, but—"

"She's about as shy as a rattlesnake," Stryker said.

"I thought she looked nice," Pinsky said ruminatively.

"I thought you went for redheads," Neilson said.

Stryker eyed him. "Who told you that?"

Neilson shrugged. "I heard around. Big redheads."

"Big redheads are what wore him down," Toscarelli said. "He *used* to be six foot tall. What he needs in his old age is a little brunette, a quiet life, home cooking—"

"That does it," Stryker said. "I'm going to beat this nagging bastard to *death*."

"Oh, yeah?" Toscarelli stood massively before him.

Stryker glared up at him, then cleared his throat. "I see you've got a new coat," he said, fingering Toscarelli's lapel. "Nice material."

It started to snow again around six-thirty. Fat, clinging flakes tumbled over one another in an effort to get to the ground first, piling up, sticking to everything. They stuck to the hunched shoulders of Richard Wayland as he staggered across the street with the other pedestrians at the busy intersection near the university.

Perhaps he staggered a little more than the others.

He slipped and lurched, reached out a hand to steady himself, and left a perfect handprint on the hood of the police car that had drawn up for the light. The compacted snow of the handprint melted slightly from the heat of the idling engine, but by the time Wayland had reached the far side of the street, the print had begun to fill in again with fresh snow.

The two officers in the car were arguing about the best place to stop for their coffee break. One place had good pie, the other good chili. Clipped to a board between them was a clear photograph of Richard Wayland. His hair was neatly combed, his tweeds were perfect, his smile warm and sincere, his handsome face showed intelligence and sensitivity.

No wonder they didn't recognise him.

KATE HURRIED UP the stairs to the English Department, aware of the snow that had started to fall during her evening seminar. All she had to do was gather up her things and make a run for it. With luck, she should be able to get out of the parking lot and onto the expressway before it got too thick. As they'd discussed Chandler's concept of the hero, she'd watched the snow gathering on the sill beyond the glass. When it had covered it over entirely, she'd dismissed the students ten minutes early, wishing them a safe journey home. She'd hoped she'd have the same.

Her footsteps echoed in the empty foyer and off the other office doors as she passed them, slowing slightly as she saw her own office door was open and the light was on. She was certain she'd closed it before going down to the classroom. Of course. It would be Richard—he had a key to her office, as she had one to his.

"Richard? Where have you—" She stepped through her office door and froze. All the drawers of her desk were opened, and the contents were strewn around the floor. Her filing cabinet drawers were open, too, their contents jumbled and muddled, with bits of paper sticking up and drooping over the sides.

"Oh, my *God*..." she said, stepping into the room.

On the far side of her desk lay Dan Stark, one knee up and his head in shadow. Except that it wasn't only a shadow that spread around his head, but blood...

From behind her there came a rustle, a movement, stealthy but quick.

In the mirror of her windows a distorted figure was reflected against the blackness outside. It raised an arm, high, high. In the hand, something glittered...

A scream rose in Kate's throat before she even turned.

And she turned too late.

TWENTY-TWO

GLARE.

She closed her eyes tightly.

Noise.

Clatter of instruments, the heavy mechanical breathing of a resuscitator, people's voices, footsteps, someone choking.

Smells.

Alcohol, disinfectant, soap, vomit, sweat.

A hospital.

I'm in a hospital, Kate thought, and immediately felt better. I'm not dead. My head couldn't ache like this if I were dead, could it? She raised a hand, or tried to, found it constricted by something. A sheet or blanket? When she lifted her head slightly to see what it was, a wave of nausea swept over her, and she vomited before she could stop herself. Instinctively she turned her head, so most of it went onto the floor. A nurse appeared from the cloudland somewhere beyond the focus of her eyes.

"I'm sorry," whispered Kate.

The nurse grinned. "Never mind, kiddo, you aimed for the floor—that's the most we ask for, down here."

"What happened?" Kate asked. "Was I in an accident?"

The nurse looked at her and raised an eyebrow. "You don't remember?"

"No. I remember finishing my class early, and starting upstairs." Kate frowned in concentration. "Did I fall?"

"No." Kate turned her head toward the new voice and regretted it instantly, both for the movement and what she saw. Stryker stood there, tweed cap pulled down nearly to the bridge of his nose, his eyes shining in the shadow like an angry animal's.

"You walked into your office and interrupted a bit of butchery. For some reason, this annoyed the killer so much he neglected to finish the job on Stark and started in on you, instead."

"Butchery?" Kate's voice was a rasp.

"Fortunately, you were saved by the bell," Stryker went on as if she hadn't spoken. "The bell and Dr. Coulter, who came along, screamed blue murder and nearly got killed herself."

"Butchery?" Kate repeated. It sounded awful, that word.

"At this rate, the only people left up there in that ivory tower of yours will be the janitors and cleaning ladies. Probably do a better job. WHAT THE HELL WERE YOU DOING WANDERING AROUND THERE ALONE AT THAT HOUR?" he suddenly shouted.

"Lieutenant, keep your voice down," the nurse said from where she was wiping up Kate's mess. "This is a hospital."

"Looks more like a battlefield," he muttered.

"It's that, too," the nurse said, standing up. "And we don't need you adding to the artillery by shooting off your mouth. What's the problem? They're all alive, aren't they?"

"Makes a goddamn change," Stryker muttered.

"I think I'm going to be sick again," Kate murmured, and found herself doing just that into a steel bowl held by Stryker, who seemed to derive some perverse satisfaction from her discomfort.

"That's right—that's this morning's breakfast," he said encouragingly. "Keep it up and we'll be back to last night's dinner before you know it." He put the bowl down and wiped her face gently with a damp paper towel conjured up from somewhere behind her. She noticed, for the first time, that under his overcoat he was dressed in a suit and tie. "First she spits on me, then she pukes. Fine romance *this* is," he muttered. "Now—can you tell me what happened up there?"

"I don't know, I don't remember. I don't know how I got here—I don't even know how *you* got here. You didn't have to get all dressed up, just for me."

"I was conducting *La Bohème* and we had to stop the performance because they said this broad was crying out my name at the hospital, so I came. I'm like that. Chivalrous." She just looked at him, and he looked away. His shoulders were hunched up. He took a cigar and began to roll it between his palms, holding it chest-high. His stance reminded her of a boxer's—he had the same habit of rising on the balls of his feet with every step. He moved off a way and began to talk into the air. He didn't light the cigar but continued to roll it between his hands. It was beginning to fray at one end, but he didn't notice. "Stark was in your office. Know why?"

"No."

"Great. While he was in there, somebody hit him over the head and cut off his ear."

"His *ear*?"

"That's right. They're trying to sew it back on now. The way it looks, the killer heard you coming, hid behind the door, and walloped you when you walked in. Ring any bells?"

She closed her eyes. Mists and fog, shadows moving, a mirror, something horrible—Dan?—and something glittering. A screech. "No, no bells."

He whirled and glared at her. "Why did you dismiss your class early?"

"Did I?" She looked at him, saw droplets shining on the shoulders of his coat. "It was snowing—is it still snowing?" It was coming back to her a little at a time. "I wanted to get home before it got bad. I went upstairs—my office door was open—I thought it was Richard, but . . ."

"What made you think it was him? Did you see him?"

She shook her head, which made it ache even more. She put her hand up and encountered stickiness. "What's this?"

"Did you see *anyone*?" Stryker demanded.

"No."

"Shit." The cigar suddenly shredded itself between his palms and showered down onto the floor. "Goddamn it, these things are made of paper these days. Paper." In disgust he kicked the shreds of tobacco under a trolley, looked up, saw the nurse glaring at him, shrugged, and knelt down to gather up the bits and pieces. He spoke, but Kate couldn't see his face beneath the peak of the tweed cap. It was like listening to a mushroom. "Well, I think Dr. Coulter saw him. She says she was coming into the foyer and heard you scream. She called out and that must have scared him off. He crashed past her, knocked her ass over applecart, and shot down the stairs. By the time she got her act together, he was gone. Jody, the kid from the switchboard, heard the fuss and found her staggering down the hall, bleeding." He stood up, his hands full of tobacco shreds. The nurse nodded toward a bin and he went over to deposit his contribution to the Keep America Clean campaign. "She's a tough old bat, I'll give her that. She told Jody to call us and *then* she collapsed."

"Is she all right? Is Dan all right?"

"They're fine," the nurse said in a voice pitched for reassuring children and small animals. "Everything's fine."

Stryker gave the nurse a pained look. "She's got some bruises and a cut lip," he told Kate. "Stark's okay too—like I said, in surgery. But they figure it will take."

"It's madness," Kate whispered. "Aiken's tongue, Dan's ear...it doesn't make sense."

"Monkeys," Stryker said, taking out another cigar.

"What?"

"*Monkeys*. You know? Speak no evil, hear no evil—like that. That's what Coulter said."

"Oh." She squinted at him. "Jane teaches folklore, you see," she tried to explain. "Folklore, the Bible, and Shakespeare. Not crime." It seemed very important that he understand, but he was going away, receding, moving toward a horizon which lay somewhere between herself and the white-tiled wall. Or maybe further. "She would think of monkeys because of...what about *see* no evil?" she whispered suddenly, interrupting herself. She meant to yell, because he was getting so far away, but it came out in a rasp. It made her angry, but she couldn't get herself organised to protest. Maybe he was going to arrest her, this time. He looked angry enough. She mustn't spit. She mustn't. "What about eyes?" She wanted to know because hers weren't working. She couldn't see a *thing* anymore. And ...

Stryker came over to stand next to the examination table. Kate had drifted off into unconsciousness again. He raised a hand and with a hesitant finger touched the cut under her left eye. It was a long, shallow cut. "You have Dr. Coulter to thank for your eyes, sweet Kate," he murmured, then stepped back quickly as the intern entered, bearing X rays. "Well?" Stryker barked, jamming his hands into his pockets and accidentally breaking the new cigar.

The intern smiled. "No fracture, just concussion. We'll keep her overnight for observation. She'll have a headache for a few days, that's all."

"She's got a cut under her eye," Stryker said.

The intern leaned over Kate's unconscious form. "Oh, yeah. Nothing to worry about."

"That's what *you* think," Stryker growled, and went out. He was back a second later. "You should put something on it. It could get infected, a scratch like that, so close to her eye."

"We'll clean it up. Don't worry about it," the intern reassured him, a little peeved to get instructions from somebody who probably didn't know a scratch from his elbow.

"If I want to worry about it, I'll *worry* about it!" Stryker yelled. "Put on some iodine, for God's sake. Would it cost so much to put on some iodine?" He went out, and the intern glanced at the nurse, who shrugged. They could hear Stryker's voice diminishing as he went down the corridor, toward the lifts. "My God, you'd think they could afford iodine in a place like this. They got these dazzling rubber plants, they got those nifty magazine racks over there, they got ducky little coffee machines, and no iodine? *Jeeeeezus!*"

After a moment, the lift doors slammed.

JANE COULTER was smouldering in a hospital bed several floors above where Kate lay in Emergency. The doctors had insisted on keeping her overnight for "shock."

"I'm not in the least shocked," she informed Stryker. "I want to go *home*. Milly will be so upset. As it is, I'll probably have to eat baked custard and chicken broth for weeks. She treats me like an infant—claims I'm 'delicate.' I ask you—do I *look* delicate?"

"You look terrifying," Stryker grinned. "No wonder he ran the hell out of there."

Her grey hair was sticking up in indignant spikes all over her head, her pale blue eyes were flashing fire, and there was a bright circle of red high on each cheekbone. "I have a loud voice," she conceded with a trace of smugness. "I developed it over the years lecturing in vast, drafty halls to bored students who couldn't have cared less about the afflictions of Job or the meaning of druidical symbols. You have to force it into them, you know. Like stuffing a turkey."

This homely allusion would have sat better on her if she hadn't been puffing on Stryker's last cigar. He pulled a chair over and sat down. "Tell me what you saw."

For the first time, she looked uneasy. "I didn't see much of anything. One cannot take in much about a cannonball as it comes at you. One minute the hall was empty, the next this figure came bursting out of Kate's office and knocked me down. He ran off toward the fire stairs." She fixed him with a basilisk eye. "I could describe his shoes well enough, as he stepped on my hand. Would that be of any help to you?"

"Not much—unless he had his name printed on them."

"He didn't. Or if he did, it was obscured by the filth adhering thereto. Very dirty shoes, they were. Like yours."

"Mine?" Stryker looked down in surprise at his well-shined loafers.

Jane Coulter leaned over slightly. "Oh—not those. The ones you were wearing on Saturday, I meant."

"Oh. You mean he was wearing sneakers?"

"*Leather* sneakers?"

"Track shoes, then. They're called track shoes."

"I see. For making tracks, one presumes?"

"Sort of." He regarded her carefully. She was talking about shoes because she didn't want to talk about faces. He was certain of it. "Kate says she thought it was Richard Wayland in her office."

The flush on Jane Coulter's cheeks deepened. "Did she see him? Actually see him?"

"No. But she said she assumed it was he because he has a key to her office, you see."

"Ah. Well, most of the office keys are interchangeable—and the locks are really a joke. It was *not* Richard. It wasn't *anyone* I know. The man was short, dark, heavy-set, and clean-shaven." Now the description came out, forcefully and clearly. "He had a very flat nose and full lips—he could even have been a pale-skinned Negro." Less and less like Richard Wayland with every word.

"I thought you didn't see him clearly."

"I didn't see the colour of his eyes, nor did I have a chance to count his teeth, I grant you." She sighed heavily. "I have been attempting to focus on him for you, Lieutenant, to imagine a photograph snapped as he came toward me. That is what I recall. And since he smelled awful. That, too, I can remember. Unwashed. Dirty. Foetid."

"I see." He noted down the description, following it with a long string of question marks. "And can you remember anything else he was wearing?"

"Something bright—ah, yes, I believe it's called a lumber jacket. Red. And a baseball cap of some kind."

"Was he carrying anything in his hands?"

"Not that I can recall."

"A knife, for instance? Papers, books?"

"I didn't notice." The colour was fading from her cheeks now, and he saw that she really was very tired. He stood up.

"Well, thank you, Dr. Coulter. I think you'd better rest now."

"What about Dan?" he enquired anxiously.

"They've brought him down from surgery," Stryker said.

"And dear Kate?"

"Fine. Concussion, that's all."

"I see. The cut on her face..." She seemed distressed. "So near the eyes..."

"Your three-monkey theory?" Stryker said. "I think it was just a cut she got when she fell, that's all. You mustn't worry about it."

"But you *must* worry about it, Lieutenant. There is some kind of madman out there, striking us down one by one..."

"As you say, *I* must worry about it," Stryker said. "*You* must rest, or they'll never let you out of here."

"Good Lord... what a thought. I shall behave."

"See that you do," he said with mock severity. "And, Dr. Coulter... thank you."

"Am I a heroine?" she asked.

"Definitely."

She sighed in some gratification. "How splendid! I've always wanted to be brave, but I never seemed to have the time for it."

Stryker grinned and left her contemplating the end of her cigar. Toscarelli was waiting near the desk beside the lifts. "How's Stark?"

Tos shrugged. "Dicey. Apparently he lost a lot of blood and wasn't in the best of health to start with. They say he'll be in a bad way for a few days—dicky heart."

"But he'll live?"

"Barring any complication, yeah."

"When can we question him?"

"Maybe not for a couple of days. They've put him in intensive care, because of the heart thing. Apparently it stopped at one point—they don't go much for that."

"Damn! That's two we've got out of reach."

"I guess that puts Pinchman in the clear—unless he sneaked out on Calder and pattered back to the campus on his stumps," Tos said wryly. "What do you figure now? Did the old lady give you a description?"

"Oh, sure, she gave me a description, all right. Short, dark, fat, wearing a red lumber jacket, a baseball cap, and dirty track shoes. Could even have been a black."

"Hey, great."

"Balls! It's snowing out—how much mud and dirt sticks to wet track shoes?"

"Well, maybe he—"

"Don't you see? She's lying. She's given me a description of a guy as *unlike* Richard Wayland as it's possible to get. He's her research assistant, she's crazy about him, she doesn't want him caught."

"But if he's going around killing people, for Christ's sake . . ."

"She doesn't *believe* that. He's her boy. He's misunderstood. Kate's the same—although I don't think she actually saw him, as she was hit from behind." He shook his head. "I wish to hell I could see what *they* see in the bastard. Have we gotten his records from the Pentagon?"

"Tomorrow morning."

"What's taking so long?"

"They say they're scattered. Something like that." He scowled down at Stryker. "I put out another APB on Wayland—they'll find him. Don't worry about it."

"Where the hell could he *be*?" Stryker demanded as they got into the lift. "What the hell is he *doing*?"

RICHARD WAYLAND sat in the doorway, next to another huddled shape, watching the snow falling into the river on the other side of the road.

"It disappears," he said.

The other figure grunted, and held the paper bag more tightly. Inside, the bottle sloshed promisingly.

"Good things, bad things, everything disappears in time," Wayland said. "Especially the minute you look away. Sneaky, that's what it is. Damned sneaky." He turned to the shape beside him. "My turn," he said, reaching for the bag. "Hey!" when the bag was withheld jealously, desperately. "My turn, I said. Or else." He produced a knife from an inner jacket pocket, a knife with a very dirty blade. "You don't want to make me mad, do you? I don't like people who make me mad—I *do* things to them." The shape whimpered and the bottle was handed over. "Better," Wayland said. "Much, *much* better."

STRYKER WAS walking the campus.

Toscarelli, following behind in the car as best he could, muttered to himself as he watched the stocky, angry figure kicking through the snow and occasionally tripping on the ridges of ice left on the pavement by careless sweepers. The pattern of snow and thaw, snow and thaw over the past few days had left the city in a dangerous state. By day, slush and trickles of melt puddled the pavements and sidewalks. Each day, the mounds of snow grew beside the roads, dirty and discoloured, turning the pavements to narrow canyons. On laws and in parks the unbroken stretches sagged and hummocked themselves into miniature glacial fields, then were deceptively blanketed afresh.

According to the weathermen, yet more snow was on the way. A big storm, moving down from Canada, was invisibly but inexorably closing in on the city.

Stryker, turning suddenly, jumped a low hill of piled snow and cut across the Mall. Toscarelli drew up at the curb and cut the engine, watching the lonely figure march to the centre of the Mall and stare, in turn, up at the front of the library, and then at Grantham Hall.

And at the snow that fell on everything.

Stryker knew that murder was the ultimate expression of ego. Whether through impulse or design, a killer struck down victims whose continued existence had become intolerable. In effect the action said, "I am more important than you, than morals, than law. You must die so I may live."

What threat had Adamson and Stark been to the killer's existence? And was he mistaken about Jane Coulter's description? Was she telling the truth, after all? *Was* it some stranger, a student, someone he hadn't considered at all because of his own conviction that Wayland, or some other member of the faculty was guilty? Had he been focusing wrongly? Had he seen Wayland as the killer merely because of his relationship with Kate? He'd heard himself insisting to Tos that Coulter was lying, and for the first time he'd seen what a wobbly edifice he'd been building over the past few days. Death was everywhere, and he'd been wrong to assume it was only where *he* looked. Death walked the streets, breathed the air, smiled behind a hundred closed doors.

"Come on." It was Toscarelli, big and stubborn and insistent. He took hold of Stryker's arm and drew him toward the car. "We'll get him."

"You're goddamn right we will," Stryker's voice was heavy with fury and revenge. It's the girl, Tos thought. The girl got hurt, and now it's personal. Now he'll never let go.

"Tomorrow, we will. Not tonight." Tos held the door open and Stryker turned for one last look at the Mall.

Death had come here before.

This Mall, this empty space, open to the black sky, the tumbling snow, the wind—it was only land. Land that had endured much. That a university was built on it meant nothing. It was temporary.

Then the fields—the land and the mouse beneath the plough.

In the village there had been short tempers and long knives.

In the town, questions of honour.

Now, in the blank-faced and dazed city, death had become vicious and secret and cold. Somewhere out there, an ego was coiled, waiting.

The one thing that remained constant, the one thing that would never change, was the warning rattle of that ego.

Don't tread on me.

Where had he heard it?

"She almost lost an eye, Tos."

"I know. Get in."

"The dirty bastard almost blinded her, killed her."

"Yeah. It happens."

Stryker's voice was grim. "Not to me. Not to mine."

But Death was everywhere.

TWENTY-THREE

WHEN KATE OPENED her eyes again it was morning, and Liz was standing in the chair at the foot of her bed, staring glumbly at her through the metal frame. "Good morning."

Kate croaked something that could have been a greeting.

Liz stood up and came around to stare down at her friend, rakishly bandaged and pale as winter. If it hadn't been for Kate's eyes and the scarlet line of the cut beneath one of them, she would have been nearly invisible against the white sheets.

"See what comes of playing detective?" Liz said with some difficulty. Kate looked so small and vulnerable lying there. How many inches had she been from death last night? Concern made her eyes flash, and Kate mistook it for anger.

"Didn't play 'tective," she managed through dry lips.

Liz took a glass from the side table and made Kate sip some water. "Well, what else was it?" she asked. If she ever met this psycho face to face, she'd demonstrate to him how she felt about this attack on her idiot friend. As it was, there was only the idiot friend to yell at. "Wandering around alone late at night—"

"I had a seminar, as you well know. I dismissed it ten minutes early, because of the snow, and went up to get my coat. That's all I did. You'd think, the way everyone keeps yelling at me, that *I'd* tried to—" She paused, remembered. "How's Dan?"

Liz turned away. "Not great. Did you know he has a heart condition? The shock brought on some kind of attack on the operating table. He's in intensive care—but they think he's past the worst."

"Oh, God. And Jane?"

"Fighting fit and demanding instant release," Liz grinned. "They want her to stay and rest, of course, but she told the doctor where he could stick his diagnosis."

Kate smiled. She closed her eyes.

Liz frowned and leaned forward. "Are you all right? Do you want me to call the nurse or something?"

"No, I'm fine."

Liz gave a ladylike grunt. "Stryker says you were lucky Jane came along. He went for your eyes, you know."

"Who, Lieutenant Stryker?"

"No, fool." She turned back and saw that Kate hadn't been told that. She was touching her face, and her fingertips encountered the cut beneath her eye. "Oh, that's nothing. It won't even leave a decent scar."

"Give me a mirror."

"I tell you, it's nothing."

"Dammit, I want to see—" Kate threw back the covers and half-swung her legs over the side of the bed. As she did, Stryker walked in on a generous display of leg and thigh.

"Get back in bed," he ordered.

"I bet you say that to all the girls," Kate snapped, reaching a toe for the floor. "I want to see my face."

"Dammit, cover yourself up," Stryker growled, pushing her back and practically hammering the sheets back into place. He turned to Liz. "Have you got a mirror in your handbag?" Liz nodded. "Then, give it to her. The more you refuse, the worse she'll think it is."

"All right, all right," Liz said, opening her bag. "Are you always so bossy?"

"Yes, he is," said Kate, watching her friend search anxiously. But when she looked into the mirror at last, her voice was almost disappointed. "Oh, it *isn't* much, is it?"

"Sorry about that," Stryker said sarcastically. "Want me to see if they've got something we can rub in it to make it worse?" He frowned at her. "Have you remembered what Stark was doing in your office?"

"No. Oh—unless he went down there to get the manuscript. I said I'd give it to him and then I forgot it because—"

"Manuscript? This the one you left the message about this afternoon?"

"That's right. It was a book of Aiken's." She told him about the girl and paying her and asking Dan for the money from the estate.

"Remember her name?"

"Considering my special subject, I'm hardly likely to forget it. Christie."

"Agatha?" Liz asked gleefully.

"No. Sorry. Mary Louise. Her address is on the envelope. I left the manuscript in my desk for Dan—that must have been why he was there. I can't think of any other reason."

"Was the manuscript there when you came in?" Stryker demanded, writing things in his notebook.

"I haven't the vaguest idea. All I saw was Dan."

"What colour was the envelope?"

"Just an ordinary large manila envelope—rather beaten up, as I recall. As if it had been reused several times. Aiken would do that—he was always pinching pennies."

"Or athletes' backsides," Liz said.

"What was the manuscript about?"

"Why are you so interested in it?" Kate asked.

"Because I haven't anything *else* to be interested in at the moment," Stryker snapped. "Did you read it?"

"Only the title—upside down. Something about the Fourth Cavalry. I guess Aiken was branching out into military history."

"All those butch, strong soldiers with their great big . . . *guns*" Liz said with salacious and comic pseudo-relish. "Wow!"

"Would he be likely to write about the Army?" Stryker asked, giving Liz a look.

Kate shrugged. "He's written about all kinds of things. It could have been the Greek Army—I might have been mistaken about the Fourth part. Why don't you read it for yourself? It must still be there."

"You can't remember anything else?"

"Nope." She eyed him. "Not about last night, anyway." She was rewarded by a slight flush on his cheekbones, but his eyes didn't change. Cold blue fire, as always.

"Okay. I'll drop back later." He went out abruptly.

"That man doesn't like me," Liz announced.

"He doesn't like anyone." Kate struggled to sit up in bed. Her head ached, but it hadn't actually come loose from her neck, so she supposed it would be all right. Grateful for such small mercies, she demanded breakfast and information.

Liz was wearing a brightly coloured handwoven skirt. She thrust her hands into its deep pockets and went over to the window to stare out. "Well," she said, "the English Department is in disarray. Deprived of their chairman, two of their most prestigious professors, and their prettiest instructor, they are rushing around babbling. 'Persecution and cruelty.' Arthur Fowler is flapping so much they're afraid he'll achieve lift-off, Mark Heskell is having a studio portrait taken in case the papers want an in-depth interview, Underhill is home writing a sermon entitled—"

"What about Richard?" Kate interrupted. "Does he know I'm here? Does he know what's happened?"

Liz looked down at her boots, tapped a toe, inspected a heel, did a small turn, but kept her eyes away from Kate's. "Richard isn't around. He hasn't been around since Monday morning. The police have sworn out a warrant against him for murder and are looking for him everywhere. If he knows about what happened to you, Kate, it's probably because he did it himself."

STRYKER WENT DOWN to the Intensive Care Unit and asked to see the doctor in charge. "I'd like to talk to Stark, please."

"I'm sorry, it's out of the question."

"Only a moment or two. I must find out if he saw the person who attacked him. It might make all the difference to catching the guy."

The doctor was dubious. "He's in a lot of pain, and heavily sedated. He's hardly conscious."

"Please let me try. Five minutes, that's all."

"*Three* minutes . . . and with a nurse in attendance."

"Deal."

The room was brightly lit and full of machines that whirred, hummed and clicked. There couldn't have been a greater contrast to the dimly lit cocoon that held Edward Pinchman, several floors below.

"Dr. Stark—can you tell me who attacked you?"

Mumbling and whispering—nothing coherent. Stryker leaned over the small figure on the bed. Stark's head was coifed in bandage, pinching his tiny features into a triangle only marginally pinker than the bandage itself.

"Who hit you, Dr. Stark?"

"Calvary," Stark whispered.

"You were reading Adamson's manuscript?"

Stark nodded, tried to speak with dry, uncooperative lips. His eyelids began to flutter.

"Who hit you, sir? Please, try to tell me who hit you. Did you see him?"

"Everybody saw him," Stark said clearly.

And then his eyes closed.

"That's it," the nurse said. "Sorry."

Stryker was standing outside the Intensive Care Unit when Arthur Fowler came bustling down the hall. "Is Dan in there?" he demanded.

"Yes, sir."

"I want to see him. Immediately."

"I'm afraid they won't let you in, Dr. Fowler. He's in a bad way... Maybe later."

Fowler produced a handkerchief and blew his nose emphatically. "Old fool," he muttered.

"Dr. Stark?" Stryker asked, surprised.

"No, of course not. Myself. There's nothing foolish about Dan Stark, except his blind faith in the goodness of man. It's all very well, these theories about weakness becoming strength and all that, but—"

"Sir?"

Fowler turned to the lifts and Stryker followed him. "Dan had a theory about people who overcame weakness being stronger than others. He kept hiring fools and witlings, despite what we said, saying they'd come all right in the end. Well, look where it's got him. It's all very well to have a faculty balanced like a house of cards as long as he's there to watch over it, but without him—catastrophe. *Catastrophe*!"

"How do you mean?"

"It is not enough that we have three members of the faculty in this hospital, and another missing altogether, is it?" Fowler demanded petulantly. "Now two more have gone off and left us in the lurch."

"Which two is that?"

"Heath and Lucy Grey-Jenner. When I came in this morning, there was a letter on Dan's desk informing him that they were getting *married* and would be back next week. *Married!* I can't tell you how *shocked* I was."

"They have a right to be happy," Stryker said.

"Yes. Of course they have—but *not* at the start of term. *And* with all this other disaster going on. I am deeply disappointed in them, and will tell them so on Monday. I'm having to assign graduate students to take instructors' classes so the instructors can take on senior classes—I have to let *Heskell* take two of Dan's graduate seminars on criticism, God help the students, and Rocheleau is teaching semantics because Underhill is sick, and—"

"Chris Underhill is sick?"

"Yes—another one out. We might as well shut down the *entire operation*!" Fowler announced dramatically. "Simply *shut down* until it's *all over*!"

Stryker thought he could have been doing the man an injustice, but he had a sneaking suspicion that Fowler was loving all of this.

"And what, may I ask, is all this about *monkeys*?" Fowler added.

"Sir?"

"Don't 'sir' me, young man. In the papers this morning. They have nicknamed this maniac with a vendetta against *my* department 'The Monkey Killer.' Why? Why? They are making all sorts of ridiculous statements...eyes, ears, tongues...it's *ghastly*. What have monkeys to do with anything? It's Heskell, I know it is, he's talked to them again, about see no evil and hear no evil...the man's a menace. He'll not get tenure from *me, oh,* no. There are reporters everywhere—" He stubbed his finger angrily against the lift button and then sucked it like a child. His hair was standing up in a halo around his gleaming bald head, and his jowls were wobbling alarmingly. "Monkeys," he muttered around his finger. *"Monkeys!"*

"I'm sorry, there's nothing I can do about that," Stryker said sympathetically.

"Oh, yes there is. You can catch him and put an end to it, *that's* what you can do. Meanwhile I shall endeavour to keep Dan's warship afloat, you can tell him that. Tell him Arthur Fowler will do his best. I'm good at details, I'll take care of the details. Tell him that. Tell him—" Suddenly the man's eyes were filled with tears. "Tell the old fool to get better. We need him."

The lift doors opened. Fowler got in and savagely punched the button for the ground floor. Stryker leaned forward and put his hand against the rubber stop of the lift doors, holding them open. "Do you know anything about a book Dr. Adamson was writing? About the Army?"

"The Army?"

"Well, the Cavalry, then. The Fourth Cavalry, I think it was."

"No, I know nothing of it. Wayland's the one you want there."

"Wayland?"

"*If* you can find the devil. I believe *he* was doing something about Viet Nam. He was a great objector, you know. Protests and all that. Although it might have been the Civil War, come to think of it, because of Whitman. They don't call it the Cavalry anymore, but they did then. I think it's in his file. A paper or a book on Whitman—Lincoln—something along those lines. I'll check for you, if you like.''

"I'd be very grateful.''

"I have so *much* free time at the moment,'' Fowler grumbled, making a note. But his eyes twinkled, perhaps with the remnants of the tears he hadn't allowed to get away. "As for Aiken, I can't imagine *him* having anything to do with it. He hasn't published anything for quite a while, of course. One *must* publish, you know, publish regularly. He's never had a great success, but…the Army? I shouldn't think so. No. Wayland's your man there. Ask him. And when you find him, would you remind him he has a contract with the university that requires him to actually *teach* in addition to everything else? He tends to forget.''

"I'll mention it.'' Stryker let go of the doors.

They closed over Fowler's red and resentful face, and Stryker stood there, staring at them, trying to clear his mind of all the muddle. He wished *he* was as good at details, as Fowler claimed to be.

He was still standing there, five minutes later, when Neilson came down the hall. "I think you'd better come,'' he said urgently. "She's in Pinchman's room, and he's starting to talk.''

"Who is?''

"The Trevorne girl.''

"Oh, Jesus—what next?''

Pinsky was standing outside the door to Pinchman's room watching for them. "I wasn't here…she went in after the nurse and began yelling at him. Nancy tried to put her out, but the old guy began to respond, so…''

They went into the room. Kate, dressed rather haphazardly in the blood-stained clothing of the night before, was bending over Pinchman's bed, calling him. The old man was still unconscious, but restless, moving around in the bed, turning his head from side to side. His face was twisted in a grimace.

"Edward, you must wake up. Tell them it *wasn't* Richard, tell them what really happened, about the cradle, what about the cradle—?''

"Kate!'' Stryker's voice was a whiplash but she neither flinched nor turned as she answered.

"He knows, he *must* know. Liz said you're after Richard, that you think *Richard* did all these things and I know he didn't, I *know* he didn't—''

"Richard," Pinchman said suddenly.

And the room became still.

"Cradle, rocking . . . endlessly rocking . . ."

"What the hell?" muttered Stryker.

"Kate . . . be careful. Richard . . . dangerous . . . stay away."

Kate straightened up suddenly, her face pale. She began to sway, and Stryker moved forward to hold her up. Her eyes, filled with horror, were locked on Pinchman's face as she shook her head from side to side, denying what she was hearing. She'd wanted Edward to wake up, but not like this. She'd wanted him to clear Richard, but everything he said was making it worse.

"The cradle, Richard . . . rocking . . . endlessly rocking . . . remember . . . nobody knows . . . Aiken found out . . . Oh, God! Richard! Get away! Get away!" The last word was a shout, but Pinchman's eyes remained closed, tears flowing from beneath the papery lids. He fell back on the pillows.

"I'm afraid that's it," the nurse said. "You'll have to stop this at once."

"But he's about to wake up," Stryker protested.

The nurse had Pinchman's wrist. "No, he's not."

"You mean—" Kate gasped.

The nurse briskly replaced the twitching hand beneath the covers. "I mean he's exhausted and can't take any further strain. His heartbeat has become irregular, I'm calling the doctor, you'll have to leave."

"*She* stays," Stryker said, indicating the policewoman who had replaced Calder on this shift.

"Yes, I know. But *she* goes." The nurse pointed at Kate.

Kate went, running blindly out into the brightly lit anonymity of the hall, past the indifferent white uniforms and the open curiosity of other visitors who turned to see the woman crying, running. Free show. Drama. The real thing. Look at that.

Stryker found her in a corner at the end of the corridor, standing by an overflowing linen trolley. She was blotting her tears with a sheet that could have come from a typhoid victim, for all she knew. He snatched it from her and replaced it with his own clean handkerchief. "You could catch something, dummy," he said gruffly.

"He was afraid of Richard," she snuffled.

"Was he?"

"Wasn't he?" She blinked at him blearily. He looked ruffled and cross and hot, standing there. As if he wanted to hit someone. It occurred to her that he always looked as if he wanted to hit some-one.

"What was all that crap about the cradle?"

"I don't know."

"The hell you don't."

"Oh, please..."

"It's part of a poem. Whitman. 'When Lilacs Last in the Door-yard Bloomed.' Right? About Lincoln's death. Right?"

She nodded miserably, into his handkerchief.

"And according to Fowler, Wayland was doing his doctorate on Whitman. He teaches modern American poetry."

"*And* the Bible as literature, *and* history of the English language, *and*..." she listed desperately.

"But Whitman is his thing, right?"

Kate didn't answer. She felt so tired, so confused, and he was so *angry*.

"I'm taking you home. I don't want you involved any more in all this," Stryker said.

"A few days ago you were begging for my help."

"Not any more. You're out of it."

"The hell I am!"

"Nice talk. *Nice* talk from a college professor."

She gave him a little more "nice talk," causing a nurse to turn around with a shocked expression. Even Stryker was a little taken aback. "You think Richard is responsible for this, don't you?" she concluded. "Well, I don't. I *know* he couldn't have hurt me. Not Richard."

"I agree. Not your devoted Richard—but somebody Richard might have *become*. Murder makes strangers, Kate."

"Not Richard," she said stubbornly.

"Your needle's stuck." They glared at one another, until Stryker sighed and looked away. "Kate," he said in a more gentle voice. "You nearly lost an eye last night. Maybe both, if Dr. Coulter hadn't come along."

"You're going to start hunting him, aren't you?"

"We've *been* hunting him since Monday," he said heavily. "Look, did it ever occur to you that he's missing because he might be lying dead someplace? No, I see that it didn't. Don't you think that's interesting? Don't you think it's indicative of something that you were never worried about *that* possibility—but only that Richard might be a killer?"

"Oh—"

"Did it also ever occur to you that when we are looking for killers, we're doing it to protect potential victims?" Stryker continued inexorably. "We're not in it for the fun of the chase, like your fictional detectives, because the chase is *not* much fun. All you guys back then, when you were protesting and screaming 'pigs' with your fat little heads full of fat little ideas about yourselves and nobody else—did you ever think about the people you might jostle in front of a passing bus, or the janitor with arthritis who'd have to clean up after you, or your parents who probably went without a lot of luxuries to pay for your education...oh, hell." He saw she looked stricken. "When I go to the scene of a crime, the first thing I see is a *victim*, Kate. And I get angry at the waste. Later, when and if I catch the killer, I see another kind of victim. And I get angry about *that*, too. Nothing is ever one thing, nothing that ever happens is just one thing happening. There's not four dimensions, there's a thousand—depending on which way you look, which eyes you use. When we started looking for Wayland it was as much for his own *safety* as anything else."

"And now?"

"Now it's for everyone's safety."

"He didn't do it."

"Kate—maybe he's a nice guy, I don't know. Maybe he's a saint. Maybe he's hurt. Maybe he's dead. And maybe—just maybe—he's a killer. You thought that too, Kate. You're thinking it now, aren't you?"

"Stop it!" Her voice was high and thin, and she turned away from the reason in his eyes. It *had* been in her mind. She hated Stryker in that moment. Hated him because nothing would ever be the same now. He'd seen the cold, dark place inside her where Richard didn't live and was not loved. A thousand images filled her mind: Richard laughing, Richard loving, Richard walking, eating, drinking, teaching, swimming, dancing...

Richard killing?

"He went to Viet Nam, after all," she said, and it didn't seem irrelevant. Only odd, to announce it like that. Anyway, Stryker knew it already.

"Viet Nam or any war doesn't *make* killers, it only trains them," Stryker said. "Millions of guys went to Nam. It affected them, taught them, scared the piss out of them—but the decent guys came back decent guys, and that was ninety-nine percent of them."

"Did you go?"

"I didn't have to. My war is here."

"And your enemy is Richard Wayland?"

"Maybe. I won't know that until I find him."

"Do you expect me to wish you luck?"

"I don't expect you to do anything but go home and stay there."

"Like a good little girl?"

"Like a *safe* little girl."

"Richard won't hurt me. I *know* he wouldn't."

"Oh, Kate," Stryker said softly as she turned away. "Don't you realize I'd like nothing more than to be *wrong* about Richard Wayland? Don't you think I know how you'll feel toward me if I arrest him? Can't you imagine what might have happened if we'd met anywhere else but over a murder? It's created a gap between us that we may *never* be able to cross."

"Very poetic." She was rigid with rage.

He looked at her for a long time, her soft mouth set in a hard line of anger, her eyes darkened by it. "Damn you, Kate," he said. "You know what I'm saying is true, you know what's been happening with us right from the beginning. Maybe from as far back as fifteen years ago, I don't know. But I'm not going to be cute about it. Damn Adamson, damn Richard Wayland—damn all the thieves who steal what might have been. And yes, I know—I'm very poetic." Pinsky appeared at the far end of the corridor, and Stryker waved him over. "Drive Miss Trevorne home, will you? She doesn't like it here."

"Sure." Pinsky beamed at Kate. "I hope you're feeling better, Miss Trevorne. That was a close call you had last night."

"I seem destined for narrow escapes," Kate said, and walked away without a backward glance. Pinsky raised an eyebrow at Stryker, who reached out and touched his sleeve. He waited until Kate was out of hearing, then spoke in a low, tight voice. "Take her home and set up a discreet surveillance. I *mean* discreet too—she's to know nothing about it."

"Okay. You afraid he'll try to get to her?"

Stryker reached into his pocket, got out a cigar, lit it. He glared through the smoke at Kate, who still had her back turned to them. "Afraid? Hell no. I'm *hoping* he'll try to get to her. It may be the only satisfaction I'll get out of this goddamn case."

"You don't mean that," said Pinsky.

"Don't I?"

"Nope." Pinsky's battered face was full of confident trust.

"Am I a good cop, Pinsky? Do I do my job?"

"Best I know." He hesitated. "Of course, I don't know that *many*."

"You're a great comfort," Stryker said.

"That's what my wife tells me." Pinsky nodded and started down the hall. "*She* doesn't mean it either."

TWENTY-FOUR

"HEY, Speedy!"

Toscarelli stood in the middle of the gym floor, turning to follow Stryker's dogged progress around the running track overhead. "Are you gonna go around in circles all morning, or what?"

"Why not?" Stryker panted. "I've been going around in them all night."

Toscarelli muttered something in an aggrieved tone.

"What?"

"I said you're a horse's ass. Neilson says he left you last night surrounded by the daily reports and the forensic reports and the case file and when he came in this morning there you were, still at it."

"An illusion," Stryker panted.

Toscarelli kept turning as Stryker pounded on with wobbling knees, sweat streaming down his face and into the towel he had around his neck. "I slept on the couch in the captain's office."

Toscarelli shook his head and turned a couple of times in the opposite direction to clear his head. "Goddammit, will you stop? You're making me dizzy."

Stryker staggered to a stop, gasping and hung over the edge of the rails to catch his breath—or to keep from collapsing—he wasn't sure which. "Any news of Wayland?"

"No, nothing yet. I see his records have come through from Washington."

"Yes—did you look at them? At the medical officer's report?"

"Yeah. And the psychiatrist's report. You got anyone covering the bars and clubs?"

"I do now," Stryker said. "Vice is helping out."

"Do you think the girl knows?"

Stryker wiped his face with the end of the towel. "I don't know. Maybe. It would explain some things, you know. Tos. Adamson left him fifty thousand, but there was nothing about him in the diaries or anywhere."

"Nothing about the girl, either, and he left her ten."

" Maybe it's old debts." He pondered this, rubbing his neck. "I *think* it's old debts."

"Listen, the hospital called. Pinchman's improved—he's coherent."

Stryker straightened up. "Why the hell didn't you say so?"

"I just did."

Toscarelli came into the locker room as Stryker was drying off from the shower. He sat down on a bench while Stryker dressed. "Right," Stryker said, grabbing his coat and scarf. "Come on."

Toscarelli looked at him standing beside the bench as if waiting for a starting gun to go off. "Did you eat anything this morning?" He was obviously unprepared to rise until he had been given this piece of information.

Stryker thought. He remembered going into the cafeteria, all right. What had happened then? "Cereal, something. I don't know. Yeah, I ate. Come *on*."

They left the locker room, Toscarelli giving his usual impression of an aircraft carrier on manoeuvres, Stryker bouncing impatiently ahead.

"This could be it, you know—he probably can explain the whole thing," Stryker enthused, over his shoulder.

"And he might just want to say hello," Tos observed majestically.

"If he *does* say it was Wayland, we'll have him cold. The case will be finished."

"Swell," Tos said, watching Stryker loping away toward the car park. He was off and running again. It was all part of Stryker's own kind of hysteria when a case was bugging him. This was the worst it had ever been, Tos thought. Neilson had noticed it. Jesus, even *Pinsky* had noticed it. If Stryker wasn't careful he'd screw himself straight into the ground and somebody would run over his head.

"Hey!" he called after Stryker. "You will take those vitamins I told you about?"

WHEN STRYKER and Toscarelli walked in, Pinchman was propped up in bed watching the door. Aside from an occasional blurring of the bright blue eyes, he seemed alert enough after his long and nearly eternal sleep. He was a nice-looking old guy, Stryker thought sadly. Despite all that had happened to him, one way and another. He felt sorry for what might lie ahead. They exchanged edgy greetings, then Stryker pulled up a chair and sat on it backwards, propping his arms across the back.

"You want to tell me what happened?"

Pinchman nodded and sighed. "I was so relieved on Saturday when you said 'stabbed,' you know. I'd come down there in terror thinking I'd killed him through some terrible mischance. I never meant to kill him, you see. I admit I struck him in my rage, but he was only unconscious when I left him. I made certain he was alive because he looked so awful, lying there. I held my cigar case to his lips and it misted over quite completely."

"You hit him with your crutch?"

"Yes. I didn't know I was going to do it until it was done. They're so much a part of me, you see. I raised my hand to him in anger—and the crutch was in it. He'd pushed me back against the desk, kept prodding me with his finger, saying he was going to tell them—and it happened. Very quick, it was. All in the rage of the moment. I have a devil of a temper when it lets go, always did, but I haven't lost control in years..." He paused. "Not for a very long time."

"Not since the last time you were arrested?"

Pinchman stared at him, then closed his eyes and sagged against the pillows. "So he told, after all."

"No, he never had a chance. We routinely sent your fingerprints to the FBI and they said that they belonged to *Edgar* Pinchman, a con man with a record as long as my arm. They were surprised at this, because as far as they knew, Edgar Pinchman was an expatriate, resident in Greece. Is that what Adamson had found out?"

Pinchman nodded. "How efficient you are, Lieutenant. To have found all that out in a day."

"It's been nearly a week, Professor Pinchman."

"A *week*?"

"We'll get to that in a minute. Can you tell me about Edgar—or Edward?"

There was a long pause, and then Pinchman spoke softly. "I was a pretty good con man, you know," he said with a smile.

"You got caught."

"Not always." The smile was momentarily triumphant. "And *never* here in Ohio." He sighed heavily. "Edward was a year older than myself, but people often took us for twins at first glance. Back home in Connorsville we were just called the Pinchman boys. It was kind of a joke with us—and it sometimes came in handy, too.

We looked alike, we talked alike, we walked alike. But under the skin we were about as similar as beans and bananas. Edward was a brilliant scholar, hard-working, dedicated. I was brilliant at getting *out* of all that, and into trouble. But Edward always stuck up for me, helped me out of scrapes, even lied for me. Lying was very difficult for him, automatic for me. We loved each other.'' He glanced at Stryker. ''People used to, you know.''

''Yes, sir. I remember.''

Pinchman smiled wryly, nodded, went on with another sigh. ''He always believed that each time I got in trouble would be the last. He never despaired or patronised me. We grew up and gradually went our separate ways. He won scholarly acclaim—I won jail sentences.'' The flickering smile went out at last, and a kind of darkness replaced it.

''Nineteen years ago, his sabbatical coincided with my release from a five-year sentence. He suggested I accompany him to Greece. I was tired, and I was grateful. There wasn't much money—but enough. We lived simply. It was very pleasant. I took an interest in his work and he said I had a gift for it. Said it was a shame I hadn't stayed on at college and, bless him, he wasn't referring to my criminal activities. I began to believe we weren't so different, after all.'' He chuckled to himself. ''The bean who became a banana—or vice versa. We used to walk in the afternoon. People don't expect that in Greece. One afternoon a truck came around a corner too fast to find two middle-aged gentlemen strolling down the middle of the road. There was nothing he could do. I lost my legs—and Edward lost a great deal more.''

''He's alive. We checked.''

''Oh, yes—physically alive. But his were mostly head injuries. He's healthy and happy—but beyond reach. Rather like a sweet and speechless child. I spend every summer with him.''

''As *Edward* Pinchman.''

He shrugged. ''It was a small country hospital. They were hardly likely to take fingerprints, were they? They simply tried to save our lives. They had two men named Pinchman, and it hardly mattered which one was which, unless one died, and it never came to that. It was weeks before I was well enough to realize they didn't know whether I was Edgar or Edward. When I *did* realize, it was after I'd learned of Edward's hopeless condition.'' Again he glanced sideways at Stryker. ''Dammit, man—I'd spent my life taking advantage of situations, hadn't I? This was a gift—a chance to begin again. And I knew that Edward would have agreed if he'd known. God knows he'd lied for me often enough when we were kids. So I accepted the role. The hopeless invalid was officially listed as *Edgar* Pinchman, and I returned to this country as Edward Pinchman."

"Just like that?"

"Well, nearly. It was damned hard work, at first. People made allowances because of my physical condition and so on, of course. I made a 'thing' out of having had my 'looks' destroyed, made it a joke, you know. That answered any curiosity about my face having changed. In fact, it hadn't changed all that much. As for height and weight differences—well—the tin legs accounted for *that* all right. Edward had been teaching in California. As soon as it was possible to do so, I started scouting out a new post. It meant losing tenure, of course, but I wanted to get away before his friends and colleagues started noticing any *other* changes that wouldn't be so easy to cover up. I knew a great deal about Edward's life from his letters and from conversations we'd had before the accident, but small details are what can trip you up. All the 'Say, do you remember's' and so on. Shared jokes, intimacies, and so on. When I got the offer from Dan to come back to Ohio I leapt at it." He smiled. "As far as I was able to leap, that is. Edward and Dan had been at school together, so it seemed quite natural to give up sunny California for old friends and home. They thought I was mad, of course, especially when I asked for a year off before starting actual teaching, using my health as an excuse. The truth was I needed time to bone up on Edward's subject and researches, so I wouldn't come a cropper over *that*. Sometimes I wondered if I could manage it at all. But Dan was so patient and forgiving." Pinchman looked puzzled for a moment. "You know, there were times when I almost thought he guessed the truth, but he never actually *said* anything."

"Dr. Stark is a very bright man."

"Yes. Well—that's it. I worked hard and I took Edward's place, and I don't think I've done too badly at it. Until now."

Stryker looked at the tired old man and felt a surge of admiration. It must have been very tough indeed. No wonder he'd been so sympathetic to Kate, who'd also had to "catch up."

The old man's eyes blurred slightly. "I told Edward what I was going to do, before I left, and why. We spent a lot of time in the gardens of that small hospital, with the bees and the flowers and the sound of oxen beyond the wall. I do honestly believe he understood what I was doing, and why—although he couldn't say so." He closed his eyes and there was a glitter of moisture along the lashes, but not enough to drop. "I like to think so, anyway. I've come to love his life. When I go back each summer, I tell him what I'm doing, which students show promise and so on. I can't continue his research, but I *can* teach. It's a kind of con game, in its ways." His head came up. "Dammit, I'm a good teacher. Even Aiken never denied *that*."

"How did he find out?"

"Chance. Pure chance. He was passing through the small town and saw Edward being taken out in his wheelchair. He saw the resemblance, asked who it was, heard the whole story." Pinchman sighed. "I didn't mind for myself, I don't have that many years left. But, for Edward . . ." He raised a hand and let it fall. "It was *his* life. His career. I've never fulfilled his scholarly promise, of course. People assumed it was because of the accident—well, and so it was—but I managed to maintain it respectably. When Aiken shot his first dart at the meeting, I knew what it heralded. Months, perhaps years of torment—and the possibility that when he'd tired of the game he'd tell Dan. He *did* have very high academic standards, you see—and *I* didn't even have a proper degree, did I?"

"What happened?"

"After the meeting, I went to my office, supposedly to work, but really to try to sort things out in my mind. I thought perhaps early retirement on health grounds..." His voice faded and Stryker could see how much it would hurt him to leave the profession he'd come to love. "As a matter of simple fact, I worried over it so much I finally fell asleep in my chair. When I woke up it was cold and very late. I'd never turned my light on, you see. No one knew I was there. But I could see a light in Aiken's office, across the hall. He'd said something earlier about making a call to the Coast. I could hear him in there, sort of humming to himself, in that wretched little way he had. I don't know how long I sat there, getting more and more angry. Then it became too much. I got up and went across and told him I wouldn't put up with his games. He laughed." Pinchman's cheeks were flushed—anger had returned. "He *laughed*. He said I'd made a mockery of Edward's career, but that probably Edward would have done the same. He said Edward's early work was rubbish, anyway. That was when I hit him. I hit him *hard*." His eyes met Stryker's squarely. "My God, it felt good. I could have gone on hitting him for hours. *Days*."

"But you didn't."

"No, of course I didn't. When I'd recovered my wits, and made sure he was alive, I went back to my office and closed the door." He was remembering now, and Stryker hardly dared breath lest he interrupt the pictures in the old man's mind. Pinchman's breathing slowed. Was he falling asleep?

"Go on," Stryker said very softly. Pinchman's eyes flew open.

"Where was I? Oh, yes, in my office, getting my coat. I didn't want to be there when Aiken woke up, you see. But before I could leave, someone came down the hall."

The hairs rose on the back of Stryker's neck, and he knew this was it. It was coming.

Pinchman saw the look on his face and quickly put him out of his misery. "No, I didn't see who it was. I'm sorry. I saw only a...shape...against the pebbled glass of my door. My lights were out, there were only the lights from Aiken's office. The person—whoever it was—stood in the doorway of Aiken's office for a moment, then went in and closed the door. I waited for some reaction—but there was none. Only silence at first. And then . . ."

"Yes?"

"Laughter. Not very nice laughter. It frightened me," he said simply. Stryker imagined him, distressed and panicky, hiding in the darkness of his own office after having assaulted someone, and hearing that sound. Pinchman was tough, he'd survived much, he had guts. Yet he'd been afraid. It must have been some laugh, that laugh.

"Man or woman?"

"I couldn't say. It was sexless. Gleeful, like a mad child. It just . . . froze me. Then there were more noises, drawers opening, grunts . . . I don't know. I just stood there, unable to move. Then the door opened and the figure emerged. It went down the hall, and I heard the elevator go down. I knew I was alone with Aiken. I waited a few minutes, then managed to open my door and look through his. I decided the other person, whoever it was, had robbed him as he lay there. And I came away as fast as I could."

"And you left him there."

"Yes, I'm sorry. I did."

Well, the blood wouldn't have reached the door by then, Stryker conceded. The old man would have no way of knowing, of guessing, even, that murder had been done while he hid in the darkness. "Tell me about the shape against the pebbled glass. Tall or short?"

"Medium."

"Colour of clothing?"

"Brown, I think. Darkish brown."

"Hat? Coat?"

"I don't know if it was a hat or...lightish. The colour was light because I couldn't really distinguish it through the glass, you see. If it had been dark I would have."

"Man or woman?"

"I told you—I don't know."

"Could it have been Richard Wayland?"

"Well, I *suppose* it could have been. The shape was never pressed against my door...it was in the middle of the hall, you see. I didn't think it was as tall as Richard, but it could have been. Oh, but no—not *Richard*."

"He took you home on Monday?"

"Richard? Yes he did."

"You spoke his name several times when you were unconscious."

"*Why* was I unconscious, by the way?" Pinchman asked. "Nobody will tell me that. They just smile and nod and say I must rest. I remember Richard getting me home, but I must say, I remember very little after that. Did I collapse? I do, sometimes."

"I don't know. You may have. When you spoke Wayland's name you seemed very upset. You seemed to be warning him or warning people about him. You said things like 'Stay away, Richard' and 'Get away, Richard.' Did he attack you?"

"*Richard?* Attack *me*?" Pinchman was astounded. "Good Lord, don't be preposterous, man. He was kindness itself. He saw how upset I was about the letter and offered to take me home."

"Letter?" Stryker stared at him. What was this?

"Yes. It was in my pigeonhole at the office. It just said, 'I saw you kill the old man and I want money or I'll tell the cops.' Crude, but effective. Good simple structure, full marks for clarity." His voice was wry.

"Did Wayland *see* the letter?"

"No. Only that it upset me. Well, it would have upset you, too, wouldn't it? Saturday morning I thought I was a goner, then you said Aiken was stabbed, and I thought I was off the hook, so to speak. Then, out of the blue, there came this letter and I was in the soup again. It was ghastly—as if Aiken had lived to torment me, after all."

"So Wayland took you home? Then what?"

"Well, he settled me in my chair and then made me some coffee. I hate coffee, but I drank a little to please him. He said he'd come back later, after classes, to see if I needed anything. I believe I fell asleep. Did he come back?"

"I came first," Stryker said. "Did you finish the coffee Wayland made for you, before you fell asleep?"

"I don't think so," Pinchman said dubiously. "As I say, I don't much like coffee, only keep it for guests. And whatever Richard's undoubted talents for relating to students, he has absolutely none for making coffee. It tasted *dreadful*."

TWENTY-FIVE

LIZ OLSON CAME UP the back stairs cautiously, opened the door to Kate's flat and stuck her head around. "Kate?" she called. There was no response, but from the front of the flat she could hear music playing, and went toward it. As she neared the archway leading from the dining room to the living room, she suddenly saw a bare foot lying very still, and her stomach contracted with fear. She ran the last few steps, saw Kate lying full length in the centre of the room, and screamed at the top of her voice.

Kate screamed too, scrambling to her feet in terror. They stared at one another for a moment, wild-eyed, and then Liz sank down onto the nearest heap of cushions.

"Oh, Jesus Christ, I thought you were dead." She'd gone as white as the snow outside, and panted as if she'd just run a one-minute mile in gum boots. "Oh, God, I thought you'd been murdered."

"*I* thought I was about to be," Kate gasped from where she'd slumped back onto the carpet. "Why aren't you at school?"

"It's after four."

"It is?" Kate looked dazedly at the clock on the wall. "I must have fallen asleep."

"Drink."

"What?"

"Get this broken woman a drink," Liz pleaded.

"I'll get both of us one. That's a really rotten way to wake someone up, you know?" Kate groused, rising and going into the dining room. "You've got a voice like the five o'clock whistle at General Motors."

"My mother always said I should be an opera singer."

"Or a hog caller." Kate returned and thrust a gin and tonic into her friend's hand. "There. Revive yourself."

There was a companionable silence for a few minutes. Then Liz scowled. "I wish you wouldn't do that."

"Do what?"

"Sit there as if you were waiting for the wall to fall in on you."

"I think it is." Her eyes filled with tears suddenly. "Oh, Liz—I'm beginning to believe it *was* Richard, after all. How can I? I *must* believe in him, I *must* trust him."

"Why?" Liz wailed. "What *is* it with Richard Wayland that causes sane women to behave like idiots? In the old days it was the same—half the girls who worked for the 'cause' were there because of him. *And* didn't he know it?"

"Just because he never made a pass at you—"

"Ah, but he did," Liz said calmly. "He made a pass at me and every other female that crossed his path. It was an automatic reaction, like salivating when you see someone suck a lemon. And he's a lemon, all right."

"I . . . didn't know he made a pass at you. You never said."

Liz raised an eyebrow. "Don't tell me it still hurts?"

"No, of course not. I was just . . . startled."

"My God, you're all the same over there in that department—you, Dan Stark, Jane Coulter—you refuse to believe anyone you *like* can be bad."

"Jane called a little while ago to see if I'd heard from Richard." Kate stared at the floor. "She asked me to let her know the minute he got in touch." She looked up at her friend. "I think she *did* see him running away the other night, you know. I think Jody saw him too."

"So do the police."

"Do they?" Kate seemed almost too tired to be interested. "She didn't say so, but she more or less implied that if it *was* Richard who knocked her down running out of my office, he'd only just walked in and found us. *Afterward.* She said didn't that seem a good explanation."

"How about a good explanation for why he ran away instead of running for help?" Liz asked in a practical tone.

"Oh, God." Kate rubbed her temples. "My head keeps trying to divide into three parts, like Gaul." She sighed. "Look, I loved Richard once. And Jane has been grooming him to take her place when she retires. And Jody worships him. Is it so strange that we keep believing he's innocent?"

"Kate, the man is dangerous. Probably a killer. You always defended him when we were students, and you're doing the same now. It's a knee-jerk reaction. We're against him, so you're for him."

"I want to hear what *he* says."

"So do the police." Liz regarded her empty glass and got to her feet. "I've got a load of papers to read and correct, and a test to prepare. I cannot stay here and get drunk with you."

"I don't intend to get drunk."

Liz looked down at her. "You should. It might help."

Kate listened in misery to the sound of Liz's steps going down the back stairs. She went into the bathroom and got some aspirin for her headache, took one, choked on the second, and was still coughing when the phone rang.

Even before she answered it, she knew it was Richard.

IT HAD TURNED bitterly cold, and the slush-melt of the day had turned into crystalline menace on both sidewalks and roads. A scimitar wind slashed between the buildings from the river—pausing for a moment, turning, cutting, and turning again with a fresh edge. Kate pulled her old sheepskin coat more tightly around her and wished she'd put on an extra sweater to make up for the two missing toggles. Her boots caught on yet another frozen runnel that snaked across the elegant black-and-white patterns of the tesselated area in front of the Civic Center. It was the latest addition to the riverfront. The snow had been carefully swept from it, but the surface was glassy and treacherous. Ahead she could see the brightly lit glass cube of an equally new MacDonald's. Within it small figures moved, like marionettes. Which one was Richard? Was he in front of the counter? Or at one of the tables? It was crowded—where did all the people *come* from? It was after eleven, the plaza itself was empty, the streets deserted—and yet the glass cube was like one of those ant farms with a front you could look through to see all the activity within.

As she slithered closer, however, she saw that distance had conferred a false respectability on the customers. Some of those in the lines were well dressed, presumably inhabitants of the apartment towers all around, looking for refreshment to consume with the midnight movie. But the ragged men hunched over their cups of coffee were only there for the glare, the warmth, and the illusion of company.

All the lonely people.

A sudden gust of wind nearly spun her around, so she had a momentarily kaleidoscopic view of the plaza. Empty—save for a car decanting men on the far side. The black-and-white pavement made them seem like chess pieces on the far side of a gigantic board.

She staggered the last fifty feet, leaning into and supported by the wind, so that when it dropped, in the lee of MacDonald's, she literally fell through the door. The turncoat wind rushed in with her. A dropped napkin did a saraband beneath the stairway to the floor above, and two french fries missed by the cleaners skidded after it. The door swung shut, and the wind, frustrated, rattled it a few times, then went in search of new victims. It was a big city, after all.

Out of breath, Kate leaned against one of the stand-up counters and looked over the people in the lines. None of them was Richard. She stripped off her gloves, joined what looked like the shortest line, and when her turn came ordered coffee and a Big Mac. She carried them up the stairs and found a table near the window, so Richard could see her when he arrived. Her mouth was full and she was beginning to regret not taking off her coat when one of the hunched figures at a far-corner table lurched up, steadied itself, and started resolutely toward her.

It wasn't until he was nearly on top of her that she realized it was Richard Wayland. He walked past, going toward the men's room, and muttered out of the corner of his mouth. "Move to the back, in a corner."

He went on and the door to the toilets clunked shut behind him. She sat there for several seconds before remembering to finish chewing what was in her mouth. He's looked awful—as if he hadn't shaved, washed or eaten in days. She gathered up her things and moved to a table that was partially screened by a planter. She smelled him before she saw him return. Bitter waves of nervous sweat and whiskey enveloped her as he dropped onto the far end of the padded bench. "Did you bring the money?"

"I brought all I had in the house. Around ninety-three dollars. Sorry, ninety-one after I bought this."

He glanced at the Big Mac and his mouth tightened. "Never could resist them, could you?" His hand closed over the money she produced from her handbag and she saw his skin was grey with ingrained dirt. There was a scab on one knuckle that was beginning to fester. When she looked into his face, she saw more dirt, and more scratches down one cheek. She was so shocked by this evidence of violence and neglect that he had to repeat his question to her.

"What happened to *your* face?" he asked, his voice rough and blurred.

She reached up, and her fingers encountered the strip of adhesive on her cheekbone. "You don't know?"

"Should I?" He was putting the money she'd brought into a pocket, absorbed by the problem of jamming it in. It seemed to evade the opening, as if it didn't want to come with him, had better places to go.

"Richard—have you been drinking?"

He looked at her with empty eyes. "Yes, I have been drinking," he said very carefully. "And I intend to go *on* drinking until I am filled up. I will vomit, and then I will drink more. Do you have any goddamn objection to that?"

"Oh, Richard," she mourned. "Why?" And then she wished she could snatch the question back, because she realized he was going to answer it and she really didn't want to know. He was a stranger, someone who had been created anew in the years between what he had been and what he seemed to be now. A war baby, born in Nam; his secret time, the years he'd refused to talk about. He'd made a joke of it. Now she knew the laughter had been merely a bandage.

"*Why*? Because I'm a murderer, that's why. Everyone says so. Haven't you seen my face and name in all the papers? I always wanted to be famous, Kate. You remember how I always wanted to be famous, don't you? We used to talk about it." He was periously close to tears. "Wouldn't that make *you* take a drink?"

"But you've been missing since *Monday*."

"No, I haven't. I've been with me the whole time, knew right where I was every minute."

"Wednesday night? Where were you Wednesday night?"

He looked at her, tried hard to focus his eyes, his thoughts, his mind. "On Wednesday night I know right where I was on Wednesday night on Wednesday night I was...in...a *bar*." He grinned at her fatuously, triumphantly, a real thought pulled out of the hat at last.

Kate stared at him, aghast. Pictures came to her, superimposed on the bleary face across the table: Richard refusing drinks because he was "allergic" to alcohol, Richard going on week-end "fishing trips" when he'd always hated to fish, broken dates, grey-faced mornings he claimed to have been awake all night with "migraine."

Richard Wayland was an alcoholic.

Was that what had been wrong with him last Friday night? She'd left him scowling in the restaurant while she went to the ladies' room, came back to find him sitting near the bar, full of smiles. Had it started then? Because later anger had returned, abrupt, unreasonable, inexplicable. He'd said it was rage against Aiken's taunts. Had it really been thirst? Had he left her, slamming the door, on his way to Aiken—or the nearest bar?

"Richard—did you see Aiken on Friday night?"

"Sure. You did too." His eyes were sly. See? he seemed to be saying, you can't catch me out *that* easily.

"I mean after you left me."

"Yep. Laughed like hell when I saw him lying there like a dummy."

"You *did* go back to the university?" she whispered.

His eyes became furtive. "Did I?"

"Did you kill Aiken?" She had to ask him, she *had* to.

"I don't think so," he said solemnly. "I *tried* to kill him—got the idea from one of your books, you know, fiendishly clever, diabolical—but I don't think I did it. That is, I don't think *he* did it." For some reason this was funny. He began to shake with suppressed laughter. "Shhhhhh," he said, looking around. "Don't make a scene, Kate."

Kate drew back. Was this the truth, or just some fantasy he was acting out? If he'd been drunk since Monday, his brain must be hopelessly muddled. "What about Edward?"

"Edward?"

"Did you take him home on Monday?"

"Sure. Edward is a nice old guy, you know? He's got no legs, Kate. Poor old bastard, no legs at all. No legs to stand on." Again, the suppressed mirth. "I took him home. He didn't *mean* to kill Aiken, you know. But he was upset and wouldn't take his pills, so I put one in his coffee. He never knew."

"You put pills into his coffee?"

He drew himself up. "Only *one*. I'm not *stupid*, you know. I was a medical orderly in Viet Nam, I know about pills. Poor old bastard needed some sleep is all. I helped him sleep. I'm a good guy too, you know. Really. I'm a good guy."

"Richard—did you come to the university on Wednesday night and take Aiken's manuscript?"

"What manuscript?"

"I don't know much about it. Apparently Aiken had just finished a book about the Fourth Cavalry, whatever that is. The girl—"

"Fourth what?"

"I don't know, really, I only saw the title. Something like that. I was going to give it to Dan, only he got his ear cut off—"

"His ear?" He kept echoing her phrases like a parrot, staring at her. "Dan's ear?"

"Did you go down to the university, Richard?"

He nodded. "I had to stop him, Kate. I couldn't let him take it, you know."

"You mean the manuscript? You mean it was something he'd taken from *you*?" She stared at him as this new possibility presented itself. "You mean Aiken stole your work? About Whitman and the civil war? Is that what Edward was talking about?"

"Stolen work? Was that it?" Richard said suddenly, sounding absolutely sober. "He thanked me, don't you remember? He had the gall to thank me right there in the car—said it was because of me that he was going to be famous. It's my fault." He began to cry. "It's *all* my fault. I didn't know he'd take it, I never thought he'd take it."

"Take what?"

"Is *that* why you got hurt? Because you read it? and Dan? and Jane—poor Jane. All my fault. All *my* fault. You'll all hate me now, and I didn't mean it, I didn't mean to do it . . ."

She'd never know the truth until she sobered him up.

"Come on, love. Let's go home," she said, standing up. She took hold of his arm and found him surprisingly docile, rising lumpishly but obediently to stand beside her. He came along, the big smile still handsome in the filthy, unshaven face.

"You're not cross with me, Kate, are you?"

"No, Richard, I'm not angry at all. We'll go home and you can have a bath, and I'll make you some coffee . . ."

"Join me in a cup of coffee," he giggled. "Do you think there'll be room for both of us?" he laughed hugely, staggering down the stairs, and other customers turned, some smiling, some scowling. Kate had never steered a drunk before, and found it as difficult as trying to push a piece of string. She got him to the door and butted him through ahead of her. She felt a jolt through his body as the wind hit him. It had been waiting outside.

And not waiting alone.

"Okay, Kate—we'll take him now."

Men surrounded them in a darkness that was all the deeper after the glare they'd just left. One shape was big—Sergeant Toscarelli—she recognized his voice. Another was small, standing to one side with hands jammed in his pockets and legs braced against the wind.

Stryker.

"You must listen to him, he—" she began, but Richard turned on her, all his merriment gone in the instant.

"You bitch," he said.

And ran.

They hadn't expected it—he'd gone from sagging clown to wild man in an instant. The wind, perhaps recognizing a kindred spirit, joined in by throwing a truly magnificent gust at them, sleet-laden and fierce.

Seen from above it could have been comical, for the wind rose up so strongly that they literally had trouble making headway against it in the vast open expanse of the plaza. Yet, with only a moment's start, Wayland had a great advantage, for he ran ahead of the wind that howled after the scattering pack of baying police. Bucketing and backing, the wind was like a great and whimsical child pushing its dolls this way and that. The ice beneath their feet made them skaters and dancers and clowns. In a moment they were gone, with only occasional echoes of shouts and cries heard above the gleeful whistling of the wind as it rose up from the plaza to the top of the nearest building and began to dismantle a television antenna.

"You followed me," Kate said in a flat, half-swallowed voice. "You watched me and followed me."

"We thought he might come to you," Stryker said, his voice equally remote, his figure still in the shadows.

"Of course." She gave a big, blank smile. "Who else could he *trust*?"

The wind had momentarily tired of its games. In the empty plaza there was the kind of stillness that follows an explosion. Empty and waiting. She could hear, in the distance, a car horn, shouting, a freighter on the river muttering its heavy way toward the lake. The coldness seemed even more bitter in this sudden stillness, and she felt as if everything, everything, was turning to ice.

Including herself.

TWENTY-SIX

THEY HADN'T STOPPED her leaving the plaza. Having served them as bait, they needed her no more. She was as free as she'd ever be, remembering the look of panic and betrayal in Richard's eyes. She knew she'd driven home, because here she was. She had thought she was exhausted—and yet, she was still wide awake, long after midnight. The wind had matured into a steady roaring presence, clacking the branches of the naked trees that lined the street. The car radio had warned of a blizzard coming from the north. As yet there was no sign of new snow. Just the invisible wind, shaking the house.

When her doorbell rang, Kate's heart jerked like a fish on the line. She went to the window and looked out, rubbing the glass free of her own brandied breath. Below, foreshortened and stomping his feet, was a familiar figure with a tweed cap pulled down to his nose.

"Go to hell," she shouted, loud enough to be heard through the window. He turned and looked up to see her misty figure behind the glass.

"Let me in. I have to talk to you."

"No," she said, and pressed the buzzer that released the door downstairs. She ran back to the sitting room and knelt on a cushion facing the wall, wiping her face on the sleeve of her ratty old robe. She heard him come slowly and wearily up the stairs. He came a couple of steps into the room and stopped.

"What happened to your furniture?"

"I haven't got any furniture, and take your shoes off before you walk on my six-thousand-dollar, handmade carpet."

Stryker stepped back into the hall, kicked off his wet shoes, and then padded in to look at her sitting there. He was reminded of Alice's caterpillar on the mushroom. He wished he knew which side would make him bigger. He certainly couldn't feel much smaller. The room was large and empty save for the cushions and a stereo unit. The Carpet, lush and rippling, like a sunburned field of wheat. "This is a nice carpet," he said carefully. "Keeps the ankles warm."

"Did you catch him?"

"No, he got away."

"So you've come here to wait for him."

"No—he won't come here, whatever he does."

"Thanks for that."

"Kate, I'm sorry. I had you watched, but it was the only way. Surely you can see that? Won't you look at me?"

"There's nothing about you I want to see."

"How much money did you give him?"

"About ninety dollars."

"*That* ought to keep him drunk for a while."

He was silent for so long that she finally turned to look at him. He'd sat down, cross-legged, in the middle of the carpet. His collar was half in half out of his pullover, his scarf was trailing down into his lap, and he had an elbow on each knee, resting his chin in his steepled hands. His eyes were closed. He could have been meditating. She didn't think he was. "If you didn't think Richard would come here, why have *you* come here?" she demanded in a quavery voice.

"I came here to talk about Richard Wayland, obviously. When did Adamson seduce him?"

Kate felt exhausted and unable to defend herself or Richard any more. She knew, suddenly, that Stryker was there to stay until he got what he wanted. If she'd had any energy at all she would have attacked him. As it was, she simply sank back down onto her nest of cushions and wept. He was too much for her.

Stryker, feeling as rotten as he'd ever felt in his life, sat very still and waited for her to finish. Her curly head was bent, exposing the nape of her neck, and her small, bare feet were tucked beside her. She looked about nine years old. When she'd reached the hiccuping stage, he went into the kitchen. He brought back a handful of paper towels, just as she was running out of dry sleeve.

"Just tell me," he said quietly. "Or listen, and let me tell you. I think I've guessed most of it. With a triangle the story is usually the same."

"Only the sexes are changed, to destroy the innocent?" she choked.

"Isn't that a little melodramatic?"

"It *was* melodramatic, that's the whole point. It was *awful*. I was seventeen. Richard was nineteen, we didn't know a damn thing about sexual aberrations and our sense of perspective was non-existent.''

"I thought Adamson kept his hands off his students."

"He did. But I guess with Richard he couldn't stop himself. Richard was his student assistant that year, because Aiken was indexing his big mythology collection. One night they worked late, Aiken took Richard out to dinner and then back to his place. He got Richard drunk and . . . bingo. Old story, right?" She looked away toward the window, where the wind was prying at the catch. "Do you remember how naïve we were then? Out here in the great American heartland, where gay still meant light-hearted, where—" Her voice broke. "I didn't know what to do. I didn't know how to help him. I didn't know *anything*. When he told me, I threw up. Can you imagine how that made him *feel*?" Her voice slid out of control.

"Take it easy," Stryker murmured.

She took a deep breath. "Richard didn't know what to do either. He quit as Aiken's assistant, of course, and Aiken didn't say anything."

"Richard could have had him fired."

"He didn't realize that. Remember, Aiken was *faculty* and we were only kids. All Richard knew was that he'd *let* it happen, that he hadn't tried to stop it. That he'd even . . . enjoyed it. So he decided there and then that he was a homosexual."

"A little drastic."

She looked up at him then, almost in supplication. "I could hardly bear to have him touch me after he told me, but we tried to make love, and . . . he couldn't. He was impotent. So he said that proved it."

"Crap."

"Oh, sure—I know that *now*. I was seventeen and I'd never gone with anyone before Richard. I didn't know what to do to make him feel like a man again . . . I didn't *know* all the tricks to make him want me. I felt ugly and stupid and made of cardboard."

"So that's why he left Richard fifty thousand and you ten. He'd hurt you both. I thought it might be that."

"He left us *money*?" She was astounded.

"Yes, I didn't know if it was guilt past or guilt present, though. Past? They weren't . . ."

"Oh, *no*. It was only that once. I was always amazed that Richard came back here knowing he'd meet Aiken again. He *hated* him."

"Wayland came back here because Stark was the only man who'd hire him with 'alcoholic' on his army records. He was given a psychiatric discharge because he persistently got drunk and started fights in the 'gay' bars in Saigon. The army shrinks said he was avenging some early incident. When I read that, the rest seemed obvious. What I can't figure is what happened Friday night to bring things to a head."

"Nothing came to a head, Friday night or any other night," Kate said firmly.

Stryker gave her a pitying look. "He admitted going back down there, he admitted seeing him lying there and laughing over him," he said.

Her eyes widened. "How did you know that?"

"That couple in the next booth were Officers Casey and Grabowski. They hate each other, so it wasn't much of an effort for them to listen to your conversation."

"They were there to *spy* on us?"

Stryker sighed heavily. "Kate, you must trust Richard Wayland to the moon and back, but I'm a cop. I don't trust anyone—especially not a drunk who might have attacked you before. They were there to protect you, in case anything happened. Like Wayland trying for your *other* eye."

It was no satisfaction to him to see her go pale. Obviously that possibility had never really occurred to her. It did now. "I...see." Her fingers touched the cut on her cheekbone. "But he asked me about this. He asked me what happened to me. He didn't *know*."

"Uh-huh. What did he go back down to the department for on Friday—this mysterious manuscript?"

"It wasn't there on Friday."

He was momentarily taken aback. "Right on; so it wasn't. Then...oh, hell. Of course. The insulin. *That* was it. But if he had a few drinks on the way, and then found him lying there..."

"Oh, no..." Kate whimpered.

"Kate—when he got drunk in Nan he beat up homosexuals. If he was drunk last Friday night and came across the homosexual he most hated lying helpless at his feet..." He stopped. "He could plead temporary insanity, I suppose, with a good shrink and a good lawyer. It could have happened just that way, Kate. Pinchman *saw* a shape, *heard* the laugh..."

She made a choking noise, held up her hand in defence.

"You're not sure any more, are you?" Stryker asked. She shook her head and wouldn't meet his eyes. A tear fell onto her knee and she hit it with a fist, again and again.

He reached into his pocket and pulled out the cigar case. "Mind if I smoke?"

"I thought you weren't supposed to smoke?"

He looked disgusted. "Now, don't *you* start." He lit the cigar, made a face, got up and went in search of the kitchen and the garbage pail. While he was out there, Kate heard him swear.

"What's wrong?" she called.

"There's a cat in your china cupboard. I thought he was china until he meowed. Scared the hell out of me."

"That's just Hodge. He won't hurt you."

Stryker came back. "Hodge was Samuel Johnson's cat."

"So he tells me."

"That's the biggest goddamned cat I ever saw. What does he weigh?"

"Twenty-one pounds. Without his shoes."

"*Hell* of a cat." He sat down again. "That why you can't afford any furniture?"

"You're sitting on why I can't afford any furniture." Kate tried to focus on being helpful. She hesitated, then spoke slowly. "Your spies . . . did they tell you that I asked Richard about the manuscript?"

"Yeah, they told me."

"And what he said? That it was his fault? I don't think he meant exactly that, you know. I think—"

"Kate . . . stop it. Stop trying so hard to make sense of what a drunk says. All through this I've had things said that don't hang together—for a department of English you sure are a lousy bunch at communicating."

"But haven't you read the manuscript?" Kate asked.

"The manuscript was taken when you and Stark were attacked. Didn't you know that?"

"No. Is that what . . ." She paused. "Is that what the killer was looking for when he ransacked Aiken's office? I thought you said that was a fake, all that pretence at robbery?"

"I'm beginning to think I was wrong." He grinned at her. "I hope you took note of that—not many people have heard me say such a thing, you know."

"If you want to know what was in the manuscript, why don't you ask the typist?" Kate demanded.

"Because I can't find her. The neighbours say she's gone to stay with her parents while her husband's in the hospital, but they don't know the parents' name. Pinsky's touring the hospitals looking for the husband." He stood up. "You're sure it was Cavalry, not Calvary?"

"Calvary?"

"Stark said, 'Calvary'—I'm sure he did."

"A lot of people mix the two up without thinking."

"The chairman of an English department?"

"Sure. It's not mental, it's physical. Calvary's easier to say, the mouth goes to it first."

"But doesn't Wayland teach something to do with the Bible?"

"Yes. But we all, from time to time. I mean, nobody's really *proven* that Cain slew Abel, you know. Or that—"

"Stop that."

"Stop what?"

"Going off in another direction. You all do that, it's one of the things that drives me crazy about this damned case." He stopped pacing and looked at her. "*One* of the things."

"What about the lilacs?"

"That's *another* thing," he agreed, still looking at her. "I think you should go to bed. You look terrible."

"Is that a proposition?"

"No. If it was, I would have said *we* should go to bed because you look *wonderful*. Get the difference?" His eyes were on her, but not seeing her. "Did he have an agent?"

"Who?"

"Adamson, Adamson. Did he have an agent?"

"Probably. Dan would know."

"Gee, thanks."

"Or his lawyer might know. Or his publisher."

He nodded. "Right. I'll check. Go to bed."

"As soon as you've gone."

"What's the matter? Afraid I'm going to steal the silver?"

She looked at him, puzzled. "Why *are* you here?"

"It's cold out."

"You're not leaving, are you?"

"Nope. This carpet will do me."

"But *why*?"

"I want to discuss Johnson with your cat." He was collecting cushions into a heap. "GO TO BED."

She got up and started out, then turned back. "*Is* it because you think Richard might come back?"

"Not exactly. It's because I don't know *what* he'll do. Any more than I know what *you'll* do next. Besides, by the time I drive across town to my place it will be time to get up again. Have you no heart, woman? No soul, no finer—"

"Good night," she said and went down the hall. She was too tired to argue with a madman.

TWENTY-SEVEN

THE BOOK was empty.

He'd put off looking, savouring the moment, for nothing. The security guard cursed and returned it to its place on the shelf among the others. Two days now, and no second payment. He'd give it another day, but if the money wasn't there by tomorrow night, he'd put the screws on.

He grinned.

Maybe his victim had sat here, today or yesterday, watching that book, watching to see who came, who took it down. Nobody ever touched that row in the normal way—it was dusty as hell.

Pretty boring subject, he guessed.

But ideal for his purposes.

The first payment had gone like a dream. The mark had put the money in during the day, and he'd picked it up during the night. No contact—no danger. But the first payment had been peanuts—just a test run. What he was waiting for now was the big one.

His grin turned to a scowl.

All right, he thought.

I'll wait.

But I won't wait forever.

TWENTY-EIGHT

TWO THOUSAND MILES to the north, above the flat sweep of Canada's arctic plain, a broad cold front was moving steadily southwards. Marching behind it in the darkness, high and wide, were the huge anvil heads of cumulonimbus clouds pregnant with ice particles. As the front moved away from the bleak tundra and into the marginally warmer forested regions of Manitoba and northern Ontario, the ice particles within the clouds began to gather themselves, merging and combining into intricate hexagonal crystals, infinitely variable, delicate, lighter than air.

As the cold front crossed the Great Lakes, even the manic energy of the high-atmosphere winds could no longer support the snowflakes which the ice crystals had become. The storm began to drop its burden.

At just after seven o'clock on Saturday morning, the first few outrider flakes began to touch down on the suburban lawns of Grantham, already coated with old snow. The darkness of the night merged imperceptibly into the darkness of a dawn that never really broke, for the clouds blotted it from the sky. The temperature dropped from just above freezing to just above zero against it. Birds disappeared under eaves, dogs and cats fled homeward or huddled where they could. The wind screamed in triumph—at last it was master of this place.

Stryker woke up on the golden carpet knowing who had killed Aiken Adamson.

THE STORM WARNINGS had gone out on radio and television, but there was plenty of traffic on the streets, particularly in the vicinity of neighbourhood supermarkets. Stryker grimaced as he drove by the one nearest Kate's place. "Let's hurry down and stock up before the hoarders get there," he said, quoting one of his father's favourite sayings.

He swerved suddenly to avoid a woman who stepped blindly off the curb, her vision obscured by the huge brown paper bags she was carrying. She never missed a step, but he nearly winged a bakery truck that had been spinning its wheels and suddenly leapt free of the slush into his path.

Other warnings had gone out too.

He'd spoken in a whisper into Kate's telephone, not wanting to wake her, not wanting to have to explain. Not yet. First, the station.

THE HOSPITAL also seemed to be stocking up and battening down. There were more nurses around, and more of the blue-coated maintenance staff than were normally evident on a Saturday morning. Already, men in white slickers were clearing areas of snow in front of the ambulance bays and putting down a thick layer of salt. Sawhorses lined the driveway, preventing stray cars finding their way into the emergency approach. Later on, victims of the storm would start to come in: the broken legs, the heart attacks, the old people suffering from hypothermia, the bruises and worse from fights and arguments that the isolation of the storm would bring out.

Stryker found Tos outside Stark's room. "Have you got the men placed?"

"Two on this floor and two on Pinchman's, in maintenance uniforms; four roving in intern whites, and four women officers nursing. Still snowing?"

"Still snowing. Worse yet to come."

"Listen—what about Neilson and Pinsky. Where the hell are they?"

"I sent Pinsky home. One of his kids is sick."

"Did he find the typist?"

"He found her, sitting by her husband's bedside at the St. Mary Ignatius Hospice. They've just found out he has terminal cancer with maybe a couple of weeks to live. She's in a pretty bad way too."

"Oh, hell. That's terrible."

Stryker nodded. He'd spent a frantic hour at the station putting it all together. "Pinsky says she didn't make much sense, but she was pretty clear about one thing. Her husband's illness is a 'judgement' on her for typing Adamson's manuscript. She told Pinsky it brought the devil into the house. She intends to become a nun after her husband dies, to atone for her 'sin.'"

"My God, what was in this damned manuscript, anyway?"

"So-called 'proof' that Christ didn't die on the cross after all but ran off with Mary Magdalen and set up housekeeping somewhere in France. There's some kind of sect based there who claim direct descent."

"That's crazy," Tos said, shocked to his Catholic core.

"Maybe. I don't know. But Adamson's agent said he'd done a real 'hot job' on it. She said it would be bigger than the 'Bermuda Triangle,' and where the hell was it? All she had was an outline and the first two chapters, which he'd sent her months ago, and the publisher was screaming for the rest. After reading Adamson's diary, I can imagine what kind of 'hot job' he did. Can't you?"

"And this is why he was bumped off?"

"I think so. But I haven't any proof yet."

"Where's Neilson?"

"Running an errand for me." He glanced at the door. "How's Stark this morning?"

"A lot better. You want to talk to him?"

"I certainly do. And then Pinchman."

THE SNOW had ceased to be intermittent and had begun to fall steadily and thickly. Driven by the wind, it stuck to walls and trees as well as the ground, moving like a river through the streets, where it frothed around the corners, met itself, and spun upward into whirlpools.

All the hospital lights were on, and across the courtyard Stryker could see a nurse and an intern in one of the linen rooms, talking earnestly. He turned back to Pinchman.

"I hope I'm not tiring you, sir."

"Oh, no. Please. Stay as long as you like. I don't suppose I'll be having many visitors once they find out who I really am," Pinchman said sadly.

"I don't think they'll mind your being Jake Laredo, you know," Stryker smiled. "According to Kate, writing Westerns and detective novels is becoming almost respectable."

"I didn't mean that. I meant taking my brother's place. I'm not academically qualified. Dan will have to—"

"Dan Stark has known about your deception for some time," Stryker told the old man. "He tells me he had great admiration for your brother as an academic—but as a teacher he left much to be desired. You, on the other hand, he considers to be a born teacher. And that, he says, is what a university is for."

"Did Aiken tell him?"

"No." He returned to his vigil at the window. The nurse and the intern had given up counting sheets or whatever they had been doing, and were locked in an embrace. He watched them idly for a moment, then turned back to Pinchman. "Stark had played handball with your brother as an undergraduate. Edward had a birthmark on one arm—you didn't. He put the rest together—he was an intelligence officer during the War. He knew a lot of things about the people he hired—in many cases, far more than Adamson knew. The difference between them was that Stark used his knowledge for good, to build up people instead of tear them down. To help them overcome their weaknesses by trusting them and encouraging them. He's a remarkable man in many ways—but he took risks. Terrible risks. I think he realizes that now."

"You mean . . . Richard?" Pinchman's voice was sad. He still found it difficult to believe that Wayland, who had always been kindness itself, would have actually tried to kill him. He started to say as much, but he noticed Stryker was not just looking out of the window now, but staring with his full attention, every line of his body taut. "Who is it?" the old man asked, leaning forward a little in the bed to see.

Across the courtyard, within the frame of a lighted window that shone out in the murky shadow of the storm, two people were embracing intimately. He was a little surprised that Stryker would have a streak of voyeurism in him, but . . . Stryker whirled around, startling him.

"You said you got a blackmail note."

"Yes. On Monday morning. It was in my pigeonhole."

"What did it say?"

"That the writer knew I'd killed Aiken—which I hadn't—and that—"

"No—what did it say *exactly*?"

Pinchman thought back. "Something like 'I saw what you—' "

"Yes, yes," Stryker crowed, glancing at the window and gesturing. "At first I thought it was Wayland's way of keeping you quiet about anything you'd seen or heard, but now . . . look."

"At what?"

"Them. Across from us. If you were down on the ground, you couldn't see them. If you were in the hall outside the door over there you couldn't see them. *But*, over here, we can see them as clearly as if they were on a stage. What's directly across from Adamson's office on the fourth floor of Grantham Hall?"

Pinchman stared at him. "The fourth floor of the library."

"Right. And if a man can send one blackmail note, he can send two," Stryker said, heading for the door. "Maybe you weren't the only one who had a little message waiting on Monday morning."

"WE MAY HAVE an eyewitness to the whole thing," Stryker said, putting down the phone of the reception desk. "According to Campus Security, his name is Sam Klusky, he's sharp but not too bright, and always short of money before payday. Come on—I've got his address right here." He started for the lifts.

"I thought we were waiting for the killer to come after Stark," Tos objected.

"McGee can handle it. Come on."

"Lieutenant Stryker?" It was a nurse at the desk, holding out the telephone. "For you *again*. This phone is not really for—"

Stryker crossed and took it. "Thanks. Yes?" It was Neilson. "Did you ask her? Did she tell you—"

"I never had the chance. When I got there she was gone."

Stryker felt something seize his throat. "Gone?" he managed to say.

"Yeah. Seems she got another call from Wayland. She went out right after that."

TWENTY-NINE

KATE DIDN'T CARE if it was a no-parking zone or not. She didn't think any meter maids would be out in this storm at this hour, and she was damned if she was going to walk any further than she had to in this snow.

Anyway, she wouldn't be long.

She had woken up expecting to find Stryker stretched out on the sitting-room carpet, but when she had padded out she found he'd gone, and left no sign. It was as if he'd never been there at all.

She'd had some breakfast and heard the storm warnings on the radio. By lunchtime the truth of the situation began to be quite clear—if the blizzard continued to build up, they'd be trapped by the snow for some time, even in the city. But, if she moved now, she could get down to the department, gather up what she needed, and be back before it got really bad. And she could pick up some groceries, too.

It took her a while to dress, and she had been halfway down the back stairs when she'd heard the phone ring. Fortunately she'd managed to get back in time.

She struggled out of the car and turned her face away from the stinging snow. Staggering a little, she went across the pavement to the doors of Grantham Hall. After the howl of the storm outside, the empty halls stretching away on either side were gloomy and a little spooky. She was alone here, among the empty classrooms and the closed racks of lockers. Behind her the wind screeched suddenly through the crack between the doors, and Kate jumped.

"Come on, get moving, don't be stupid, it's still daylight," she told herself sternly.

She leaned against the wall of the lift as it grumbled its way upward (it had sounded like a crabby old man from the day it had been installed). Where was Richard in this storm? In a nice warm bar somewhere? She hoped so, for his sake.

When she emerged from the lift, it was into a curiously silent and mantled world. All the windows of the foyer were curtained with snow, which had begun to gather in folds at the bottom of each expanse of glass. Successive accumulations had slid down the warm surface and looked like velvet curtains hung upside down.

Through the glistening web of moving snow she could see the dark bulk of the library, closed now. The snow curtains were between, shutting her in and the wind out. The sensation was claustrophobic, and she felt very alone.

Maybe this hadn't been such a good idea after all.

As she hesitated by the lifts, Kate heard a soft noise. The sound of a stack of papers slithering to the floor, followed by a rat-like rustling. She took a step backward, kicked the aluminum waste bin with the heel of her boot, and nearly sent it over.

The scrabbling stopped abruptly. Kate stood there, listening to someone who was listening to her. Something cold crawled up within her, stealthily touching her arms, legs, spine. She took another step backward, toward the lift, and then another, with legs that were suddenly stiff and uncooperative. She pushed the button and the doors opened—oh, blessed doors.

She got in and pushed the button for down, pushed all the buttons, desperately, willing the door to close. But it was so slow. So terribly slow.

And someone was coming.

The doors were moving now, arthritically slow, closing at last. Now there was only a crack remaining as the footsteps came closer and closer. She heard the button outside being pushed, again and again. She pushed the buttons inside, again and again. Confused by conflicting instructions the door hesitated, closed, and then began to open again. Kate stared at the slowly widening gap.

Oh, traitorous doors!

TOSCARELLI REPLACED the receiver of the radio set and grabbed for the dashboard just in time to brace himself for another bone-jolting impact. "Jesus!" he yelled. "If you're going to play three-cushion shots with this car, maybe you'd better let *me* drive. At least I always remember to hit cheap stuff."

"The curb is cheap," Stryker said, accelerating slowly but insistently into the next swerve and narrowly missing the back end of a bus that suddenly began to glide toward them like the *QEII*, wheels spinning. The windscreen wipers groaned under each successive load of snow as they swept laboriously across the glass, dumping their icy load and further impacting the mass that had gone before. Their sweep was getting shorter and shorter, and the gap where momentarily clear vision was possible was narrowing fast. Stryker, his glasses sliding down his nose, leaned forward and clutched the wheel with both hands, concentrating.

"Did you hear what Neilson said?" Tos asked.

"I heard."

"You think it means anything?"

"I don't know. I hope not." He cursed under his breath, turned into yet another skid, and grazed the bumper of a car coming the other way. They both blew their horns, waved their arms, but kept on driving. It wasn't the first dent, it wouldn't be the last, and the traffic was too jammed up to pull over and exchange insults, anyway. In fact, the traffic was bumper to bumper and slowing down every minute.

"Where the hell are they all *going*?" Tos muttered.

"They're coming back—look at all the grocery bags in the back of most of them," Stryker said. "It's not that there are so many—it's just that the goddamn road is down to two ruts each way."

The radio signalled again. The voice told them in laconic tones that the security guard's phone didn't answer. They'd been ringing repeatedly. He should have been there. But he wasn't taking calls.

"Maybe he's in the john," Tos said, putting back the receiver.

Stryker's hands tightened on the wheel. "Maybe."

Suddenly the traffic came to a full stop, pinning them firmly between an oil truck and a delivery van. "Oh, God! *Now* what?" he screamed, pounding on the steering wheel.

KATE STOOD in the doorway of the office, staring at the maelstrom of papers scattered from open drawers and file folders and torn notebooks. They made a treacherous carpet underfoot, slipping over the polished tiles, drifting and skittering in the wisps of wind that leaked through the badly fitted windows.

"Did you ever *see* such a mess?" tsk-tsked Arthur Fowler, beside her. "Is nothing sacred? Are we to be subjected to constant harassment and vandalism until this department is totally destroyed? Can the police do nothing? Can they do *anything*? I'm beginning to wonder."

"They're doing their best," Kate murmured, crossing the office to look out of the windows at the storm. She pulled the window a little more tightly shut, cutting off the draft. "When did you discover this?"

"Just a few minutes ago. I came to get some work to do over the weekend. We may be closed down because of the storm and some things *must* be dealt with before Dan comes back. When I got out of the elevator, I thought I heard someone running down the hall toward the fire door, but when I got to the corner, there was no one there. I saw the door of this office open, walked down and found this." He looked a little pale, and swallowed. "Thank God, it was *only* this. My God, I might have been killed myself!"

The realization came suddenly, and he looked as if he were going to faint. "Here, you'd better sit down," Kate said, putting out the desk chair quickly. Fowler flopped into it, his face shiny with the cold sweat of fear. He began to shiver. "Do you suppose it was . . . the Monkey Killer?"

Kate stared at him. "The what?"

"Haven't you been reading the papers? They're all full of it. Speak no evil, hear no evil, see no evil. Aiken's tongue, Dan's ear . . ."

And my eyes, nearly, Kate thought. "I think Lieutenant Stryker said something about that," she said. "Jane's theory, wasn't it?"

"*I* don't know." Fowler said fretfully. "Are you certain that window is closed? I'm freezing." He wrapped his arms around himself. "I think we should call that Lieutenant Stryker and tell him about this," he said, nodding at the ransacked office.

"I expect you're right," Kate agreed. The phone was on the end of the desk. She picked it up gingerly, and as she did so, glanced out of the window. A figure she recognized was going across the Mall, bent against the wind, head down in the snow. But the library was closed, no one could get in. What was the point of . . .

Then she saw another figure. One she also knew. And it was following the first, which had by now reached the library itself and was tugging at the doors.

Which opened.

And closed behind it.

A moment later, the next figure did the same.

Two people had just gone into a locked, closed library.

She picked up the whole phone and took it to the end of the desk nearest Fowler. "You call him," she said, scribbling the number she had memorised on a scrap of paper. "I've just seen something very odd in the library, and you'd better tell him *that*, too. All right?"

"You're going to just *leave* me here?" Fowler asked, annoyed.

"I'll be right back. You just call Stryker, Arthur, and everything will be all right." Kate nodded encouragingly and went out. Fowler listened to her footsteps going down the hall, heard the doors of the lift open and close, heard the whine of the motor as it began its grudging descent.

"Well *really*," he huffed, glaring at the phone. "You'd think I was a common *secretary* or something."

STRYKER BANGED out a frustrated rhythm on the steering wheel. The snow was hissing around them, but the only motion the car made was a slight rocking in the wind, for the traffic hadn't moved forward in the last six minutes. "The hell with this," he burst out, reaching down for his gloves and starting to pull them on. "The hell *with* it. You stick with the car, call us some help, break out of this as soon as you can. It isn't far now." He opened the door and it slammed shut again almost immediately, driven back by the wind. It nearly took his foot off. "Jesus." He put his weight behind the door and forced it open again, nearly losing a hand this time as he got out into the wind and the door snapped its jaws shut once more. He gesticulated to Tos, who was yelling at him through the closed window. The wind was so strong he couldn't hear a word, but he figured he knew the gist of it. He should button up his overcoat, or something. The snow was stinging on his face, and his glasses had coated over. He took them off, jammed them into his pocket, and started toward the curb, gingerly stepping over the icy ruts. He grabbed hold of a parked car and edged between it and the next to gain the pavement beyond. He looked back and saw Tos's shadowy shape edging into the driver's seat of the sedan, while talking into the radio receiver. The engines of the jammed and stationary cars sent out plumes of exhaust that rose behind them until they reached roof level, then the wind snatched at them and tore them apart.

He started to move along the pavement, head down, hands half outstretched to warn him of obstacles. The snow was already caking his eyelashes. He'd turn into a side street as soon as he could and maybe make better progress tacking diagonally, rather than trying to follow the main streets. For the moment, he had to lurch like some half-blind crab, painfully encountering every streetlamp and telephone pole ever put up. His ears and nose began to ache, and he wondered what the weather was like in Miami right then. His chest was aching too, the wind going down into the Brussels lace he'd once used for breathing. He tried to move more quickly, but he lost traction and slipped. He wanted to run, but all he could do was slide. He wasn't moving much faster than the car had been, when it had moved at all, and there were still so many blocks to go.

ARTHUR FOWLER shook his head at the telephone. "I want to talk to someone who is working on the university murder case, not someone in traffic control. Are they *all* out?" He listened to the harassed voice on the other end of the line. "I appreciate that there's a storm on, young man, and that everything is all 'balled up' as you insist on telling me, but we have snowstorms every year. Surely this hasn't come as a complete surprise to—"

The other voice interrupted yet again. Fowler's face was getting red. "Well, then, if not Lieutenant Stryker, then Sergeant Toscarennie or whatever his name is. Toscarelli, thank you. No? There were two more, then. Good lord, doesn't anyone write these things *down* in your department? Ah, I thought as . . . yes, I'll wait." He sat gazing out at the swirling snow, tapping his fingers and humming a small, angry tune. "Yes, hello? Neilson, yes and—Pinsky. That's it. Fine. Either one will . . ." his voice trailed off, disbelievingly. "Out and off-duty? Young man, is there *anyone* there? Well, obviously, you're there, I know . . ." Another interruption. "No, I don't think I will leave a message, thank you. I'm certain it will take you too long to get enough alphabet blocks together to handle it. Good day."

Fowler slammed the phone down and glared at it. Now he'd have to go all the way down to the main office to find the phone books. Pinsky? Pinskie? Pinski? Pensky?

Honestly, it was too much, he should *never* have come in.

STRYKER STOOD in the vestibule pushing the button marked Klusky, and getting no joy. The snow caking his clothes was beginning to fall off in clumps onto the worn linoleum, and a puddle was forming around his feet. Another was forming inside his shoes.

The inner door flew open and a short fat woman wearing three cardigans glared up at him, the curlers on her head practically standing on end in indignation. "Whatsa matter, you don't take no for an answer? Knock it off with the bell, first the phone now the bell, my Chester's asleep in there and it comes through the ceiling like a fire alarm, Klusky ain't in, he went out an hour ago, because the storm was getting worse, and he said if he didn't go then he'd never make it, they counted on him, I'll bet they do, *hah*, who counts on him counts on their fingers and *toes*, don't ring that bell no more or my Chester comes out here with a poker, biff, on your head, buddy."

The door slammed and Stryker was once again alone in the tiny vestibule. He felt as if a very strong wind had just blown around him and he almost touched his head to see if his hat was still there.

It was. Klusky obviously wasn't.

Once more into the snow, dear friends.

And the university was at least fifteen blocks away.

EDWARD PINCHMAN lay against his pillows, trying to ignore the pain. He was accustomed to ignoring pain, but from the opposite direction. His head was throbbing, but he hated to call a nurse for such a small thing. They were so very busy with everyone else. Why, somebody could be dying in another room! Or having a baby or a haemorrhage! What was a little headache, compared to that?

Since Stryker had left, borne on the wings of sudden insight, he'd been left totally alone. Not even the young policeman who used to sit by his bed was there now.

Would Dan really overlook his deception? He found it hard to believe, and yet Stryker had been very unequivocal. Of course, if it got out, he'd have to leave, but if Dan and the police kept quiet... He sighed. It always depended on other people.

If he'd behaved as he should after striking Aiken, if he'd even opened his own office door a crack when he realized the other person had come in, the attacks on Dan and Jane and sweet Kate could have been avoided. On himself, too, for that matter. But he'd been a coward, he'd have to face that. An absolute, snivelling coward, always looking out for Number One.

He hadn't changed. He wasn't Edward, no matter how hard he'd tried, all these years. If he could have given Stryker even one tiny thing to go on, but no, not a clue, not a sight nor smell nor taste nor sound had he remembered that—Suddenly he sat up away from the pillows, staring out at the empty room.

"Good God," he said.

PINSKY OPENED the door to admit the snow-caked figure that half fell into Grantham Hall and led him to a bench in the study area.

Stryker peeled the snow from his face and hair in a thick layer that held together like a frozen bandage, only breaking at the last moment into lumps that showered down around his numb feet. Beneath the snow, his skin was white, and his eyes red-rimmed and watering. He kicked his heels one by one against the bench supports to dislodge the clumps of snow that had built up on his shoes.

"What are *you* doing here?" Stryker managed to croak at last. "Has something else happened while I was giving my first and last performance of Nanook of the North?"

"Well, yeah, it has," Pinsky said. "Sort of."

"Tell me."

"Well, Fowler called me at home and I don't live so far away as all that so I skied over here—"

"You what?" Stryker suddenly became aware of Pinsky's knitted bobble hat.

"Skied over here. Like cross-country? Anyway, I made good time because they've just been waxed, and there's a hell of a mess upstairs..."

There was a fresh blast of wind from the doors and Tos came in, his black overcoat piebald where the snow clung. He took off his hat, banged it against his side, then spotted Stryker and Pinsky. "I put on the light and the siren and drove on the pavement until I hit a mailbox. It just came through on the radio. Is she here?"

"I've just been telling him," Pinsky said patiently. "There's a hell of a mess upstairs, and Mr. Fowler is getting pretty upset. He thinks something might have happened to her, because..."

"To who? Whom?" amended Stryker, remembering where he was.

"...she's gone in and she hasn't come out," Pinsky finished.

"Who?" Stryker demanded, torn between trying to catch his breath and wasting what little he'd managed to get back on a scream.

Neilson came in, bringing more snow.

"Is she here?" he asked.

THIRTY

THE SECURITY GUARD sat facing the windows.

The snow, whirling beyond the glass was like one of the crystal balls that children have, which they shake and shake again, watching the snow dance wildly.

But he wasn't watching the snow.

Occasionally the Mall cleared for a moment, and Grantham Hall would be visible, its windows blank, no lights on.

But he wasn't watching Grantham Hall.

The light from outside was growing fainter and fainter as the blizzard clamped down. The light gleamed with a pearly sheen on his face. On his mouth. On his nose.

And on the two bloody sockets where his eyes had been.

THIRTY-ONE

AFTER THE HOWL and hiss of the blizzard outside, the darkness and silence of the library seemed absolute. Kate, panting after her struggle with the storm in crossing the Mall, stood still in the gloom and tried to regain her senses. The drip of the melting snow hitting the floor around her seemed unnaturally loud. She could hear her own breathing, the rustle of her clothing, and the small struggles of the wind at the door behind her. Her face felt raw where the wind had scoured it. Having made the dash from Grantham Hall full of concern and zeal, she now felt hot and shaky inside her bulky coat. It was very warm in the library.

Her eyes slowly adjusted to the faint suffusion of light coming from behind her through the doors, and from the clerestory windows, set high on the walls. The area here at the entrance was all right.

It was that big blackness ahead that worried her.

The library was large; four stories of shelves ranked the width of the building like an army carrying knowledge in close formation.

They were in here somewhere—but where?

And why?

She took off her coat, for it was stifling her. They must keep the heating on all weekend in here, she thought, for the sake of the books. And the snow was insulating the building as it had Grantham Hall, so that everything within was very quiet. Very quiet.

She heard a laugh.

A sudden laugh, far off and strange.

And then voices.

Somewhere upstairs, the next floor or the one after that. She had to find the stairway, then, somewhere in the centre of the building. She would have sworn that she could have found it blindfolded, so many hours had she spent in this place. And yet, within ten steps of leaving the semigloom of the entrance area, she walked straight into the first tier of shelves hard enough to raise a welt on her forehead. She steadied herself against the cold metal of an upright, her fingers resting against the ribbed spines of the books beside her. This part is Medical, she thought, trying to orient herself. I'm somewhere between Apparatus and Appendectomy, probably. Onward into Blisters and Boils. Somewhere water dripped, and a clock made a mechanical click overhead, moving the minutes along.

An icy finger of snow detached itself from her hair and slid down her neck under her collar. She shivered, felt for the edge of a shelf, and guided herself along it sideways, until she came to a break. If she kept her hands outstretched, she probably wouldn't run into anything else.

Almost immediately, her foot encountered something that sprang away, and she pitched forward between the shelves, landing on her knees and outstretched hands. The thing she'd fallen over slid away—one of the rolling step stools the librarians used to reach high shelves. It had moved like something alive, like an animal in the dark. She found she was panting again, and her heart was making more noise than the wind outside. The rush of her own blood and breathing was nearly deafening her.

So loud . . . you'd think someone would hear.

She clamped her mouth shut with a snap and moved into a sitting position against the shelves. All right, she'd been an idiot to follow them, she accepted that, it was just the kind of thing she hated in the movies. It was so *stupid*.

The temptation had just been too great.

And anyway, Arthur would have called Stryker by now, so she'd be all right. All she wanted to do was get close enough to hear what they were saying, see what they were doing.

And perhaps to stop Richard from killing again.

It had all gone too far. She'd been wrong to protect him, lie for him. But she could do this one last thing. She didn't think he'd do anything in front of her. Or to her. And if she could keep him talking long enough, Stryker would arrive in time to take charge. She must do this sensibly. The darkness had been getting to her, that's all. This was a place she knew well, nothing frightening about it at all.

Well, hardly anything.

She got to her feet and began to move cautiously toward the staircase again. After a moment, she found that if she closed her eyes it was actually easier. She could concentrate more. She moved slowly from tier to tier of shelving, feeling the grit of polish compound beneath her shoes, smelling the books and the paste and the metallic chemical odour of the photocopier. Ah—then she was near the stairwell. Yes—across the gap and her hands were on the painted bricks at last. She slid along, facing the wall, until she came to the doors.

As soon as she pushed one open, the voices became louder. Still indistinct, but louder. One low and reasonable, the other high and almost demented. That's right, she thought, keep him talking. One by one, her feet found the steps, and she gripped the wooden banister tightly, leaning against it and the wall for support. Now was not the time to slip.

She pushed open the doors to the next floor, and knew she'd been right. They were here—in English Literature, of course—beyond the inner doors on the right, in the stacks. The shelves were higher there, and set closer. The metal shelves, with their burden of books distorted the voices, and as Kate moved along, feeling her way toward the sounds, she found that they seemed to be moving too. Sometimes she could almost make out a word, and the next moment the voices were blotted out, leaving only tatters in the river-rush of the wind around the building.

She reached the next set of doors and separated them slightly, her ear closer to the slit, almost jumping when a voice spoke suddenly from only a few feet away.

"*Too* kind. I could read between the lines, well enough. I don't blame him, he has a responsibility to his firm, it isn't often something like Aiken's book comes along for a small house like that. Don't you see? He didn't say it, he'd never say it, but there was a question in his mind. It occurred to him that I had perhaps tried to edge into *Aiken's* field. That I was a me-too, a follower-on."

"You could have refuted that . . . surely . . ."

"I would be on the defensive, I had no proof that I had been working for so long on the thing, no more than Aiken himself. There was only the work itself, collated and annotated."

"You could have sued—"

An inarticulate cry, some animal stepped on, some gross but invisible injury beneath the skin. "You *still* don't understand, do you? George didn't say it, but the message was clear. *My book was dull.* Just as I've always been dull, no matter how I tried to be otherwise. All my life I've been considered *sound.* Solid and worthy, like some large, ugly table. Aiken's book was controversial, clever, it danced and sang in its bitchy, snide way. Anyone reading it would sniff new blood for the chat shows, he would become a media darling—"

"That's just popular nonsense, that's not the same as being—"

"Sound?" There was something like a sob. "He didn't need it, you know. *He* didn't care whether fourteen desiccated professors in various universities nodded their heads over the work and said, 'Brilliant,' he didn't care whether there were dry monographs on this point or that in some little journal with a circulation of nine. And *neither did I* when it came down to it. Looking at his book, I saw how it could have been done, perhaps even how it *should* have been done, to reach the most people and change them. And suddenly that mattered to me very much. Once, just *once* to have someone say to me, 'How *clever* you are! Not sound, not sensible, not *dull*.'"

"But you could have published—"

"Oh, no, Aiken saw to that, too. I was a fool. I kept everything to myself, told no one what I was *really* working on. Not even you, in the end. It had taken me years to accumulate and organise my references and facts. It must have taken Aiken an hour to walk down the hall one evening, read through my files and my notes, and perhaps another hour to photocopy them. That was bad enough, but what he did with it was worse. Even for Aiken, much worse."

Kate suddenly felt cold and sick. The voice rose madly, was not the voice she had known and loved at all. It was as shrill as the wind outside, with as little control and as little direction. She had to stop this. Surely, between them, they could stop it. She pushed open the doors and the voice became clearer, the tone even more chilling.

"I don't understand—"

"I found his first draft in his files, after what he said in the car that afternoon. The office keys are virtually interchangeable, and what he could do, so could I. It was my work, my research, but put together in an entirely new way, Aiken's way, shallow and salacious and cruel . . . but witty. Oh, I knew what George meant, all right. It would *sell*."

"George?"

"My publisher. I'd sent my manuscript off three weeks ago, and I got his letter back on Friday. He was amazed—and dismayed. If he'd only known I was working on this . . . but he'd already commissioned a work on the same subject from a colleague of mine, and was expecting the completed manuscript within the next week or so. He didn't feel he could profitably publish them both. He was very kind."

There was a pause, and then the voice went on.

"I was an ugly child, you know. And there was never much laughter in our house. Virtue was its own reward, and a thin gruel it was, too. One didn't put oneself forward, one didn't brag, one didn't flaunt. Hard work and..." The voice scraped, viciously. "And no ribbons."

Kate felt her heart contract. She understood, and with understanding came a foolish, dangerous compassion. She spoke, through the half-open door, her voice light in the darkness.

"Richard?"

Silence, sudden and total, and then the sudden rustle of movement—feet sliding along the floor, a thump, silence again. Kate spoke gently but firmly. "Look it's no good, the police will be here any minute. They *know*, Richard. You can't do any good with more talk..."

She stood in the dark, waiting for a reply.

"Richard?"

She could hear heavy, asthmatic breathing now, somewhere within the network of shelves. Footsteps again, sliding along. "Who's there?" a voice asked.

"It's Kate, love. You need help. You can't go on killing people and hiding..."

"Oh, yes I can," the voice said, almost gleefully. "Each time, I've been clever. Each time that something has gone wrong, that wasn't my fault, I dealt with it. I knew it was Edward who had knocked Aiken out when I saw him get a note just like mine on Monday morning. He had to be dealt with and was."

"Edward is alive, and awake. He'll say you came to his apartment after, Richard."

"He didn't know." Again came a laugh, a low chuckle. "He was already asleep when I came in, it was just a matter of making the sleep a little deeper, and then getting him over to the stove. He's not so heavy, he's only half a man, after all."

"But *I* know," Kate said. "*I* know how you did it."

"Clever little bitch," the voice said, right beside her, and a hand fell onto her shoulder, grasping it painfully.

Kate screamed and pulled away, crashing into a shelf, slid along it to an opening, and went through and ran along, trying to put some distance between herself and the horrible touch of that hand, the rasp of the mad voice, the smell of wet fur, stale tobacco, fresh blood, and lilacs.

Where was Stryker? Why didn't he come?

She dodged down another narrow space between the shelves and ran straight into Richard's arms. He wrapped them around her and pinned her arms to her sides, put his face close to hers, his mouth touching her ear. "How the hell did you know we were here?" She started to speak but he put his hand up to her mouth. "We've got to keep moving...was that true? About the police?"

She nodded, against his chest.

"Okay..." He began to back down the space, taking her with him, pressed close against his chest. There was a step on the other side of the shelves and he pulled her down to the floor. Silence, except for the whine of the wind and their own breathing. Slowly, slowly, they stood up and began to move again, toward the doors.

There was a sudden movement from the other direction.

A quick, scuttling movement. Richard gave a grunt, stiffened backwards, a hiss of breath sliding out from between his clenched teeth. The darker shadow beyond him sprang back. Richard turned toward it, slowly, and Kate saw that he had something in his hand.

A gun.

As his finger tightened on the trigger, his other hand flailed impotently at the thing that was stuck in his ribs, but before he could fire, darkness overcame him and he went down. The shadow beyond him darted forward like a spider to a fly in its web and picked up the gun. Kate could see the dull glint of its muzzle, even in the gloom.

"Now you, my dear. You complicate things, but I have no doubt I shall work out something. I intended Richard's death to look like suicide after killing that damned guard, but I suppose—"

"No," Kate said. "Please...stop it *now*, before—"

"I *will* work something out, I tell you, I always have before. You all underestimated me...oh, yes you did."

Suddenly the voice shrieked upward as Richard, lying on the floor, grabbed at a thin ankle and pulled.

"Kate! The gun! Get my gun!" His voice was weak, but it still had command in it, and Kate tried to obey. She leapt forward over Richard's body and lunged at the off-balance and swaying figure. She tried to reach the gun as the arms flailed wildly.

The shape screamed, she screamed, the wind screamed.

It was like wrestling with an animal, literally, a fur-covered, maddened animal sticky with blood. Richard's blood? The guard's? Her own? Kate didn't know.

The gun went off, she felt the heat sear her leg as she pounded and lashed out at the thing she'd once called a friend and that was now trying to kill her. They fell against the steel shelves, and books avalanched from above. They went down, and Kate felt her hands close over the gun that was still clenched in a bony hand. The gun was hot, its muzzle burned her, but she had to turn it away before it fired again. She twisted, hard, away from herself and against the bones of that other wrist. She felt them giving, grinding against one another, and heard a scream of rage and pain in her ear. She hit out blindly with her free hand, wanting to hurt for Richard's sake, wanting to kill for Edward's sake, wanting to destroy for her own sake, wanting, finally, to just survive and live, and thinking of nothing but that. They rolled and struggled in the darkness with the wind howling outside, until there seemed to Kate there was no up or down or sideways but just this grunting, panting thrust of will against will, body against body, in the dark, in the warm angular dark.

The lights came on suddenly, blinding them.

The terrible weight was dragged from her, and Kate was no longer struggling alone. Dazed and breathless, she was dragged to her feet by Stryker's strong and impatient grasp. She stood in the space between the shelves, swaying and gasping, blood on her hands and face and in her hair. Richard lay in blood, and he lay so very still.

She looked at Stryker, whose eyes were filled with fury and the beginnings of relief. He patted her all over as he'd pat a dog, searching for wounds or broken bones. He thought the blood was hers. He kept saying over and over, "Are you all right? Are you all right?"

She tried to speak, to tell him she was fine, but nothing came out except a sort of croak. He stood there with his jacket open and his sweater torn, his hair on end and dripping wet snow, his eyes and nose red in a white face.

He looked wonderful.

He held her together, because she started to fall, he kept telling her that it was all right now, that it was all over, that she was safe. But even his voice couldn't drown out the terrible, tearing, endless sounds of Jane Coulter's screams as she writhed and kicked and struggled between Toscarelli and Neilson.

They went on and on and on and on and on.

THIRTY-TWO

"WHERE IS THIS?" Kate asked, looking around in confusion at the gleaming antiques crowded into the small room.

"My place," Stryker said brusquely, taking her coat and throwing it over a chair. "You weren't fit to go home alone." He turned away from her bewildered face. "I'll make some coffee. You should eat something. When you've had a rest you'll feel better. Anyway, there's the storm."

"Oh, yes...the storm." She nodded vigorously, as if he'd explained everything.

When he came back from the kitchen, he found her sitting on the end of the chaise longue, staring into space. She looked at him when the mugs clicked on the coffee table. "Richard will be all right," she assured him, as if he'd been worried.

"Yeah, I know." He thrust a steaming mug at her and walked away to straighten a picture, taking his own coffee with him, unable to settle, yet.

"What will happen to Jane?"

"What usually happens to people who are nuts. Not my problem, really. I only catch them, get them off the streets."

"Or out of the ivory towers."

"Whatever."

Kate sipped at her coffee. "I didn't even *know* she was writing a book about the Crucifixion."

"Wayland did. He'd helped her with some of the editing. Sometime in the past year, he must have mentioned it to Adamson, perhaps only in passing. But enough to make Adamson curious."

"She must have realized something of what he'd done when he thanked Richard in the car that day, going downtown. Thanked him for making him famous," Kate mused. "I wasn't paying attention. I never did, when Aiken went on like that."

"Dr. Coulter paid attention, all right. And then she got that letter from her publisher, on Friday. She simmered about it, and when the taxi was taking her back to the parking lot after her other meeting, she probably saw the light on. It was like a beacon, that light, drawing all the moths to his flame. There was a lot of traffic at Grantham Hall that night.''

"And I was sitting at home, eating cookies with Liz," Kate said. "Do you have any cookies?"

"I'll look in a minute. You know, she *saw* Richard running away. At first she must have thought *he* had knocked Adamson out. When she saw Adamson, her enemy, lying there, she went crazy. When it was over, *then* she began to think. She got everything out of his files and hid them in her own files—"

"Like 'The Purloined Letter' . . ." Kate mused.

"Yeah. I think it was after that was done that she decided to go back and cut out his tongue. She was tough enough to do that, but too much of a lady to unzip his pants and cut off what *should* have been cut off if she wanted to convince us it was a homosexual killing. I should have realized then that it might have been a woman."

"But she was fine the next morning."

He scowled at her. "You were *all* fine the next morning. You threw words around and performed like troupers, dazzling the dumb cops." He was gratified to see a fleeting smile cross her blank face, and went out into the kitchen to find some cookies. He came back with some bread and butter, the best he could do. *He* hadn't had a chance to go to the supermarket to stock up, had he? He watched until she took a bite, then resumed his walk around the room.

"You can imagine her shock, *and* Pinchman's, when they got those blackmail notes on Monday morning. *He* fell apart, and your kindly Richard took him home. By then Richard was in a pretty bad state himself. He knew he was on the verge of a binge—he'd been fighting it off since Friday night, when he'd come down to undo the trap he'd laid for Adamson."

"What trap?"

He told her about the insulin. "I think he just wanted to make him sick, to tell you the truth. Anyway, he saw Adamson lying there and probably thought he'd already taken the 'insulin' and was in a coma. He ran off. Then your dear sweet Jane came along."

"We thought she was wonderful."

"Maybe she was . . . once. But her work had become an obsession, and her jealousy of Adamson was the last straw. With every setback, she got worse. Poor Wayland didn't realize he was handing Pinchman's keys to a killer—he just wanted her to go along and make sure the old man was all right."

"He would have given them to me, I suppose, if we hadn't quarrelled," Kate said sadly.

"Maybe. But he had no reason not to trust Jane Coulter, she was a good friend. He went off on his binge thinking he'd done the right thing. And she went to Pinchman's apartment and tried to pin the thing on *him* by making it look like suicide."

"She used the gravy baster," Kate said.

"Yeah, I know she did. We had the bulb tested and found traces of coffee and barbituates. You figured that out the day you came to the apartment, didn't you? You squeezed the bulb and smelled the coffee—but you thought Wayland had done it. You handled it all over, made certain no fingerprints were on it but yours, knowing I'd seen you pick it up."

Kate looked at the floor. "I'm sorry."

"Are you?" Stryker clenched his fists. "I suppose I might have done the same thing in your place. All she had to do was make up a strong solution of coffee and barbituates, stick the thing into Pinchman's mouth, and squeeze hard. He was asleep—even if he'd choked a bit the stuff would have gushed down his throat."

Kate sighed. "There was no roasting pan in the drainer, you see. Why a baster if he'd had nothing to baste?"

"Uh-huh." He looked at her bleakly. "He was asleep, but he might have caught the scent of lilacs, as he had the previous Friday night. It didn't register then—but I gather he called the station today and tried to tell me about it. I might have put it together from that, but by then I'd gone after the guard. Too late, though. She got him."

"Poor man," Kate said softly.

"Stupid man," Stryker said harshly. "Adamson was one kind of blackmailer, he was another. She got them both."

"Yes, but—"

"*And* she was trying to frame your precious Richard," Stryker said harshly. "When the typist turned up with that manuscript, she knew she couldn't strike again without another scapegoat. She had to get it back before anyone read it. She didn't want to hurt Dan or you, so she tried for this weird 'three monkeys' thing. Maybe she caught sight of those three monkeys on your desk, I don't know. Anyway, she did what she had to do, then knocked herself around and screamed for help. She knew damn well I'd never buy her description of her 'assailant'—she was *counting* on me not accepting it and assuming she was covering up for Wayland. You thought so too." Kate nodded miserably as he went on. "Then Wayland walked into her trap by calling her up after you'd told him about the manuscript. I don't know how she convinced him to go to the library with her..."

"She didn't," Kate said. "She went in first. I saw her—and then, a few minutes later, I saw Richard following her. He must have gone to her office, found the things of Adamson's she'd hidden in her files, and known the truth. He followed her to confront her, or maybe she'd told him about the guard. But *I* thought he was going to kill her. You'd convinced me, by then, that he was the killer. You really had." Her eyes filled with tears, and she blinked them back.

"She would have gotten to Richard eventually," Stryker said. "If not at the library, then later—but she *had* to kill that guard, and kill him in a way that connected with the other two attacks. She kept trying to force things into a pattern she'd thought up *after* the first killing. That's why it rang so false, somehow. If it had been a *true* pattern, she would have killed Stark and you. But she didn't."

"She liked us," Kate said, and the tears ran over. "She *liked* us." She looked up. "She liked Richard, too."

"Yeah, but in her eyes he was the cause of it *all*. If he hadn't talked about her work, her precious work, to Adamson, none of this would have happened. That justified *his* execution. Everything she did was justified in her eyes because it was done to protect her Work. I think she actually thought that if she plugged all the holes, she'd eventually be able to go ahead with her own book and never be caught. That's what gets me about you people—words mean more than reality to you. Ideas come before people." He went over to stare out at the snow. The wind had dropped somewhat, but still the snow fell thickly, and already had coated his car into a white hump by the curb. He could just make out the uneven dips in the snow that had been their footprints as he'd helped her from the car to the house. They'd been hours at the hospital, waiting to hear if Wayland would live. He supposed Richard would look like a big hero to her now. A man worth saving, while *he* was just another of her golden boy's persecutors. The mean cop, as always. He could have taken her home, he supposed. It had been a selfish impulse to bring her here. He'd just wanted to see what she looked like with his furniture.

Kate joined him at the window. "We seem to be marooned," she murmured.

"No... it will stop soon, and the ploughs will be out. I can run you home then. No problem."

She moved away. "I see. Everything over. No problem."

"That's it."

She glanced at him, standing so stubbornly by the window. His shoulders were slumped. He looked tired. Her eyes fell on his reading glasses, lying on a table by what was obviously his favourite armchair. There was a book of poetry beside them. So this was the big, bad terrifying cop who'd chased her through all those dreams. Rilke said that perhaps all our dragons were really princes waiting to be kissed. This particular dragon hadn't been kissed, except by time. He was no prince, either. Just a man, doing a job that had to be done. She'd hated it, once, but she understood it a little better now. She still didn't like it, but it was what he did, and he did do it well. He *cared* about doing it right. That was important.

And what about herself? Still ready to right the world's wrongs, was she? With her double chin and a few grey hairs and practically no ideals left to warm her through the night? What right did she have to call *him* a dragon?

"You said that this was making a gap between us," she said.

He turned. "This and everything else, Kate. There'll *always* be a gap between us. I am what I am, I'll never change."

"Maybe that's because what you are is what you *should* be," she said. "I'm not certain what I am yet."

He looked at her and tried to shrug off the things that were shackling him. Her fight to protect Richard, Richard himself, always there and no doubt more than ready to go on leaning if she'd let him, her "ivory tower" world, even her vulnerability and her insecurity. So much held him back, and he didn't want to hurt her. Not again. "It's very risky, Kate."

"Because of the gap?"

"Because of the gap."

She took a deep breath and measured the distance with her eyes. "I make it about ten feet. I'm willing to chance it if you are."

They met halfway.

A JOANNA STARK MYSTERY

DARK STAR

MARCIA MULLER

A splash of red. From her peaceful Sonoma Valley home, art-security expert Joanna Stark can't escape the crippling fear that Antony Parducci—thief, art dealer, dreaded enemy and onetime lover—is nearby, hot on the trail of a newly discovered Van Gogh. Then a worthless but significant painting suddenly disappears from Joanna's own collection and she knows Parducci has left his calling card...challenging her to a deadly game of cat and mouse.

But when Parducci's dead body is found splayed in her living room, Joanna becomes a pawn in a much more sinister scheme—as past secrets, a priceless painting and a desperate killer create a masterpiece of murder.

"Joanna Stark, female sleuth, is brazen, courageous, feminine, but most of all convincing."
—*Mystery News*